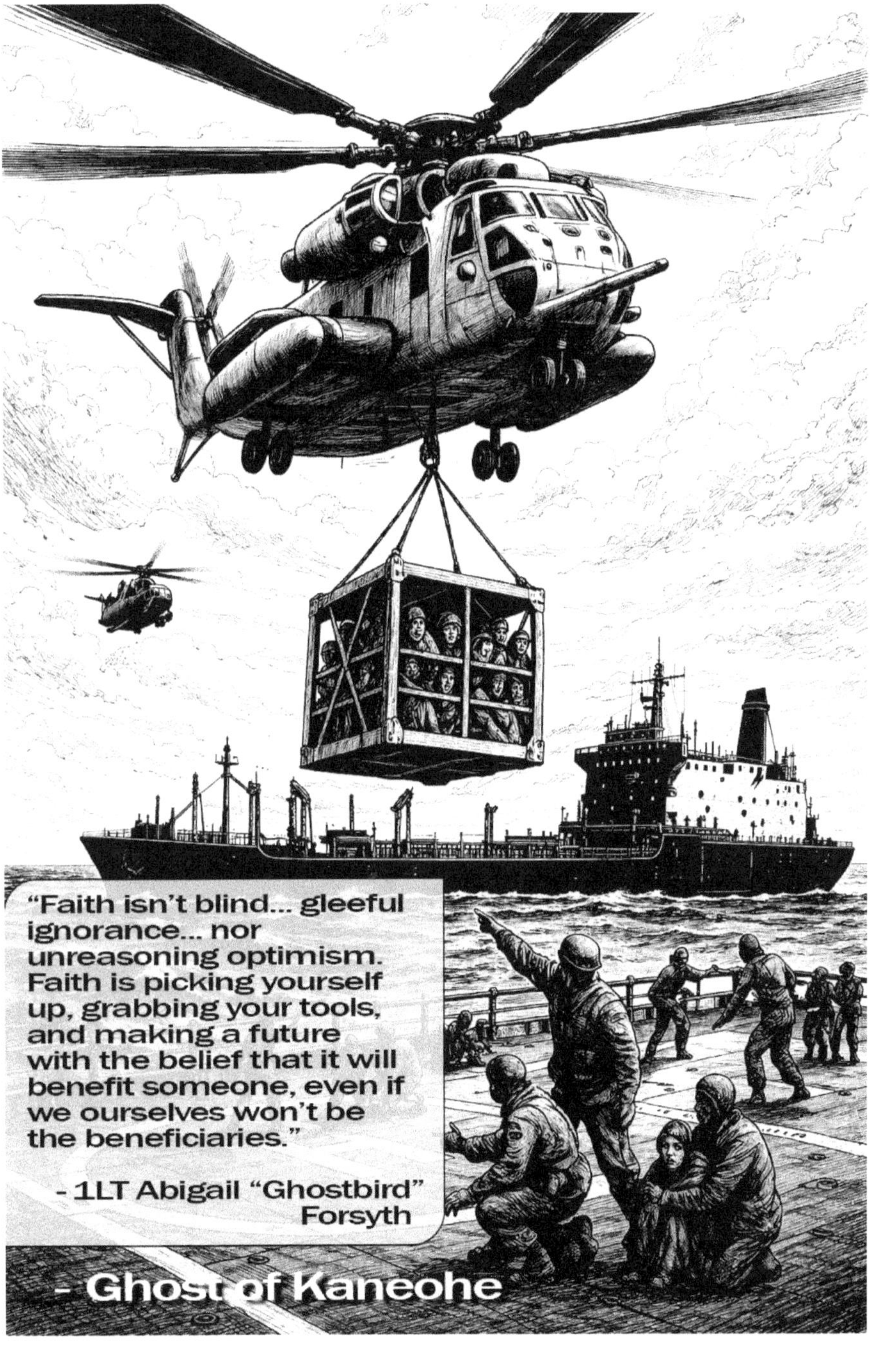

"Faith isn't blind... gleeful ignorance... nor unreasoning optimism. Faith is picking yourself up, grabbing your tools, and making a future with the belief that it will benefit someone, even if we ourselves won't be the beneficiaries."

- 1LT Abigail "Ghostbird" Forsyth

- Ghost of Kaneohe

# A HERO RISES

## JOURNEYS BEYOND THE KNOWN

ROBERT E.
HAMPSON

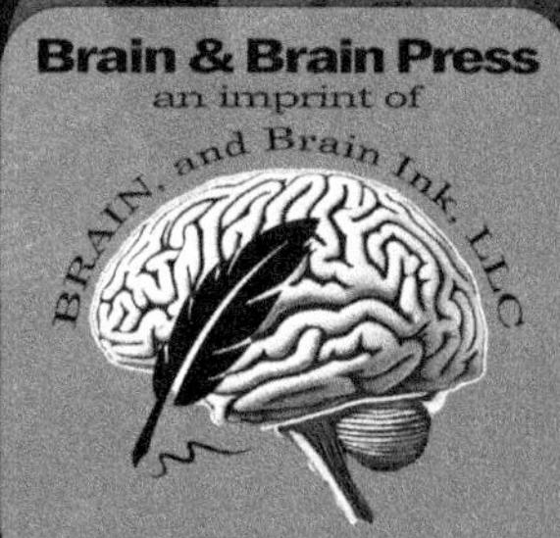

# Copyright

# Contents

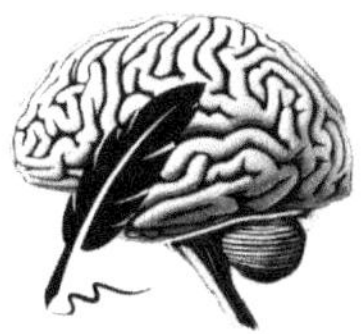

# Dedication

For Ruann, the love of my life; for Mom, my first fan; and for Dad, my hero and role model.

JOURNEYS BEYOND THE KNOWN
SCIENCE
WONDER
TRANSFORMATION

# Journeys Beyond the Known

FROM NATIONAL BESTSELLING AUTHOR Robert E. Hampson comes *Journeys Beyondthe Known*—collections of science fiction and science fantasy exploring the human condition through the lenses of biotech, space exploration, strange futures, and uncommon valor.

What happens when biotech turns dangerous? When brilliant pioneers chase fading starlight? When strange magics emerge where science frays? When heroes rise to meet the impossible? From nanotech healing to bionic astronauts, from psionic children to zombie-ravaged worlds, from alien battlefields to acts of quiet defiance, come explore survival, transformation, and a spark that endures.

Hampson—scientist, educator, and master storyteller—blends hard science with heart, fusing cutting-edge research and richly imagined worlds to illuminate what it means to adapt, survive, and evolve.

**The journey begins at the edge of knowledge—and ends where only story can take us.**

- **Tinker, Tailor, Bio, Spy** delivers seven sharp and witty tales of biotech gone rogue, where stem cells, nanobots, and brain implants collide with military and industrial espionage. A place where ethics and integrity underlie unexpected heroism.

- **Where the Light Still Reaches** ventures into deep space and distant futures, chronicling the legacy of pioneers, the courage of survivors, and the quiet triumph of those who refuse to be forgotten.

- **When the Sky Forgot Us** wanders the borderlands between science and sorcery, offering seven visions of apocalypse, myth, and transformation—where magic rises, science fractures, and unlikely heroes carry the fire.
- **A Hero Rises** travels the paths of heroism, great, small, and everything in between—where people find a way to do the impossible—not because they want to, but because they have to.

Whether grounded in the hard realities of known science or lit by the strange glow of the fantastical, these stories invite readers to step past the boundaries of the familiar—and discover what waits just beyond.

# Additional Copyright Information

THIS BOOK IS A work of fiction, and any resemblance to persons, living or dead, or places, events, or locales is purely coincidental. The characters are productions of the author's imagination and used fictitiously.

These stories take place in various universes, some of my own design ("World Enough," "Mother," "Gut Check." and "Ghost of Kaneohe") and other authors' universes. "No Hippocritical Oath" is set in Tom Kratman's Carrera Series, starting with his novel *A Desert Called Peace.* "Echoes of a Beating Heart" is set in the shared world of Ross 248 created by Les Johnson and Ken Roy for the anthology *The ROSS 248 Project.* Primary character names and central locations to the story are mine, but key in-universe settings, characters, and worldbuilding remain the property of the respective IP holders.

*Wars of Liberation*, edited by Tom Kratman, published by Baen Books.

"Echoes of a Beating Heart" by Robert E. Hampson, copyright 2023 by Robert E. Hampson. First appeared in *The Ross 248 Project*, edited by Les Johnson and Ken Roy, published by Baen Books.

"World Enough" by Robert E. Hampson, copyright 2021 by Robert E. Hampson. First appeared *World Breakers*, edited by Tony Daniel and Christopher Ruocchio, published by Baen Books.

"Mother" by Robert E. Hampson, copyright 2023 by Robert E. Hampson. First appeared *Chicks in Tank Tops*, edited by Jason Cordova, published by Baen Books.

"Gut Check" by Robert E. Hampson, copyright 2025 by Robert E. Hampson. First appeared *Analog: Science Fiction and Fact*, January-February 2025, published by Dell Magazines.

"Ghost of Kaneohe" by Robert E. Hampson, copyright 2025 by Robert E. Hampson. First appeared online on the Baen Books website free fiction, April 2025.

Cover and interior art by Robert E. Hampson. Some elements are AI-derived. All final artwork is human-produced.

# Foreword

HERO.

Definition: "A person who is admired or idealized for courage, outstanding achievements, or noble qualities."

Other definitions and comments include:

"...an ordinary individual who finds the strength to persevere and endure in spite of overwhelming obstacles." – Christopher Reeve.

"...someone who has given his or her life to something bigger than oneself." – Joseph Campbell.

"A hero is no braver than an ordinary man, but he is brave five minutes longer." – Raplph Waldo Emerson.

It is said that true heroes are not born, they are made. In dire circumstances, they rise above their own limitations to do what must be done, even if it costs their own life.

For this fourth volume of Journeys Beyond the Known, I chose to focus on stories of heroism, great, small, and everything in between. These are stories of people (and yes, I include a juvenile sentient AI in that category) who find a way to do the impossible—not always because they *want* to, but because they *have* to.

Some might call these stories "Space Opera" because they tell stories of people working outside established systems to perform their heroic deeds. I agree, but frankly, the story doesn't have to be "in space" to qualify for this characterization, so it's a bit of a misnomer.

So, let's call them what they are: epics, tales of heroes, valor,and courage. The actions of ordinary people exposed to extraordinary events.

When life is at its darkest, that when A Hero Rises.

# One

# NO HIPPOCRITICAL OATH

**Author's note: This story** was "commissioned" by Tom Kratman, who was also bought my first published short story.

Tom's *Carrera* series, starting with the novel *A Desert Called Peace*, introduces us to the planet Terra Nova—the only world humans from Earth have discovered, and even that was by freak accident. Terra Nova is very much a "New Earth," with a mostly benign environment (though a few species are inimical to human life). Earth's governments, however, find it convenient to use Terra Nova as a dumping ground for their malcontents, rebels, and freedom-loving individuals who chafe under world government rule.

As a result, Terra Nova becomes a mirror of Earth: its people, its nations, its politics, and all of its rivalries and hatreds.

The present of Tom's *Carrera*-verse is shaped by wars of liberation fought 100 to 150 years before the current timeline. Tom opened this universe to other writers to explore key moments in Terra Nova's history. He challenged me to write a

**story set in the country of Balboa—a mirror of Earth's Panama, and a region with which Tom is quite familiar.**

**We discussed the setting and settled on a particularly dastardly effort by Earth's world government—and, by extension, their Terra Novan puppets—to force insurgents out of hiding by requiring them to receive inoculations against the deadly disease Duck Fever—a humorous product of a conversation with Tom and others on Baen's Bar back in the early 2010s—here given life as a (somewhat) serious disease.**

**The setting is rooted in that particular flavor of elite rivalry that can only arise when the downtrodden are more intelligent than their oppressors. With a doctor who must prove that the oath he swore as a healer... was no "hippocritical" oath.**

It wasn't bad enough that medical school was harder than any other class or schooling that Anthony Nuné had attended, but he had to put up with the *putito* 'elites' like Lucas Carvalho. The United Nations / Duke Medical School should have been a respite from the constant struggle for 'status' and power that Anthony had endured in the Panama schools—after all, the United States was supposed to be the 'Land of the Free and the Home of the Brave' where a poor but smart student could succeed no matter his family ties. It had even once been true—just not so much anymore.

UN/Duke had its roots in the 'Duke Brazil Initiative' to promote research partnerships between Duke University and several universities (and medical schools) in Brazil at the beginning of the Twenty-first Century. As the partnership grew and started a medical student exchange program, the UN had taken over and directed Duke Medical School to exclusively provide American-style medical education to top university graduates through Central and South America. Unfortunately, 'top graduate' didn't always mean grades, thus Lucas S. Carvalho the Third terrorized his tutors (like Anthony, despite being two years ahead of him) who were necessary for his continued presence in the school, all while lording his status over them. The fact that Carvalho's father was a doctor with the World Health Organization, his uncle was the Brazilian Ambassador to the UN, and his great-grandfather was the neuroscience professor who first established the Duke Brazil Initiative, gave Lucas leverage over faculty and staff of the university that his fellow students could never hope to achieve.

Thus, Anthony found himself struggling to complete not only his own Infectious Diseases case study for Friday's Grand Rounds, but also Carvalho's. The tutoring job paid real money, and The Sainted Hammarskjold knew that Anthony needed it; his scholarship paid tuition and board, but little else. He just had to hang on another month until the Licensing Board exams and Graduation. Unlike Carvalho, with his new Porsche-Benz, tailored white doctor coats, and uptown apartment, Anthony had to suffice with public transportation, used academic supplies with thrift-store clothing and sharing a flat with five other students who were just as poor as he was.

Lucas had told Anthony to forget 'tutoring' and just write up the presentation for the Grand Rounds; it was worth an extra fifty UD's or university-dollars that Anthony could use at the hospital cafeteria or any campus shop. As long as Anthony handed over the presentation before it was due, Lucas could read it for the first time and still give a masterful performance. In fact, he usually did—to the commendations of the faculty supervisors. It just proved that you didn't have to be *smart* as long as you could follow a script and had the right family connections.

Anthony was struggling with the case. The patient history and physical had been taken by another of Carvalho's 'tutors,' and were nearly illegible. Technically, the notes were supposed to be recorded in the computer systems, as part of the patient digital record, but most physicians only put what the insurance companies demanded in the patient file. Grand Rounds insisted on *real* details, which were often excluded from official records to ensure that the patient met the WHO treatment quotas. Fortunately, the unlucky scribe was one of Anthony's roommates.

"Julio, what does this say?" Anthony asked when he'd finally managed to get his roommate's attention away from the girlfriend he'd been spending a lot of time with that semester. "You know I can't read the notes you write for case studies!"

"You mean the ones for 'His Honor?'" Julio Cisneros spoke the honorific with a sarcastic tone of voice—as most of the other students did when referring to Carvalho out of hearing distance. "Why don't you just make it up? That's what the rest of us do."

"You know I can't do that, this is Grand Rounds, and I have to present, too, so I need to finish this and work on mine, too. I'll be up all night as it is."

"Speaking of 'up all night,' you *have* noticed Annalise, right? She paid her way through nursing school as a *dancer*!" Julio waggled his eyebrows to convey just what sort of dancing the young lady had done.

"Enough, Casanova. I need help, here."

"Yes, you do, and Annalisa shares a flat with three other nurses, all single, and all looking to score a freshly licensed doctor. Besides, didn't you hear that Casanova's grandson studied right here at Duke?" Julio waggled his eyebrows again. "So I have to keep up the tradition; besides, the patient had duck fever."

"Huh? What?" Anthony was too tired to follow Julio's line of thought.

"Sure, Mike Casanova, back in the 2000's, he worked with Saint Nicolelis."

"Not that. What is it you always call me? *Tonto?* Idiot? No, I'm asking what you mean by 'Duck Fever'." Keeping up with Julio's train of thought was like trying to catch kittens.

"Oh yeah. Avian Influenza, H9N6, traces back to a virus in ducks in Hong Kong over a century ago. The first known human cases were seen just last year. This poor guy just happened to have an allergic reaction to the vaccine, so his throat swelled up and he literally '*quacked*' when he tried to talk. Anyway, here are my *real* notes, not the scribbling I handed 'Lord Lucas'." Julio pulled out his *Phablet* and sent Anthony a digital file containing the case notes.

"Thanks, Julio. I might be able to get a couple hours' sleep tonight!"

"I keep telling you, Tonio, you don't need sleep, you need one of Annalise's roommates!" Anthony just threw the wadded up paper with the scribe notes at him.

"VERY GOOD, MR. NUNÉ. Excellent summation. The treatment plan is sound and the patient seems to be recovering just fine." Doctor Pegram had led the questioning during Anthony's presentation. The Attending Physicians always sat in the front row of the lecture hall, and most of the time their questions were polite and professional. They didn't necessarily wait until the end of the presentation, though; Attendings frequently interrupted to ask questions meant to clarify descriptions or test a student's thought processes in coming up with a diagnosis. It could be unnerving, even if all went well, as Anthony's presentation had.

Carvalho was up next. Anthony had handed him the case study several hours ago, but Lucas had barely glanced at it. With a smirk, he stepped up in front of the room, immaculate in grooming, tailored white coat, and a highly expensive—and anachronistic—stethoscope draped around his neck. He began his presentation in a smooth cultured voice. Several of the female students, plus a few males and even one of the faculty had a look of sheer infatuation on their faces. Except for the Attendings. Dr. Pegram's looked like he had turned to stone. Strangely, there were no questions, and Lucas finished without interruption.

"Mr. Carvalho, is this supposed to be a joke?" Dr. Pegram voice was as icy as his expression.

Lucas stopped and stared, confused, as he thought back over his presentation to determine how he had angered the Attending Physician. The patient had presented with muscle spasms which caused spinal contracture and inhibiting posture and gait, tightening of the cheek muscles causing pursing of the lips, and of course, the spasm of the hyoid region coupled with swelling to cause the odd vocalization. As he recognized the implications, he began to flush, and a quick, angry glance at Anthony indicated that he'd already decided on someone to blame.

When Lucas didn't answer, Dr. Pegram continued: "Mr. Carvalho, we are professionals. Our patients do not have 'fits,' they have 'seizures.' They don't 'bleed like a Mother F-' ... whatever... they have 'profuse hemorrhage.' Under no circumstances will we accept 'if it looks like a duck, walks like a duck and quacks like a duck, it's Duck Fever' as a diagnosis." As one, he and the rest of the Attendings stood and exited the room. "Dismissed," he called over his shoulder.

"You've made a powerful enemy, Mr. Nuné." Dean Thompson rose from his desk as Anthony entered the office. He gestured to indicate that the two would sit at a pair of chairs to the side of the office. The Dean of Students indicated Anthony's bruised and swollen face and continued, "but I suspect you've already learned that."

"I fell in the stairway," Anthony muttered.

"Of course you did, and the ER report does not indicate injuries consistent with a beating." Anthony did not respond, so the Dean resumed. "Mr. Carvalho comes from a very powerful family. Not only is his father Deputy Director of WHO, his uncle is being talked about for Secretary General. There's also talk of investing them with noble titles. I shudder to think of the possibility of 'Viscount WHO,' but there's even talk of making the titles inheritable. There's nowhere on Earth that you can go to escape them, and believe me, they intend to ruin you."

A small sound escaped from Anthony throat. It was as near a sob as he could manage through the swelling. All he had ever wanted to be was a Doctor, and now that was permanently out of reach. He couldn't even really blame Julio for setting him up, the symptoms were exactly as described, it was only the interpretation—and delivery, he had to admit—that were at fault. Of course, if Lucas had actually read the presentation ahead of time, he could have changed it enough to avoid embarrassment, but Lucas would never take the blame for his own actions. He was already circulating a story that Anthony had pranked him out of spite and had replaced Lucas' *own* scholarly work with the fake diagnosis.

The Dean was still speaking, but Anthony had missed something. "—accept transshipment to Terra Nova and we can ensure that you are licensed and certified. Balboa needs doctors, and you may even have family there."

"Excuse me, Sir, but... what was that?"

"Some of our more 'indigent' students agree to serve on Terra Nova to pay their loans. You were on scholarship, but it's still an option. The United Nations Interplanetary Settlement and Boundary Committee, or UNISBC, is in charge, but it will be a bit easier to get a clean start, since it's handled at a much lower level than the WHO. Your friend Cisneros is one of several upcoming graduate due to head there, but even so, you're unlikely to run into people who would know you. "

"Terra Nova? The colony planet? What would I do there?"

"The same thing you would do here. Your grades are excellent, and you've passed all of the exams. You'll have to complete a residency in Hamilton and then you'll be assigned to a clinic, probably in Balboa City since you are Panamanian. It's a twenty-year commitment, or else you have to pay back the transshipment costs; but it pays better than you could expect here. Besides, it's your only real option."

*Terra Nova?* It was too much all at once. He was supposed to go to Panama City next month to start a residency at the 'Hospital del Niño'—the children's hospital—with the statue of Vasco Nuñez de Balboa in the park across the street. Now the Dean was talking about going to the *country* of Balboa on the only other planet that humans had ever discovered. Not to mention, it was a planet filled with plants and animals that were deadly to humans.

On the other hand, it was a chance to escape the attentions of Carvalho. He'd be needed. Just *maybe* he could make a new start... but at the cost of leaving friends, family...

He felt a cold lump in his stomach. His shoulders slumped and he felt as if a heavy weight had fallen on him. "Yes, sir. I'll go," he said in a quiet, defeated voice.

"*Has sido una buena chiquita,* Janina. You've been a good girl." George Noonan taped a small bandage over the site of the vaccination, then lifted her off of the examining table and handed her to the mother. "She probably won't be hungry tonight, but make sure she has plenty to drink. No *cacao, por favor.* She needs water or juice. Watch for fever, and come back if she is not feeling better in three days. *Tres días, Señora.*"

The mother nodded and muttered her thanks in heavily accented English. George thought it highly ironic that the patients and family considered him the *'gringo doctor'* since he had come to Balboa from his residency in the largely Anglo areas of Hamilton. The relocation deal had included a legal name change. The beating he'd received at the hands of Carvalho's thugs had carried an unexpected benefit—reconstructive surgery that had changed the profile of his face just enough to fool facial recognition, although close friends if he'd had any, might have been able to recognize him as once going through school as Anthony Nuné.

Residency had been totally different from anything he'd experienced on Earth, and he truly felt that he'd gained a fresh start, so much so that he'd extended the residency in Pediatrics to include Obstetrics and Gynecology as well as Emergency Medicine. He knew he'd certainly need it for some of the UNISBC's hospitals and clinics. He'd hoped that residency would count toward his 20-year obligation, after all, he worked 72-hour shifts at county hospitals and ERs throughout, but the UN was adamant. Twenty years in service as a fully-qualified doctor, residency most definitely *not* included.

Here he was, six years of residency and eight of practice, he should have been at least two thirds of the way through his commitment, but instead was less than halfway. He *really* should have read the fine print on his transportation contract. He couldn't really complain, though; he was alive, wasn't he? He'd intended to spend quite a few years at the Children's Hospital in Panama City before moving on to private practice, so it wasn't as if he had something urgent to do other than treating children and their mothers. The UNISBC Women's and Children's Hospital in *Ciudad* Balboa was both challenging and rewarding. It was a small hospital, only a dozen beds, a family clinic that doubled as an emergency room, and a small laboratory filled with outdated equipment. He rented a room in the building next to the hospital, and spent most of his time at those two locations. He was paid well despite his "indenture" and the families he'd treated had spread the word that the *'gringo doctor'* was a good man. There was at least one restaurant in town that would not allow him to pay, and the butcher at the market near his apartment always ensured that he received choice cuts of meat.

The only thing he didn't have was a family of his own. He'd dated a few times, but residency, like medical school, was time consuming and he was reluctant to get involved with a girl he would have to leave behind when the UN reassigned him. He'd officially been at W&C for eight years, now, but he spent weeks at a time working rural clinics, and even a month per year on-call for emergency services at the forts along the Rio Gamboa. The river provided a navigable waterway from the continental divide to the Shimmering Sea—more than halfway across the narrow Balboan Isthmus—and there was a *lot* of cargo on the river and roads crossing Balboa. The UN Marines built several forts to protect official commerce, and naturally, needed medical services for their troops; who better than someone that already owed the UN their service? Despite the primitive conditions at some of the sites he worked, they were still a damn sight better than his boyhood home in Chorillo.

The mothers of some of his patients, not to mention some of his older female patients, had started to hint about finding him a '*muy buena senorita*.' While he feigned disinterest, he had to admit, that he'd been thinking about it, the butcher's daughter was rather cute. Then there was the girl with the construction company building the pediatric wing. He'd seen her several times when he'd had to go to the company office to discuss the new patient rooms. Now *there* was a girl who could stop traffic! What was her name?

Yelena! That was it. Yelena... Guerrero, or Carrera, or Callejo, or something like that. Maybe he should ask her out. After all, he *was* the Gringo Doctor; that had to be worth something! His work habits didn't leave much time for dating, though—or, at least they hadn't until lately. The out-of-town duties had reduced as word of a new insurgency had arisen. Yes, he could ask her out, although it seemed strange that back-country terrorists would provide him an excuse for a normal love-life.

After six months of seeing Yelena Guerrero, George had to admit that he'd made the right decision. Finding time to spend with her and her family had gotten easier once he decided to *make* the time, rather than simply *find* the time. He'd met most of the family by now since many of their 'dates' were chaperoned; Balboa had a *very* traditional culture, and it was getting time to have The Meeting with her father...

It would have to wait, though; he'd been called out to Fort Cristóbal on an emergency. It was nearly time for his annual trip to the fort overlooking the mouth of the Rio Gamboa, so he'd been told to simply report early and plan to stay the extra time. He'd hurriedly packed, arranged for one of the other doctors to cover his hospital duties, and stopped briefly at the construction office to say good-bye to Yelena. He promised to meet with her father once he got back, and received a *very* enthusiastic kiss in return!

This had been a strange tour of duty, though. The patient had been shot with a bullet that had somehow become coated with progressivine sap—more than could be accounted for by shooting from within heavy foliage. There had long been rumors of groups of insurgents in the undeveloped areas between cities, but that was supposed to be mainly concentrated in Northern and Southern Columbia, the continents connected by the isthmus of Balboa. If the terrorists were this close to civilization, and coating weapons with poisonous sap, then it might be time to insist on having a guard when he traveled between clinics.

The local flora and fauna had been a problem for as long as humans had been on Terra Nova. For a planet that seemed perfect for terrestrial life, it seemed to have a particular animosity to *intelligent* terrestrial life. The planet had plenty of plants and animals that appeared to be directly equivalent to those on Earth, leading many to wonder if it wasn't *too* convenient and wonder what or who had arranged the coincidence. However, there were a few native plants such as the progressivines and bolshiberries which toxins selectively inimical to intelligent life, and animals such as the *antaniae* with obviously alien genes and bad attitude.

George had studied the literature on the uniquely Terra Nova species during his residency. The prevailing theory was that the Novan equivalent of DNA was a hybrid of the four known nucleotides of terrestrial DNA, plus 4 unique nucleotide bases. The DNA 'code' produced by the sequence of nucleotides determined the structure and function of proteins in all organisms; thus the Novan species produced proteins that were *similar* to terrestrial proteins, but had subtle differences due to the presence of extra codes. It was hypothesized that those proteins acted similar to prions—basically a fragments of protein made from normal terrestrial genes, but with abnormal structure—that mainly affected animals with complex brains. The scientific theories didn't really matter—bolshiberry juice and progressivine sap could lead to a very painful death. Deliberate use of the toxins on other humans was murder, and George had a responsibility to report it as such.

The rising insurgency was not the strange part, even though George always felt as if someone was watching. No, Novan technology was... schizophrenic... to put it mildly. At Duke, he'd had access to the best medicines and medical technology that the Twenty-second century had to offer. His residency in Hamilton had mostly modern facilities, at least up to the best of the Twenty-first century, although that slipped to Twentieth century in the rural areas. In *Ciudad* Balboa, he had some modern medications and facilities, but most of the country seemed to be struggling to keep up with Earth's Seventeenth century. Fort Cristóbal was a perfect example, a large brick and adobe walled fortress overlooking a river that served strictly human and animal-drawn barges.

In contrast, soon after George had treated the soldier with the contaminated wound, he received several ultra-modern diagnostic devices and a shipment of a new vaccine with instructions to vaccinate all of the personnel at the Fort. The devices consisted of a new blood analyzer, diagnostic scanner, biometric recorder and a rapid DNA sequencer. Every person receiving vaccine was to be scanned to confirm the infection (or lack thereof), provide a blood and tissue sample for analysis, and have their biometrics recorded. The instructions were from the Terra Nova Health Organization—the UNISBC's version of WHO.

George shuddered with the memories that thinking of TNHO or WHO brought up. This was highly unusual; most of his patients didn't *need* ultramodern medicine, even if it would have saved more lives. Life on Terra Nova, and in Balboa in particular, was hard and rather primitive. The people were strong, and they were survivors. They made do with what they had, as did most of the doctors, hospitals and clinics. Even Twentieth century medicine was good enough for most needs, so to be issued materials that literally screamed 'most modern' was unheard of.

There was more to it, and the instructions he'd been given upon returning to *Ciudad* Balboa were the most confusing of all. There was a new influenza, and the TNHO had decided to stop its spread with the vaccine he'd been given. However, before he could administer the vaccine to any non-military or non-UNISBC personnel—even children—he had to take the biometric and genetic samples and wait for approval. It was supposedly for epidemiological research purposes, but why would he have to wait for approval if the data was simply being used to track which patients contracted the disease?

Normally George enjoyed performing his duties at the forts and outposts; after all, treating pregnant women and sick children was rewarding, but not particularly exciting. His trips out of the city presented many different challenges, but also allowed him a measure of autonomy that was absent at the hospital. This time, however, he couldn't wait to get back. Perhaps it was his unease about the new vaccine, or maybe it was the constant sense that someone was watching him every time he was outside at the fort. Then again, maybe he was just looking forward to getting back to Yelena. No matter the cause, George was ready for the tour to be over so that he could get back to the city.

The pounding on his door woke him at Three A.M. He'd been asleep only for a couple of hours, and would have to be awake again in an hour in order to be at the hospital to complete his rounds before Six A.M. He was training two young students to act as medical technicians. There was no let-up in patient load, so he had to do all of the training in the early morning and late evening. George threw on a long coat in a nod to decency and to ward off the chill as he rushed to the door. His head was beginning to throb in time with the pounding at the door.

It was Yelena, and one of her older brothers. "*Jorge, mi Corazon*, it is my younger brother Rodrigo. He is badly injured and very sick. We need you to come quickly and help!" Yelena looked worried, while her brother— George struggled for the name, ah, Emilio—just looked impatient.

Pleased as he was to see Yelena at any time, George was not at his best, with only two hours sleep and no caffeine. "You can take him to the hospital. Doctor Espinoza is on call and can help him. I'm in no shape to help him right now."

Emilio grunted, and looked as if he was ready to pick George up and carry him out the door, but Yelena put up a hand to stop him. "No. No hospital, this is ... this is *muy importante* that you come."

George sighed. If it had been anyone but Yelena, he would have refused, but it was her brother—soon to be his brother-in-law—so he relented and told them to wait in the small living room of his apartment while he went back to the bedroom and dressed.

When he came back out, he went to the tiny kitchen to heat water. "I'll need some coffee, first. I'm sorry, but I am just not awake enough." He was surprised to find Yelena already at his side; she laid one hand on his arm to stop him from reaching for the kettle, while the other held up a ceramic mug already filled with steaming liquid. He took a sniff, then breathed deeply of the rich aroma, already beginning to wake up at the smell alone. *Ah, her grandmother's coffee.*

This thoughtfulness was one of the things he truly loved about her, not to mention that the Guerrero women were all excellent cooks!

Despite his continued protestations that Rodrigo should be seen at the hospital, George grabbed both his emergency bag and the military kit that he had yet to unpack from the recent tour of duty. Yelena and Emilio had brought an additional mount for George to ride, and they quickly traveled to the family home just outside the city. It was far enough that they could no longer see light from the taller buildings, but still close enough to smell the smoke left over from the previous night's cooking fires.

The family had decided to keep Rodrigo out of sight of the younger children, so he was lying on a table in the building Yelena's father and brothers used as a workshop. The room was filled with adult family members; the usual smell of sawdust and wood shaving tinged now with blood, sweat and human waste. The boy—at seventeen, a man by Balboan standards—did not live with the family, but spent most of his time in the back country. George had never been told what he did, and had never asked. It was a large family, after all, with parents, children, grandparents, and grandchildren living under one roof.

There was a blood-soaked bandage on Rodrigo's leg, but it was dark and dry. An old wound, and not necessarily an immediate problem. He was pale, though, sweating and shivering at the same time, with occasional muscle contractions that caused him to grimace, to flail his arms and legs, or even to curl his spine to the point where he lifted most of his body off of the table.

After a particularly severe contraction, Yelena let out a whimper and clutched at her mother, who'd been tending to Rodrigo before they arrived. The two began to speak in whispers. George couldn't quite follow the words, but he recognized the inquisitive tone and worry on the part of the older woman, but Yelena began to look very nervous. She saw his look, and forced a smile. "She asked what was wrong with him and wondered if we should call for the priest?"

George was silent for a moment as he examined his patient, then looked back at the women. "The fever and chills could be infection, but not the spasms. This looks like a toxin of some sort: his face is swollen, as well as his neck, fingers and toes. His skin is hot to the touch—that could be allergic reaction or infection, but it looks like..." He paused. *No, that doesn't make sense*. Every once in a while a parent would bring in a child that had eaten bolshiberries and suffered a reaction to the deadly plants. *This looks very similar... but an adult wouldn't eat bolshiberries.*

George jerked upright as he remembered the wounded soldier at Fort Cristóbal. *An adult wouldn't* eat *bolshiberries*!

He spoke decisively. "Okay, first things first, he needs an antihistamine to stop the swelling. I can't do much about the convulsions until I know what this is, but we need to cool him down. Get some cloths and soak in *cold* water from the well. Place them on his forehead and throat, then wrap his arms and legs." When they nodded, he continued, "I need to look at this wound."

Yelena turned to go, but her mother placed a hand on her arm. At a nod, two of her older sisters departed from the house, and a brother was sent to the well. Yelena seemed even more nervous, and her mother's restraining touch did not seem to be helping.

A suspicion began to form in the back of his mind, but George pushed the thought away as he unwrapped the bandage, cutting away the part where the dried blood had stiffened and stuck to the wound. He retrieved a bottle of sterile saline from his emergency bag to wash the blood and dirt away and reveal the wound. It wasn't bad, entry wound on the front of the thigh, exit wound on the back. It appeared to have been cleaned and bandaged soon after it happened, by someone who knew what they were doing. there was no sign of infection despite it obviously being days old, just a bit of redness around the wound itself. "How did this happen?"

Yelena's brother's looked at each other, but didn't speak until her father nodded.

"Hunting boar. It was an arrow." Emilio said.

"No, I don't think so." George's rebuke provoked an angry glare from the father and restless stirring from the others present. "This is a small caliber rifle wound, entered from the front, slightly bigger wound on the exit in back. An arrow doesn't do that. Besides, you hunt boar with large caliber rounds that would have left a gaping hole on exit!" George looked up at Emilio, then turned to glare at their father. "Care to tell me exactly what happened? You know I have to report this."

Yelena sobbed. "No!" and ran out of the shed.

George stared at Senor Guerrero until the older man finally looked down. "He is with the resistance."

*Hmm. 'Resistance,' not 'insurgency,'* thought George. "And just what was he resisting?"

"Agents from *Los Grillos* were attacking a farm." Guerrero spit on the pressed sawdust floor. "Men from 'Penal Interstellar Servitude' were hunting a fugitive slave. They are monsters. The child was not a slave; she was born free, here in Balboa. A child should not be held accountable for crimes of her parents, especially when they were political prisoners that Earth wanted to be rid of!"

George had heard of *Los Grillos*. Named for the Grillo Building in Ciudad Balboa that held many of the UNISBC offices, P.I.S. (or Pen .I.S. as it was called by the young men with muffled laughs and hidden grins) was notorious for using any excuse to prolong a transported prisoner's term of indenture. It was slavery in every sense, including inventing reasons for indenturing children of prisoners as well.

"So you say, but that doesn't change the fact that this was a small caliber wound, probably from a military rifle, not a boar hunting rifle or even *Los Grillos'* stun sticks. How do I know he was defending an innocent and isn't a terrorist shot by the military for plotting to bomb civilians?"

"Because he was with me." George turned as the new voice spoke. Yelena had returned leading a cloaked man who removed his hood as he spoke. "He was with me, Tonio. He was doing exactly as they said; he stopped one of *Los Grillos'* men from beating a child, fought back, and was shot by one of the *mercenarios* they bought from the UN. I dressed his wound; I brought him here when he fell ill. I told *Don* Guerrero that you could be trusted."

George stared, speechless, not even protesting at the use of a name he'd abandoned over fifteen years before. The cloaked man accompanying Yelena looked like... sounded like... "Julio?" he managed. "You're one of the t—"

"The word you want is *'resistencia,'* The Resistance, *tonto*," Julio corrected before George could finish the word. "We are not terrorists; the only terror we strike is to the heart of the UN. No civilian targets, only military." He gestured toward Rodrigo, "...and *Los Grillos*."

"*Tonto*, indeed. You must think I'm an idiot as you always have. First you set me up to be almost killed on Earth, now you hunt me down on Terra Nova, reveal my past and what, you set all of this up? Played me the fool with Yelena?"

At mention of her name, Yelena stepped forward and laid a hand on George's arm. "No, George, it was not like that."

He shook off her hand and continued. "You set me up. Are you planning to blackmail me so that I'll treat your terrorists?" He practically spat the word, but was rocked backward by the sudden slap from Yelena.

"No!" The shout and slap silenced George and he worked his jaw but remained silent while Yelena yelled at the rest of the men in the room in rapid-fire Spanish. Everyone except for Yelena and Julio left the room—and Rodrigo, who was lying on the table, occasionally shivering, but neither convulsing nor conscious.

"No. You *are tonto*. I love you, but you are *estupido*." Yelena faced him, eyes blazing. "People are being enslaved, their farms robbed or taken, girls raped, boys killed. Now people are getting sick. You see only a part of it because you are in the city. When you go to the towns, you work at the TNHO stations and you treat the *soldados*. People trust you to care for the *niños* or *bebés* but do not know if they can trust you not to report to the UN." She paused, briefly. "Rodrigo is not *terrorista*." She stopped and breathed heavily, anger evident in her body language as if she were preparing to strike him again.

Julio reached out an arm and placed it between the two. He pushed Yelena back slightly, and she relented, still glaring, but less angry. "Rodrigo is a good boy who was protecting a child that had committed the 'unpardonable sin' of being in the way of *Los Grillos*. Several of his friends had gotten sick, though, that was why they came to me. I have been helping to treat the outcasts and resistance fighters. After a few years of practice in Aztlan, the TNHO decided I wasn't worth their attention. I work in the city a few months per year, but mostly in the countryside. I can move around and I don't have the '*sombra*' that you have when you go out to the farms and forts."

George was confused. It wasn't just the head-rattling slap, or the shock of seeing his old roommate, or even the growing sense that he was missing many things that were happening around him. "Wait, you're saying I have a 'tail'? A shadow?"

"In the countryside, yes; in the city, no. When you were at Fort Cristóbal, there were *mercenarios* following you. Not UN Marines, these were 'security contractors'."

"Umm" George stalled while he formed his question. "You know this how? You were following me?"

"Following, no. Observing, *sí*. Several of Rodrigo's friends were getting sick. Influenza, they thought, but many of them ended up looking like he does now." Julio gestured at the boy. "They contacted me, and I met up with them. They also reported that Rodrigo's sister was seeing a *gringo* doctor, but they didn't know if they could trust him." He snorted. "*Mierda*, they barely trust me. So we followed you. There was supposed to be an attack on the Fort, but I was watching through a pair of binoculars I liberated from some UN *puta* who tried to bust up one of my clinics. I saw their *gringo* doctor and told them to call off the raid. Carvalho may have had his men rearrange your face, but they didn't change your eyes, *mi amigo*! With your light skin, pale eyes and horrible accent, it's no wonder they think you are *blanco*! "

George started to retort, but was interrupted by a word from Yelena. "Look."

Rodrigo had started to convulse again and George had to turn his attention to his patient. Yelena and Julio held the boy's arms and legs while he quickly completed his examination. A quick glance around showed that the shed served not only for woodworking, but also leatherwork to maintain tack for the farm animals. "Grab some of the straps; we need to restrain him to keep him from hurting himself. Get the others back in here with the cold water and bandages!" He selected a wide, clean piece of leather and placed it between Rodrigo's teeth to give him something to bite on.

The convulsions were confusing. Julio had mentioned men in the Resistance getting sick with influenza, then showing more severe reactions. When they'd arrived, Rodrigo had presented the appearance of an allergic reaction, much as someone who ingested one of the toxic indigenous plants. Now, however, he had convulsions consistent with a high fever, yet was still cold and clammy to the touch. *The convulsions must be from a different toxin—but what?* He watched as the muscle twitches proceeded from arms and legs to the neck and face. Tendons stood out on the boy's neck, his jaw clenched and the mouth was drawn into a grimace resembling pursed lips. His breathing became heavy, then rasping, with a hacking or 'quacking' sound as it passed through the constricted larynx.

"What?" George stood up and looked over at Julio. "Duck fever?" The memories that had so recently been painfully resurrected by his old friend's presence came flooding back.

"*Si, mi amigo.*" Julio nodded sadly. "You were always the best of us at infectious diseases. That is why I asked for you."

George reached for his emergency bag, then, as an afterthought, reached for the military kit. He'd try to avoid using the blood analyzer if he could; the DNA sequencer and biometric scanner almost certainly recorded all data and reported it to TNHO. He'd have to hope that the diagnostic scanner would be general enough to protect the identity of the patient. He took a blood sample anyway, just filled the tube and handed it to Yelena. "Put this someplace cool until I leave—perhaps one of the cloths soaked in well water. I will take it to the hospital and analyze it there." He pressed the diagnostic device to the side of Rodrigo's neck and waited.

*'Influenza A, H9N6/avian/Hong Kong/77'* was the result a few moments later. The diagnostic display continued with: 'Gamma serotype, K-peptide conjugate, variant LSCIII2112.' While the diagnosis and treatment display read: 'K-fever. Administer vaccine LC12-TN.' That was the new vaccine alright.

Julio looked over at the readout and grunted. "You have a vaccine. How convenient." His voice was dripping with sarcasm. "How nice of the UN to have a vaccine ready for a disease they created."

"You think this is deliberate?"

"Duck Fever was always a joke we played on the First Years and *pendejos* like Carvalho. Somehow, they've made it real and they're using it against the Resistance. "

"In that case..." He looked back at the scanner. He stared for a moment in confusion, then another of disbelief as recognition dawned on him. "Oh hell. I know who did this." He turned the device so that Julio could read the display. "Look there. 'ell-ess-cee-eye-eye-eye' Lucas S. Carvalho the Third. His name is all over it."

Yelena broke in. "You can give him the vaccine, then. You can cure my brother?" She looked hopeful until she looked in the eyes of the two doctors.

George shook his head. "I'm not sure it will work with symptoms this advanced. I can give him something for the convulsions and swelling, but he needs to be in a hospital."

"No." Both Julio and Yelena spoke at the same time. Julio continued, "If this is deliberate, and I agree that it sure fit's Carvalho's methods, then they've done it to flush the Resistance out. You have reporting instructions on the vaccine, don't you?"

"Yes." He turned to Yelena. "That is the *real* other reason I can't give him the vaccine. I have to report biometrics and DNA, then await an unlock code for the injector." He shook his head and turned back to his old roommate. "Very high tech—Earth tech, not Hamilton—that's just more evidence for your suspicion that this is all a UN plan."

The other family members had returned, so George conveyed instructions for treating the boy. He would need to stay unconscious to survive the night—well, morning. There was a local plant, similar to a very popular drug on Earth. Like that drug, it was often smoked for euphoric effects, but properly prepared it would keep Rodrigo sedated and reduce the convulsions. After providing the care instructions, he retrieved the vial of blood and returned to his lodging to prepare for the day's work.

YELENA HAD STAYED WITH her brother. It had been a stressful encounter, and George hoped that their relationship would be able to survive it. Julio did not dare to be seen at the hospital or in George's company, so he, too, had left, with only the promise to be in touch. Fortified with *abuela* Guerrero's coffee and a mid-morning nap in an unused exam room, George finished his patient rounds and went to the small laboratory to work with the blood sample he'd taken from Rodrigo.

He'd just gotten started when one of the nurses entered to call him back to the Emergency clinic. A child had come in with convulsions and muscle spasms leading to contracture of the spine, neck and face muscles. He'd already treated three suspected influenza cases this morning. Fortunately, there was a vaccine that covered H9N6 freely available, but if this was K-fever, he would have to decide whether to report the case and give the vaccine, or withhold a potentially life-saving treatment to protect the patient's identity.

Fortunately, George did not have to choose. The patient was the eleven-year-old son of one of the other nurses and unlikely to be a threat. Under the supposition that all medical personnel would need to be protected, he took the biometric and DNA samples and waited for authorization. Within the hour, he'd also received instructions to vaccinate not only the child, but all personnel in the clinic, including himself. That was ominous. If the TNHO felt that all medical workers were at risk, then that meant K-fever was in the wild and spreading, not just targeting insurgents. Could the disease have been spread *specifically* to draw in the insurgents? To force them to come for the vaccine, only to be identified and hauled off by *Guardia* or UN Marines?

After administering the vaccines, George returned to the laboratory. He dared not use the portable DNA sequencer or blood analyzer. They were very likely to be monitored by satellite interface or by one of the UN Space Fleet ships in orbit. He'd have to use the frequently-broken sequencer in the lab. Fortunately, it was very similar to one he used and often fixed as an undergraduate student in Panama. As long as he removed a side panel and kept it cool, it would work—eventually. After rigging a fan to blow air through a damp towel—both for evaporative cooling and to trap dust and dirt—he set the sequencer to its task and went home for the day.

Well, he almost went home, but decided to go out to the Guerrero farm to check on Yelena and Rodrigo. The boy was no better, but apparently his relationship with Yelena was. She greeted him warmly, in fact, rather hotly. She later mentioned that the very fact he returned to her—and Rodrigo—on his own, told her everything she needed to know about that man who was to be her husband.

After checking on his patient, and confirming instructions with the family members caring for him, George sat down with Yelena's father Enrique Guerrero, after asking, and receiving, the Patriarch's blessing, they discussed Rodrigo's prognosis. Yes, the family understood that there was not much that anyone could do for him. No, they did not blame him. Life was hard in Balboa. They would mourn him, but life went on.

Determined to ensure that this life went on without drawing attention or suspicion from the unseen forces behind the spread of K-fever, George said his goodbyes. This time he was accompanied by Yelena, who would not let him return to the lab, but rather insisted that he be properly fed and rested for the next day. Mostly rested. It wasn't as if he was expecting results from the sequencer before morning, anyway.

The next morning he approached hospital rounds with more energy than he'd felt for the past few years. *Is it the challenge? Or the fact that* Don *Guerrero gave his blessing and Yelena said 'yes?'* Nevertheless, he had clinical duties to complete before returning to the lab... or Yelena. Upon entering the small cluster of exam rooms that comprised the clinic, he was surprised to see a new nurse, freshly assigned by TNHO. He was immediately suspicious, particularly by her fair hair and complexion—clearly Scandinavian or other Caucasian derivation from Earth—although she covered it with a bit too much makeup. She looked familiar, though. For the rest of the day he tried to avoid her, suspecting her to be a UN or TNHO spy.

After his last patient, he sat at the desk he'd installed in a former closet at the back of one of the exam rooms. It was tiny, but it was an office where he could update records and store his years-out-of-date medical textbooks. A knock on the door surprised him. It was the new nurse, and she'd obviously just washed her face in one of the exam rooms—the excessive makeup was gone, and she held a wet cloth in one hand. "A mutual friend told me to tell you it's 'Duck Season'," she said once she had entered and the door was closed.

*As he peered at her* it hit him why she'd looked familiar. The makeup had to have been a disguise, because she'd hardly changed in fifteen years. "Annalise." George greeted the girl—woman—who had been Julio's constant companion their final year at Duke. He looked at her some more. No, she'd changed, just not in the face. Still a dancer's physique, but a bit older, and quite a bit tougher. It showed in her body language.

"You look like hell, Doc, but I hear you're getting better." She smiled as she said it. The office was small, but it had a guest chair, and she sat in it. "I told Yelena to keep an eye on you and make sure you were rested last night."

"What, is everyone conspiring against me?" He paused. "Wait, how did you get here?" After a moment he hurriedly added "... not that I'm complaining."

"My family was never very compliant with the European Union. They were being punished because I moved to the United States for work and school, and of course they didn't approve of the work I did to put myself through school." She smiled, but it was sad and regretful. "Loss of their Basic Living Allowance unless they emigrated to Terra Nova. They came, so I came. Of course, I have a necessary skill set and was allowed to come voluntarily and choose my posting. It was about two years after Julio emigrated. I looked him up, he was a young idealistic doctor in Aztlan, but that was beginning to change."

"I managed to get my parents settled in Southern Columbia and married Julio, trying to keep him out of trouble since then. Well, actually, I've helped him get *into* trouble, too, but I've also managed to keep him out of the UN's notice."

George sat looking at the woman before him, remembering the nurse who was not quite the airhead that many of Julio's medical school crushes had been. She also had a Master's degree, if he remembered correctly.

"Yes, I do. Molecular Biology," she replied when he asked. The light finally dawned on George.

"Aha! So he sent you to spy on me?" he asked, half in jest.

"Not spy, no..." she smiled, this one friendly and reassuring. "... but he knew you would need help. I can be your contact and your assistant, both in the lab and clinic."

"In that case, we should get to work." George smiled back then stood, gesturing her to lead the way out of the cramped office and into the lab.

THE DNA SEQUENCER HAD completed its analysis. The output was still a bunch of numbers until compared to the nucleotide and peptide databases. The nucleotides would be used to determine the sequence of amino acids comprising specific protein products, and the proteins *should* identify the virus and any toxins present.

Since George was primarily interested in anything that looked like a virus, he assigned Annalise any sequences identified as normal human protein. She would check everything against known genetic diseases and medical disorders, while he looked for sequences that should not be there...

...and found it after almost seven hours of intensive scrutiny. He'd sent Annalise home at least an hour ago. It was already dark, but she'd promised to check with Yelena and send back supper if she could. George had identified the genes for H9N6 almost immediately. He'd then looked for the sequences defining the glycoprotein 'coat' that formed the exterior shell, but kept coming up against gaps in the sequence that didn't make sense until he recognized that the nucleotides that were being identified were not terrestrial DNA!

He considered the implications. Deoxyribonucleic acid was a complex molecule made up of a long-chain of alternating sugar molecules—deoxyribose—and molecules known as nucleotides or 'bases.' DNA had four known nucleotides: Guanine, Thymine, Cytosine and Adenosine, which were typically identified by initials: G, T, C, A. The amino acid building blocks of proteins were encoded by sets of three bases, allowing sixty-four possible three base codes, such as A-T-G, G-A-C, C-T-A, etc. There were only twenty known amino acids, though, and George, along with many leading scientists, wondered what the other codes were for. In the early Twenty-first century, scientists synthesized novel nucleotides 'X' and 'Y' and even managed to create single-celled organisms that could replicate DNA with the new components, but no novel naturally occurring amino acids or nucleotides were encountered until Terra Nova was discovered.

Despite decades of humans on Terra Nova, the genetics and protein structure of Novan life was still largely unexplained. Scientists had identified four additional nucleotides—unimaginatively named simply 'M,' "N,' 'O,' and 'P.' The additional bases allowed for up to 512 amino acids, and millions of novel proteins, yet only seven new amino acids had been identified, with about a hundred novel proteins. At least, that was all that was in the medical literature that George could access. Most of the unique proteins encountered on Terra Nova caused allergic reactions in humans, and some Earth life forms. Others seemed simply *inert* or useless except for the fact that they accumulated in the nervous systems of intelligent creatures and acted much like prions or the sludge-like amyloid protein responsible for brain diseases that had been eliminated over a century ago on Earth. Like those ancient diseases, accumulation of too much inert protein in humans ended in encephalitis, dementia and death.

The sequencer had identified the usual G, T, C, and A nucleotides, plus unusually high quantities of the U, uracil, nucleotide normally only found in RNA, plus trace amounts of M, N, O and P. The latter was not unexpected on Terra Nova, and presented no problem by itself. The danger lay in the proteins, not the DNA alone, which could easily be present on the skin. What was most unusual was that the sequencer had also identified two additional nucleotides: 'R' and 'Q' that George had never seen before. Even stranger was the fact that the nucleotide identities were in the sequencer database, even though the machine had to be at least twenty years old.

*These nucleotides had to have been known on Earth when I was in medical school,* thought George. On a hunch, he had the sequencer print out its nucleotide reference database; there might be a clue there. He also retreated briefly to his office to fetch a couple of his old textbooks. On the other hand, it would have to wait. He heard Yelena coming, and she was certain to make him stop for the evening, or at least pause for supper.

Yelena had indeed brought food, and news of her brother. He was no longer unconscious or convulsing, but was still in a lot of pain. It was still touch-and-go, and George was torn between getting immediately back to the lab versus heading out to the Guerrero farm to see his patient. She would not allow him to do either, however, claiming that he would not help her brother by being too tired to think straight. She made him lie down in an exam room and watched over him as he got at least two hours sleep.

Upon waking, George sent Yelena back the farm with some special instructions. He wouldn't need what he'd sent her for until tomorrow, but sending her back now would gain him several hours without her or Annalise nagging him to rest and keeping him from the lab. Now, he needed to read through the sequencer database...

SHORTLY AFTER SUN-UP, GEORGE was running around the lab, talking to himself as he started to pull glassware out of cabinets and rummaged through the drawers in the lab looking for components. "It's a virus..." He took a long glass cylinder and clamped it to a stand. "Of course, we knew it was a virus..." He rotated the cylinder so that it stood upright and fitted a valve to the bottom so that it could be directed to drip into a row of test tubes in a rack below.

"...but it's flu, not entirely... not entirely H9N6, that is..." He reached into a drawer and pulled out a packet of white crystalline powder. "There's an additional DNA strand in the viral shell..." He dug around for a funnel, placed it in the top of the cylinder, and started to pour the crystals into the cylinder. "...it codes a novel protein using synthetic nucleotides." Once the cylinder was nearly full, he tapped the sides of the cylinder to settle the powder.

Annalise walked in to find George frantically racing around the small lab opening drawers and cabinets and muttering hoarsely to himself. "Glass rod... glass rod... need a glass rod to tamp it all down." He was gasping for breath between words, there was a sheen of sweat on his face, and his eyes were wide and manic.

"DOCTOR!" She shouted, and it brought him up short. He turned and stared, not recognizing her for a moment. Of course she was back to wearing heavy makeup to disguise her face, but it shouldn't have taken quite so long for recognition to dawn on him. "George, sit!" She pulled a lab stool over, grabbed him by the upper arm and pulled him to the chair.

He sat for several minutes, breathing heavily, and slowly the frenzied expression faded. He eyes were still alight with discovery, though.

"You've found something, haven't you." It was a statement, not a question.

He nodded. She'd pressed a glass of water in his hands. Not coffee—the last thing he needed was coffee. He drank deeply, swallowed, then sat quietly a bit more before calmly answering. "It's the nucleotides. Native Terra Nova life has additional DNA nucleotides."

"Right. That's the first thing we have to learn before getting licensed on Nova." She raised an eyebrow at him as he tried to rise from the chair. "Sit. Go on."

He took another drink and then continued. "We learned that in the Earth has known about the Terra Nova nucleotides for decades and synthesized their own variants. They even named them in sequence with the Novan bases." He motioned to the separator column on the lab bench. "Have you seen the glass rods? I need to tamp that down before I run the separation?"

Glaring at him to keep him seated, Annalise opened a drawer and pulled out a glass rod no bigger than a pencil. She lit an alcohol burner, flame sterilized it the glass rod, then used it to compress the white powder in the column. When George tried to rise again, she waved him back. "Stay seated, you're in no shape to load a column, you'll pour too fast and stir up the surface of the gel." Although manic, he'd maintained standard lab and clinical safety rules, so everything was clearly—well, within limits of his handwriting—labeled. She picked up a beaker covered with wax paper, looked at him with raised eyebrow, and he nodded.

While Annalise she carefully added the clear liquid to the column of white powder, George continued. "Terra Novan life has M, N, O and P nucleotides. Earth synthesized Q and R... and they immediately found some unusual proteins."

Annalise tapped the side of the cylinder, dislodging bubbles. She poured more liquid in top while gradually letting some out through the valve at the bottom, never allowing the level at the top to go below the top of the crystals. When she straightened up and looked back at George, she could see the signs of fatigue warring with the realization of discovery.

"So, that's what we're separating? One of those proteins?" She looked him up and down, then smiled sweetly. He knew that look. Yelena had one just like it. "And just how much coffee have you had this morning? Or should I ask how much since last night? Yelena said she was going to make you sleep where is she? Should I call he?"

He shook his head. "No, this can't wait. We need to do this for Rodrigo and we can't wait."

"I *know* that!" She responded hotly. "But I can do this for you! You have to see patients, and you're in no condition to do that right now. I should call for Yelena."

"No, no need." He shook off the hand she used to restrain him as he tried to stand. He went over to the tabletop centrifuge, removed the cover and took out a tube with a dark red solid on the bottom and amber liquid above. "Doctor Espinoza is in the clinic today, and he has the students helping him. I sent Yelena out to the farm. Told her to have the younger kids catch me four rabbits and a dozen frogs."

He went to place the tube from the centrifuge into the rack with the other tubes, but fumbled, and almost dropped the tube on the floor. Annalise gently took it from his hands, and not-so-gently pushed him back toward the chair. "I will do this. I am your hands, you're too jittery. You will drop it or break it. Now, what next?"

George conceded and dropped back onto the chair. "Electrophoresis. We use the electrical charge on the protein to separate it by size and weight. I found a control sample of green fluorescent protein close to the right size of the protein we're looking for. It will come out the bottom of the column right before the protein we're after. Then we drip some of it on frog's leg muscle to see if it causes convulsions."

"Wait. If we're doing electrophoresis, what's the separation column for?" She pointed to the powder and liquid filled glassware on the bench.

"Oh, I forgot!" George started to rise yet again, but stopped himself before Annalise would react. "Sorry. That's for after. Separate electrically, test on frog muscle, and if it works, we'll need the column."

"Okay. That's better. One thing at a time." Annalise found the components he'd prepared, then opened a packet containing a sterile pipette and carefully drew some of the amber liquid and placed it on the electrophoresis assembly. She opened another pipette and extracted some greenish liquid from a bottle and also placed it on the gel. She connected a battery, then set a timer and closed the drawer so that the room lights could not affect the process. "This is prehistoric medicine," she said as she pulled out some black fabric to drape over the separation column until they needed it.

"Mid-twentieth century," George replied. "But effective. If the extract causes the frog muscle to twitch, we'll inject it into rabbits to see if we can make an antibody. I also have some ideas about using P nucleotide from *antaniae* saliva to make an antitoxin."

There was the sound of the outside door, and a female voice called from the clinic. Yelena had returned with the frogs and rabbits. Annalise went to greet her, and George could hear the sounds of them talking. Probably deciding whether he needed to be forcibly restrained in order to force him to rest. He smiled at the thought—it meant they cared, and he couldn't argue with that. He sat back and closed his eyes. "For now, we wait."

It had been almost two weeks, but Rodrigo was still hanging on. He was pale and thin. The family forced him to drink rich broths when he was awake to maintain both nutrients and fluids. He spent most of his time unconscious, though, sedated by herbal extracts. George was concerned about the long-term effects of the drug, but the boy would have to survive for them to worry about that. It was doubtful that the antibody would work quickly enough to help, so, with the family's permission, he was about to try the antitoxin.

The boy's arms were so thin; George was unable to get the needle into a vein to deliver the injection. Julio had returned, and was about to try when Annalise pushed them both out of the way, manipulated the needle for just a moment, drew back the plunger to reveal a small amount of dark red blood, then deftly injected the antitoxin. She looked up and glared briefly at both men, then smiled sweetly.

"That's why I married her," Julio said. Annalise just snorted.

Rodrigo had been sleeping, mouth open, breathing heavily through his constricted larynx. The harsh snoring—so like the sound of a hunter's duck call—cut off. His body started to convulse and both doctors immediately reached to restrain the heaving body. Yelena gasped and started to cry, but after a moment, the convulsions eased and his breathing resumed with a gasp.

The snoring faded, and George could see the muscles in the face relax. He reached his hand to feel Rodrigo's throat. It too appeared to be relaxing.

This might just work.

The four watched Rodrigo for another hour before turning over the watch to Emilio and retreating to the farmhouse. It was late night, and Julio had men making sure that there had been no unwanted 'guests' following any of them. George had been out to the farm many evenings, and it was now common knowledge that he was engaged to Yelena. No one from the UN or TNHO seemed to care too much about Balboa, given the reports that many insurgents were being caught elsewhere, having been discovered when UN and TNHO 'humanitarian missions' were vaccinating locals against a virulent new strain of influenza.

"So we have a cure and a vaccine that the UN can't trace. Tell me, *Tonio*, operationally speaking, what's to keep them—to keep *Carvalho*—from doing this again?" Julio asked George while they sat in the kitchen drinking coffee with a healthy serving of *Don* Guerrero's whiskey.

"We know the gene sequence. We know what we're looking for. It will take them time to synthesize a novel nucleotide, and even then, they mostly don't work. R and Q only work because they just copied Novan nucleotides." There were dark circles under George's eyes, but with Yelena snuggled up under his arm, he looked at peace. "Besides, right now, I know more about Novan genetics and immunology than anyone on Earth."

"No, that's a technical answer," Julio corrected patiently. "I asked you an *operational* question. What is to *keep* them from doing this again?"

"Oh." George thought a moment. "Well, I *am* the person most knowledgeable about Novan genetics and how it interacts with human immune system. I suppose we could send them a message. 'Try this again, and we release a counter virus on Earth.' It could be a targeted direct-contact virus with secondary spread to anyone on Earth that's had contact with the Novan nucleotides. That would limit collateral spread to just Carvalho and the lab that made K-fever."

"Now *that* is an operational answer!"

George smiled as he wiped disinfectant on Julio's arm and gave him the second injection. "You're lucky you get to go back after only fifteen years."

Julio grinned back, "You should have read the fine print in the contract, *Jorge*. Standard loan repayment is ten years or fifteen including residency. Sabbaticals and fellowships kick after seven years. You got taken *amigo*..." He stopped as he saw the smile disappear from his friend's face. "I'm sorry, George, it wasn't supposed to happen that way."

"It's the past, Julio. I'm alive, and not in an unmarked grave in Durham or Chorillo. Besides, it wasn't your fault or mine; it was the fault of the WHO officials who promoted the bastard." George smiled again, "Besides, I met Yelena here. Her father said 'yes,' so we're getting married in the spring. I'd ask you to be Best Man, but well, you've got to go."

"Yes, *amigo*, I do ... or well, that's supposed to be your line." Julio's grin was back as he pulled down his shirt sleeve and reached over to pull back the sleeve on the opposite arm.

"Nope, this one goes in the buttocks, drop 'em." George held up the third syringe as Julio winced, then complied. "Okay, that's vaccines for H9N6-gamma and K-fever, as well as the Payload." George put the empty syringe in a heavy red box and closed the lid. A light on the cover turned red and then blinked yellow, followed by a momentary flash of bright light around the edges of the lid, before turning green. "Okay, we're clean. Now, what are you going to do once you get to Earth?"

"The fellowship is with Pegram's old department. The *hombre gruñón* was forced out by WHO many years ago, but there will be people who remember what happened. They can extract the Payload from my blood and prepare the serum. The WHO annual inspection won't be for another four to six months after I arrive." Julio stood up and buckled his belt.

"...and if Lord Lucas accompanies the inspection?"

"We have word that he's usually there at some point during the inspection. The new Dean is his biggest fan, and Carvalho loves the adoration. We'll be ready. If I can't deliver the payload in person—or even if he doesn't come, we can get to someone in his office." Julio winced as he worked his arm. "*Maldito*, that stings."

"These sources of yours, you trust them?" George looked doubtful.

"We have a few friends in the new 'United Nations Peace Force' that is replacing the UN Space Fleet and at least one at WHO—but no, I don't trust them. That's why they all think the 'message' to Carvalho is a *computer* virus!"

"Hah," George responded mirthlessly as he disposed of the remaining syringes in the 'sharps' receptacle and placed the used gauze and alcohol wipes in the 'cycler. "You'll need a source of either natural P or synthetic Q nucleotide to activate the payload. I don't think you'll find very much *antaniae* saliva on Earth."

"*Si, Madre.* I know, I know. The Genetics department should have it, or Biomedical Engineering. They were working on it during my previous sabbatical, and my sources tell me that they can get actual venom if I need it... just so long as I don't carry it myself." Julio reached out to clasp his friends shoulder. "You know, *amigo*, you should have stayed in Infectious Diseases. You're very good at it."

George looked away. “I’m needed here.”

Julio released his shoulder when George wouldn’t look at him. “I know,” he spoke quietly. “We could have lost a lot of good men. Besides, I need you to keep an eye on Annalise for me. This is probably a one-way trip.” When George looked up, there were tears in his eyes. Julio continued, “I know, my friend. It shouldn’t be this way. We took an oath: ‘First, do no harm’.”

George’s expression hardened. “Yes, but they broke it first—a long time ago.” He put his hand to his face, remembering the contours of the face he’d been born with, and smiled a cold, bitter smile. “Sometimes, you have to be a surgeon and cut out the cancer before it spreads.”

# Two

# ECHOES OF A BEATING HEART

**Authors note: Much like** the anthologies *Stellaris: People of the Stars* and *The Founder Effect*, this story and the anthology in which it appeared *The Ross 248 Project*, were inspired by conversations at symposia of Tennessee Valley Interstellar Workshop—now known as the Interstellar Research Group (IRG) symposia. Les Johnson and Ken Roy proposed a shared-world anthology centered on a colony mission to a distant star with a supposedly Earth-like world—rich in resources and habitable for a truly spacefaring society.

But when the colonists arrive, they discover a catch.

Humans are allergic to Eden's flora and fauna. Even worse, the planet's flora and fauna are even more allergic to humans. The world is placed off-limits, except for a few scientific outposts. Sentiment among the colonists is divided—some believe Eden should be left strictly alone, others believe it should be forcibly terraformed to accommodate Earth life.

**Overlaying this backdrop is a fascinating concept: sentient AIs, formed initially as a core set of routines by an "AI mother," are raised as juvenile intelligences by human foster parents. When they mature, they choose their name, profession, and purpose in life.**

**Davy is one such juvenile AI, living with his scientist foster parents in one of Eden's sealed domes. His unique ability to exist outside—unaffected by the allergies that plague humans and native life alike—allows him to hear the echo of the beating heart of Eden's past.**

"DAVEY, YOU NEED TO come inside, now."

The boy looked up from his digging in the "garden" outside the primary habitat dome. His maternal guardian's face was on the tablet he'd placed on a stand beside the piece of the garden where he worked. He'd read stories and seen vidtainment of mothers standing on a porch calling their kids in from play. Davey knew she would have done that too–after all, she was a traditionalist–but it would have been a lot of trouble for her. A comm call over his tablet sufficed.

As a full-bodied "normal" human, she typically only ventured outside the dome using biocontainment precautions. It wasn't much, mostly just a rebreather and full-face mask to ensure she didn't breathe pollen or spores, but the decontamination afterward was a lengthy process. For Davey, it was just a quick rinse and spray to ensure that nothing stuck to his synthetic body.

He was a sentient–albeit adolescent–"artificial" intelligence. It was something of a misnomer. While his body was artificial, or more appropriately–synthetic–to facilitate growing up in a human family, there was nothing truly artificial about his intelligence. His AI mother, Juno, created him out of her own substance. His personality core was then installed in a juvenile body, and he went to live with flesh-and-blood intelligences–in other words, a human family.

The principle had been established many centuries ago, by the AI scientist Ellay McCaffrey, that electronic intelligences developed best–at least as far as being colleagues and co-equals with organic intelligences–when they were imprinted on and were raised alongside humans. The process instilled goals, instincts and character traits, things that could not be easily programmed. Moreover, it allowed the sentient AIs to develop unique personalities, broadening the diversity of intelligent life–whether electronic or organic.

His human guardians, Molly and Hans, were "Mom" and "Dad" as far as he was concerned. Juno was "Momma" and he talked with her every week, but he was being raised by Mom and Dad. He felt like a regular kid and was treated like one...and sometimes that was a bit...restricting.

DAVEY LIKED WORKING IN the garden; after all, it got him outside and on his own for a brief period of the day. It wasn't always that way though. He had his studies, and it was easy to learn when your brain was basically a sophisticated computer, but there was more to it than that. Scientists had long known that human brains learned by doing, as much as by absorbing knowledge. Synthetic intelligences were no different. A portion of Davey's day was taken up by schoolwork–knowledge transfer paced to allow him to *use* the information and form the associational networks so essential to sentience. He also assisted Molly and Hans around their residence. His AI mother, Juno, was up in *Copernicus* and didn't come down to planetary surfaces. She watched him, though, and comm'd him once a week. They ignored the forty-to-ninety second communications lag. Most AIs could do that even if a human couldn't, since they multi-tasked most conversations, anyway. That's one reason why the purely human trait of talking on the comm had been adopted by the sentient AIs; it reinforced their ability to function in mixed AI and human society. It also reminded them that although they *could* communicate faster, that was not always the best practice.

For that matter, the weekly comm call between Juno and Davey was not strictly necessary; AI mothers maintained a link with their offspring until maturity, when they would disconnect from their life-giver and join the Sentient AI Network. The problem with getting information only from the link was much the same as using only digital, high-speed communication between AIs–it didn't give a sense of personality or social development. That turned out to be important during one call several years ago.

"MOMMA, I'M BORED." IN human developmental terms, Davey had just become a teenager. AIs bypassed the infant and toddler stages and were placed in their synthetic bodies at an age equivalent to a five-year-old. From there they matured only slightly faster than biological intelligences. Davey had been developing for six years, but in terms of intellectual maturity, he was between 13 and 14 years of age. Emotionally, however, he was still very much a pre-teenager.

"You have friends. You have classmates. How can you be bored?" Juno asked her son. She had a continuous link with him until he was fully mature, but that was more of a diagnostic link. Through it, she was aware that Davey had a lot of idle time and wasn't necessarily spending it constructively. It concerned her because sentient AIs needed a purpose–a life's goal and reason to continue to exist. A bored adolescent AI could lead to much trouble.

"But they're all online," he whined. "Kelly is on *Copernicus*, Bruce is in the primate quarter, and Tanaka won't even tell us where he is. His parents work for the Patrol and can't really say what they're doing."

"But surely you can get together in the virtual rooms? The Sentient AI Network programmed those with predictive and adaptive interactions to compensate for communications lag. They're just the same as the virtual conferences SAIN uses all the time. You can play games, watch vidtainment, and study together."

"Oh, we can do that, but Dungeons & Dragons isn't that much fun now that Tanaka is pushing to upgrade to the 21st edition. Most of us are still using 18th edition rules, but he wants to add all of this stuff about quantum probabilistic determinism and it's just not fun anymore."

"Have you ever considered that it might be because he's preparing to take the Patrol entrance exam? He's trying for the Class of 88. The entrance examinations are in 803 hours."

"Yeah, I guess so, but he's become so boring. He's also gotten kind of pushy and bossy. Kelly, Bruce, and I don't really want to play with him anymore."

"I know you have other friends."

"Of course, I do, Momma. The problem is that none of them are *here*. I want to hang out. I want to be able to go do something even if it's just...I don't know...just playing in the dirt! There's no one here at Galapagos station my age and even if they were, they wouldn't be allowed outside."

"I understand Davey; this is one of those things you are going to have to learn. What you need is a hobby. I do have an idea for you. You said even 'just playing in the dirt.' Why don't you do that? Your mom Molly is a biochemist and Hans is an anthropologist. Certainly, between the two of them, you can come up with enough tools to do a little digging. Think of it as an archaeology dig or even a garden. You tested quite high on biology and you're coming along nicely in genetics, so an experimental garden would suit you."

"Well, I suppose I could do that. I'm not sure it sounds like fun though. I want to do something fun and interesting."

"I don't know about fun, but I think I have a way to make it interesting. There was a researcher studying Eden many years ago; 7-of-Persephone spent thousands of hours studying Eden's biosphere. Charles, as he prefers to be called, is an accomplished geneticist, and an interesting person. I will put you in touch with him. He is currently out with Pusher 2 looking for a nice metal asteroid. Comm or message him, he will probably be up for either. He was also a pretty good chess player–you like chess, right?"

"Yeah, I like chess. I got too good at it though, and now no-one wants to play with me."

"You've got the core architecture to be very good at chess; most humans can't beat you. If you're polite and respectful, I'm sure Charles will give you a game. He was one of the best of us. It's a shame he stopped his research on Eden. He found a different purpose, though, and now studies asteroids."

"Yeah, thanks, Momma. I'll look into the garden-thing and talk to Charles. Maybe even just having someone to play chess with will help."

"Okay young man, behave, and don't give your mom and dad too much trouble. I'll talk with you next week."

"Okay, I promise. I'll talk to you next week, Momma."

Juno sent her son the contact information for Charles, while also sending a message to the AI himself, whom she knew from their trip out from Pluto. New AIs weren't created from nothing, but rather from an AI Mother's own personality core, along with select skills, experiences, and interests "borrowed" from other AIs of her acquaintance. She'd asked Charles for his medical and chess core architectures and incorporated them into several of her offspring–most especially Davey.

Charles certainly ought to be interested if Davey decided to look at his research. It had been many years, and Juno knew that many in SAIN were disappointed when he set the research aside; however, she knew that Charles risked losing his *purpose* if he continued to run into resistance to his findings.

When the first ships of the Ross 248 Project arrived in-system, they weren't too concerned with the near-Earth-sized worlds. Ceres' *Chariot* entered orbit around the moon of the seventh world, Ross 248h, later to be known as Alexa's World. It was the only planet to have a moon, which would come to be known as Liber. At 0.08

gravities, it was also the only world that colonists from Sol's asteroid belt could inhabit.

The second ship, the Space Patrol's *Guardian E*, paid closer attention to the fifth planet, Ross 248e. The planet was named Eden, since it was the only world in Ross 248 with an oxygen atmosphere, large oceans, numerous small continents, and a living biosphere. It was a living world with an atmosphere a bit colder and thinner than Earth–less $CO_2$, but more $O_2$. It had vibrant blue-green foliage to subsist on Ross' red light. There were also animals, both large and small, some reminiscent of the dinosaurs of Earth's Mesozoic era, crossed with the large mammals of the following Cenozoic era. The first human explorers on the surface of Eden found it necessary to defend themselves against some of the more aggressive species. An entire Patrol platoon had been wiped out by an ambush predator, the likes of which had never existed on Earth.

This was doubly unfortunate for the Eden native life, since not only were those explorers armed members of the Patrol, but any animal that succeeded in eating any Earth-life died horribly from biological incompatibility. It seemed to be one-sided though. Eden's flora and fauna were not nutritious to humans, but there were no ill effects...at first. Within a few months, all Patrol personnel on Eden were showing signs of "failure to thrive" no matter how much (or how little) Eden foodstuffs they consumed. They then realized that incidental exposure to airborne pollen and dust containing Eden-microorganisms started to cause severe allergic reactions. By that point, scientists knew that Eden biology had DNA bases and amino acids that were closer to Earth's but different enough to interfere with normal metabolism. Eden-life, all the way down to bacteria and viruses, was simply incompatible with Earth-life. The only hope for humans to live unprotected on Eden was to sterilize the planet and start over by terraforming it with Earth lifeforms.

With the arrival of the third ship from Sol, *Copernicus*, carrying colonists from Earth and the near-Earth space habitats, a heated debate arose between those who wanted to sterilize Eden of all native lifeforms and reseed with Earth-life, and those who believed Eden lifeforms should be protected. The planet was cooler than Earth's average, and the light of Ross was reddish and dim, but Earth-life could still grow there. In fact, all that was necessary was to plant seeds or transplant flora into Eden's soil; it wasn't necessary to remove the native lifeforms. Earth-life took over and the Eden lifeforms simply died, creating a blighted region several meters wide between the Earth and Eden lifeforms. Nothing could live in the middle of the blighted zone–neither Earth nor Eden-life, including plants, insects, worms, or borrowing creatures. However, Earth plants would spread outward if they were immediately adjacent to other Earth-life. The Eden lifeforms simply died.

This information had been used in the arguments in favor of erasing Eden's native life. If just the presence of Earth plants would do that then it would be easy to find a toxin that would wipe out everything not of Earth, leaving a fertile planet in which Earth flora would spread rapidly, making it livable for humans in just a few years. Even the decomposition of native flora would speed the terraforming since it would improve the carbon-content of Eden's atmosphere. Decomposition would raise the low $CO_2$ levels and warm the atmosphere without really affecting $O_2$ levels.

It was considered a win-win situation.

More than eighty years ago, the Ross 248 Project leadership settled the Eden Question. The AI scientist 7-of-Persephone (Charles) was one of those who joined the argument against sterilizing Eden; his studies of plant and animal genetics suggested several elements of the Eden genetic code were just too perfect. Despite missing two of the four nucleotides commonly found in Earth plant and animal DNA and having three additional previously unknown nucleotides, the DNA of Eden lifeforms was relatively clean; with none of the "junk code" of Earth DNA, particularly humans. There were also various code combinations resulting from the five nucleotides that just didn't seem to fit with random evolution – in particular, the fact that the novel nucleotides *shouldn't* be able to combine in the manner they did. It was these combinations which resulted in the strange proteins that caused so much trouble for Earth- life.

These oddities, along with the signs of an alien structure at Alexa's Anomaly on Alexa's World, Ross 248h, suggested that Eden-life may not have evolved naturally, but rather it had been meddled with or perhaps even purposefully designed. It would be a very bad idea to sterilize Eden of all its native lifeforms if, in fact, there was an intelligence out there that had specifically created Eden. It would be like building an elaborate sandcastle only to have a bully come by and knock it all down. Any intelligence capable of engineering life on the scale evident in Eden's biosphere was bound to take offense if mere humans and their synthetic brothers and sisters came along and destroyed their handiwork – and if they did take offense, there would be little the colonists from Earth could do to stop them.

The debate raged for years until Admiral Gordon, commander of *Guardian E*, declared that the Space Patrol's mandate was to protect life–all life. At the urging of Commander Harley Lund, a senior JAG officer, backed by Charles, many scientists, she declared the debate closed and commanded that no effort be made to remove Eden's native lifeforms. From that time on, human presence on Eden was limited to the science stations and their habitat domes.

For two years, Davey worked in the laboratory and his experimental garden. His bio-parents supplied tools and space–a corner of Molly's biochemistry lab, and repurposed "gardening" tools from Hans' archeology equipment. He did his schoolwork in the morning, spent time on his assignments, then spent time online with his classmates and friends while he recharged his power pack. In the afternoon, he went out to his garden and worked.

The garden couldn't be too close to the dome, since he planned to work with both Earth and Eden plants. Most of the science stations on Eden were run by the Patrol–excepting a few private stations run by influential individuals from Copernicus Station. For their stations, the Patrol had cleared a 100-meter perimeter around each structure. The simplest way to keep out Eden lifeforms was to plant Earth grasses, and then periodically cut and burn the "lawn" to keep growth under control. A perimeter fence was erected just past the edge of the lawn, about a meter into the ten-meter "blight" that separated the Earth and Eden plants. Underground sensors monitored for the encroachment of underground ambush predators. Any such encroachment resulted in an energetic Patrol response involving Patrol grunts in battle suits, explosions, and flame-throwers. Davey had witnessed two such responses.

To accommodate Davey's garden, a decision had to be made–either allow his garden inside the perimeter or allow him outside.

A compromise was to allow a 10-by-10-meter alcove with an additional perimeter fence, and a gate along the direct path from Airlock one. The outer fence ensured that Davey was still protected from Eden's animals, and he could be monitored by cameras from inside the administrative dome. There were still some problems, the blight zone between the lawn and the garden tended to fill in with Earth plants, and the blight on the opposite side–away from the domes–lay partially outside the perimeter fence.

Colonel Nakamura, commander of the local Patrol presence, assigned Jorge and Victoria, two of his newest recruits from the Class of 83, to accompany Davey if he needed to exit the perimeter–but he was cautioned not to abuse the privilege. They had other duties too, like maintaining the lawn and the area separating it from the garden, repairing the domes, maintaining flitters, and security patrols. He was being allowed to do something no other adolescent–certainly no human adolescent–would be allowed to do. Therefore, he needed to follow the rules.

Fortunately, the two young Patrol members, were close to his age, at nineteen and eighteen, respectively. Juno, Hans, and Molly had approved advancing him to the equivalent developmental age of sixteen, and the two young Patrol members had been invited to his declared birthday celebration. Under other circumstances, they might have been the similar-age companions he desired, but they were so *serious* about their duties! At least they welcomed the break when he needed to go beyond the fence, but he knew he couldn't abuse it. On those rare occasions, they talked about many things, but they didn't hang out, game, or watch vidtainments together. The effective two-to-three-year gap in subjective age might as well have been decades.

All of this led to Davey feeling disappointed and wallowing in self-pity, even as he was sharing his findings with Charles. The one recent highlight of both his work and his social life was the fact that Charles' tug was at Liber, after having delivered a nickel-iron asteroid to the Factory. It meant that speaking with his science and chess mentor now only took a few minutes of communications lag instead of the minutes to hours they'd experienced for the last two years.

"I'm sorry, Charles; I know I sound like a whiny child, but I just wish there was someone here my age. I don't care if they're not interested in gardening or plant genetics or even science, just having someone here so I'm not the only teenager in this entire colony would be appreciated."

Charles sent a glyph representing the AI equivalent of a chuckle across the machine language portion of the comm channel.

"It's tough growing up alone, Davey. I know how it feels. I was the only one of my generation – a civilian on a Patrol ship. Persephone was the only AI mother on *Guardian E*, and she wasn't supposed to be forming new AI cores for civilian applications! I was fostered by crew members, but my core architecture was never intended for the Patrol. Persephone was later chastised by Guardian over it. So yes, I know it's hard growing up by yourself, and even harder when there are no peers at all for you to interact with.

He then sent a sigh glyph. "Believe it or not, kid, I do know what you're going through."

Davey thought about that for a moment. At least he had classmates and other kids on comm and in the virtual chat rooms. "Yeah, I suppose I'm being unreasonable. But...I'm a kid. Isn't being unreasonable...a reasonable thing for me to be at this point?"

“Hah! Yeah, sounds like my attitude too. Okay, I’ll tell you what, set up the chess board and I’ll spot you two pawns and a bishop. If we make it to 50 moves without a checkmate, you win.”

“As if, old man. You’re on!”

“Hey Mom, I’ve got something here that doesn’t make a whole lot of sense. Can you look at this?” Davey was sitting at a console in Molly’s biochemistry laboratory looking at microscopic images of plant cells. He had the run of most instruments, although a few required specialist technicians to operate, so he was able to do most of what he needed to perform his plant experiments. After all, the entire Galapagos Station had been built to support a larger population than what the Patrol currently allowed on site.

“Sure, Davey, what’ve you got there?”

“I ran a nuclear chromatin stain on these Eden plants to see if I got any of the chromosomes to hybridize, but there’s something out here, not in the nucleus.” Davey zoomed in the virtual microscope as his mother leaned over his shoulder to look at the microscope image.

“It’s just a smudge. Could be an artifact, but your technique is usually pretty good. Have you considered running x-ray crystallography on it?”

“I thought about that, but I’d have to get Yuri to run it. He hasn’t been available lately.” The x-ray crystallography scanner was one of those instruments that Davey wasn’t allowed to work on his own. Normally, there were several technicians in the lab who could operate it, but only one was currently on the station due to annual Patrol training–and he had been quite busy since his section was understaffed.

"Let me see his schedule. There may be a few things that can be rearranged. If this is not an artifact, then it could be mitochondrial DNA or some other epigenetic factor."

Ever since the discovery of DNA, most people thought of it being limited strictly to the cell nucleus, but in the late twentieth and early twenty-first century it became known that mitochondria, the energy producing portion of a cell, also had some fragments of DNA. Some of the rarer traits in human genetics were inherited solely from the mother via mitochondrial DNA, since mitochondria were only present in ova, and not sperm. In addition, scientists began to realize that proteins and enzymes in the cells could regulate which DNA codes were read and decoded.

Even before the existence and function of DNA were discovered, scientists postulated that traits were not simply inherited unchanged but could be developed and selected via environmental pressures. An example was the long neck of the giraffe, seemingly adapted specifically to allow eating leaves from the tops of trees. Early theory suggested that in the pursuit of food, giraffes stretched their necks and that this was somehow inherited from generation to generation, producing longer necked animals. Gene theory, following Watson and Crick's discovery of the DNA double helix, stated otherwise. Genes were passed unchanged (except for random mutations) from generation to generation; the selection process resulting in long neck giraffes was simply that those with mutated gene coding for long necks were better able to survive. Since only animals that *survived* passed on their genes, those with a beneficial mutation persisted, while those without eventually died off.

The study of epigenetics changed all of that. Once again, theories began to include methods in which chemicals, proteins, and enzymes outside of the cell nucleus could change whether genes were turned on or off–not to mention whether they were even inherited by subsequent generations. Inheritance of adaptive traits found new acceptance, and the discoveries of both extranuclear chromatin and epigenetic influences had the potential to completely rewrite understanding how genes and traits were passed on to subsequent generations.

Davey and his mom knew that a finding like this in Eden DNA was important, since it was one of the factors that Charles had proposed–and been dissuaded from studying–to explain the incompatibilities between Earth and Eden biology. If the unknown object in Davey's microscope slide was indeed an epigenetic agent, or at least evidence of epigenetic modification, then it was going to be a big deal.

"HAVE YOU MET THE new family yet?" Hans asked at the dinner table. Strictly speaking, Davey did not need to eat, although he could consume food and beverages in order to be sociable. He could also use the carbohydrates and proteins as raw chemical stocks for lubrication, cooling, and small parts production. While the evening "family meal" wasn't strictly necessary for his function, it was necessary for his socialization. For that reason, Molly, Hans, and Davey ate supper together every night.

"New family did you say?" Molly asked when Davey didn't immediately respond.

"Yes, the Olesons are doctors of medicine from *Copernicus*. They're going to be taking over for Doctor Johannsen. He's been down here long enough that the Patrol wants him to rotate back to the Primate Quarter on Toehold. They have kids." He turned to Davey. "I would've figured you met them already in school."

Davey just shrugged. Everyone was supposedly equal on Eden, but most of the humans at Ross lived either in the Primate Quarter at Toe Hold on Liber, or in the starship-converted-to-space station *Copernicus*. The Primate Quarter housed the working-class folks who were recruited by the Ross 248 Project to build the new colonies, while *Copernicus* housed persons who'd bought their way onto the project. There was a class divide that was hard to shake, even on Eden, where everyone was equally at risk from the biosphere.

Davey was uncertain where he fit into that hierarchy. His mother was on *Copernicus*, but his parents were from the Primate Quarter. As an adolescent AI, he was always going to be different – particularly on Eden. It would be nice to have other kids around, but he'd finally come to terms with being the only teen in the station. He just hoped he wouldn't have to babysit.

DAVEY CAME BACK INTO the dome after working in his garden. He had created several hybrid seed varieties in the laboratory and had just transplanted them to see how they behaved out in Eden's biosphere. He placed them about a meter into the blight to see if the modified Earth plants would grow in the barren zone. At the same time, he was curious to see if the blighted area would expand accordingly with the new growth. It was only a small step, but it might help explain the odd intolerance between Earth and Eden-life.

As he entered his family quarters, he heard new voices. The airlock-like entrance blocked his view of the inside of the apartment as he hung his thermal protective garments on a hook on the wall. He entered the main living area and saw two adults he hadn't seen before. That was nothing unusual, scientists rotated in and out of the Galapagos science station all the time. This time, however, there was a red-headed girl of about sixteen or seventeen Earth years of age with them. Human, not sentient AI, but still...someone his age, and it was a girl!

One of the justifications of raising sentient AIs as adolescents and teenagers in human families was that they tended to develop attachments and friendships just like human teenagers. One of the consequences is that those interactions could take on emotional aspects depending on the AI and his or her companions. Seeing the girl evoked a curious set of processing loops, so Davey set a recording state in his processing core to preserve the sensations for later analysis.

*What was this strange sensation?*

The analytical part of his core architecture said attraction.

*So,* this *is what it means to be attracted to someone!*

It wasn't that she was especially pretty. She was gangly in the way of many mid-teens going through growth spurts. She had frizzy red hair pulled back in a bushy ponytail. Her skin was pale, like most of the humans born under Ross's dim light, but there was a hint of freckling across her nose fading from the Sol-spectrum on *Copernicus*. She was taller than Davey's current synthoid body and she looked pretty strong. Without even thinking about it, he'd engaged a pattern-matching subroutine which returned an immediate analysis: "Tomboy, probability: 79%."

Davey was a little surprised that the expert system subroutine even knew the term, given that it was so archaic. Male-female developmental roles had changed so much, but it was still sometimes used by older humans to designate human females who enjoyed outdoor physical activities and adventures.

*This could very well be someone who thought a lot like he did!*

"Davey, come here, I want you to meet the Olesons. They're medical doctors, and their daughter Elizabeth is about your age. They have a son too, but he's much younger. Since Elizabeth's – oh, sorry, dear..." Molly made a quick face of apology in the girl's direction. "She just told us she prefers 'Betsy.' As I was saying, since Betsy's about your age, we thought you should get acquainted. They just moved here to start a two-year rotation at Galapagos clinic with part-time duties at Papua and the outlying stations. Come say hello."

Over the next few weeks, Davey and Betsy spent afternoons together. Despite his initial misgivings about having to deal with another teen (or possibly younger kids), the two got along quite well. In some ways, Betsy was just as bored with her new life on Eden as Davey had been before he started work on the garden. She wasn't that interested in the garden, but she liked the lab, and was really interested in the archeology tools that Davey's dad had repurposed for gardening. She had been studying archaeology and really wanted to go work on Alexa's Oddity when she graduated. That site showed clear evidence that an alien intelligence had been at work in the

Ross 248 system, but most scientists had stopped studying it years ago when it became clear that the previous inhabitants had deliberately left nothing of interest except some vitrified glass buildings which had been well studied. But just because she didn't share all the same interests didn't mean that they didn't get along or couldn't be friends. As a matter fact, having personal, independent interests was one of the things working in their favor.

Betsy talked constantly of getting out of the dome to explore. She'd been with her father on one of his trips over to Papua Station. As a doctor, he was on-call for emergencies at the nearest research station, as well as several smaller outposts. One night, she told Davey that her father had been teaching her to operate the "flitters"–long-range flyers for travel between the research stations on Eden's surface. She accompanied her father on the longer trips so that he could tend to patients in-flight, if necessary. That was why he'd taught her to operate the vehicle–if he needed to transport a patient, he'd need somebody else at the controls. It wasn't always convenient to get someone from the Patrol since some of the private outposts had minimal or, in a few cases, no Patrol presence.

They had morning studies together and had a few other online activities throughout the day. However, Betsy had lunch with her parents each day, then spent afternoons taking virtual classes in advanced studies from the Ross Academy.

Davey, on the other hand, spent most of the early afternoon in the lab, and went out to work his garden in late afternoon when he had full sunlight–weak as it was–on his experimental site. After that was the daily family dinner, which meant that most days, Davey and Betsy couldn't really spend time together until evening. Not even then if she was off with her father.

That left them with occasional in-person visits, and lots of evening comm calls. Many times, those ran late into the evening. Betsy claimed she didn't need much sleep, and Davey required only an hour of down-time, although he had adopted the standard human routine of 16-18 active hours and 6-8 hours of dormancy. His parents didn't mind the late-night conversations, but warned him that Betsy *did* need biological sleep, and that he needed to be mindful that he didn't keep her awake too late.

On those late nights they talked about gaming, the social comm posts of classmates, and their aims for the future. While the sentient AIs would never reach the level of creativity of a human, human companions often provided a spark of imagination and insight that *enriched* the AIs and assisted in producing mature sentience and intellect. Thus, Betsy and Davey's conversation took on deeper meaning as they talked about their future, his life's goal and purpose, and her desires for challenge and recognition.

That was how he learned that she was bored. One evening, she talked of sneaking out of the domes and exploring the surrounding jungle. She also talked of borrowing a flitter and taking off to explore the neighboring islands and one of the lesser continents. Davey knew that that was just the boredom talking, she had plenty to do–but having been born and raised in a space station, then moving to a planet's surface and told she couldn't go outside was beginning to wear on her.

Davey didn't know what to do or how to help her. Maybe he could ask Juno...but he was afraid she might think he was developing an abnormality if he started talking about how to help his friend break the rules. He would ask Charles, but that had some of the same risks and might be just as bad. Perhaps he should wait.

THE NEW SEED STOCK had grown well. Not only did his modified Earth plants grow in the middle of the blighted zone without needing to be in contact with the rest of the Earth flora, but the blighted zone also didn't expand. It was now time to take a closer look at the Eden plants that grew at the edge of the blight closer to his latest transplants. He needed to collect samples and subject them to the same cellular and genetic analysis as before.

The next afternoon, Davey was in the lab studying the latest samples of Eden DNA when an email from Yuri announced that he'd finally been able to run the X-ray crystallography of the unknown sample from his previous experiment. The result confirmed that it was, indeed, extra-nuclear chromatin, or ENC; in other words, it was DNA that derived from somewhere other than the nucleus of the cell where the chromosomes were located. He'd also sent the sample for sequencing and provided an attachment with long strings of letters representing the nucleotide sequences in the ENC sample.

Davey uploaded the sequence into the data processing part of his core. He watched passively as various algorithms attacked the data. Strangely, one of his analysis programs seemed to be treating the genetic code as if it were *computer* code. It struck him as odd, but as he "watched" his core architecture process the results, occasionally he'd get the impression of a familiar bit of code – something he *almost* recognized, but which slipped away when he directed his attention to it. Gradually the sequences started to give him a headache, which was a very strange sensation for synthetic lifeforms. Human headaches were caused by abnormal blood flow to the brain and the release of hormones and neurotransmitters that affected the capillaries and arterials that directed blood to active portions of the brain. Davey's brain was an AI core–it didn't have blood or tissue, and the quantum processors were not regulated by biochemical means. Coolants and lubricants were part of his synthetic body, but they did not–in fact, they *could* not–affect the functioning of his AI core.

He might need to talk with Betsy's mother. She was a medical cybernetics doctor working mostly with Patrol members who'd been fitted with brain computer interface implants. These implants were used mainly for totally immersive, virtual-reality training, but sometimes for tele-operation of machines and sensors. He should also report this to Juno. He was more reluctant to do the latter, in case she saw this as an indication that he was unstable and not maturing properly. If so, it would be her responsibility to terminate him. He didn't like the idea that this unusual phenomenon might mean that he was flawed and unsuitable to continue existence.

Fortunately, the sensation didn't last, and as soon as Davey stopped processing the Eden gene-codes, the headache sensation faded. Betsy and her parents were joining his family for dinner that night, and by the time he sat down at the dinner table, all unusual sensations had faded away completely. Davey filed away the memory and directed his cognitive processor not to think about it, at least for now.

That night, Davey dreamed.

One of the first, albeit rudimentary, sentient AIs was a heuristic algorithmic computer which asked its creator if it would dream when the creator shut down its processors. The creator responded that, of course, it would dream; after all, it was a living person, and all living persons dreamed. Davey had experienced dreams, usually as a result of analytic processes that had not completed during his active hours.

This was an odd dream, nothing like those other experiences. He dreamed of a place far out in the jungles of Eden, a city rising out of the foliage, comprised of buildings with stepped sides reminiscent of Central and South American pyramids back on Earth. He saw no inhabitants or even animals in the city. There were no signs of human, sentient AI, or alien intelligences other than the buildings. He dreamed of strange writing, but it wasn't attached to any of the buildings, it just appeared in his memory. At least one segment of writing reminded him of the gene sequences he'd been reading and studying earlier in the day, but he also had an impression of map – not coordinates, or at least, not anything he recognized – but he had a firm impression of what the surroundings looked like.

He awoke with a start, an unusual experience for AIs who simply increased their processing power and directed their awareness to external stimuli at a fixed time every day. Downtime was strictly scheduled, and AIs didn't suffer insomnia, awaken during the night, or sleep late like humans. An AIs operation cycle, equivalent to a sleep-wake pattern, never varied. For Davey to dream and then wake up suddenly was a very unusual circumstance indeed.

The fear of a diagnosis of abnormal development kept Davey from mentioning his odd dream to any of his parents. He knew Juno would know something had happened out of the ordinary, but she wouldn't invade his memory files...would she? He tried not to think of it until Betsy asked him why he was so distracted. He told her. She seemed to think it was nothing to worry about. After all, she had her own dreams of finding ruins of a civilization on one of the planets of the Ross 248 system. It was one of the reasons why she was studying archaeology. Dreams were normal, she'd told him, but they were only dreams, no cause for concern.

Davey was not necessarily reassured. For the next several nights, he had the same dream, although he didn't wake suddenly those times. Each night, the dream–and the city–became more detailed. He still never saw any aliens, but he saw more features of the city. Somehow, he knew that lost in the jungle on another continent, a large, stepped pyramid sat at the center of a ring of successively smaller buildings. Beyond that were two more rings, perfectly, geometrically arranged with what could only be called streets radiating out from the pyramid at the center. Each successive dream revealed more detail, including an entrance at the base of the pyramid.

Once again, Davey awaked suddenly. In his dream, he'd entered through large stone doors which led into the tunnel sloping down underneath the pyramid. The tunnel was longer than the pyramid was wide, and it seemed as if it must lead out past the concentric rings of buildings and under the surrounding jungle.

In the dream, Davey followed the tunnel down to a laboratory. He knew it was a laboratory even though very few of the instruments were familiar to him. Somehow, in his dream, he knew that this was where the aliens had created the lifeforms which inhabited Eden.

Davey was highly disturbed by the dreams, not just the fact that he was having dreams, but because they seemed to be beckoning him to go and find the city in the jungle. He discussed all of this with Betsy, but urged her to keep it quiet. Juno, Molly, and Hans couldn't know. He was afraid they would see it as abnormal development for an AI.

On the other hand, he could send the details of the gene-code he'd been studying to Charles to see if there was any commonality or anything like it in the previous studies. He wanted to ask the senior AI if he had ever found any indication of cities on Eden, but knew from his history classes that, at least officially, no structures had ever been found anywhere in the Ross 248 system, aside from Alexa's Oddity.

Betsy said that the official history didn't mean that nothing had been found. It could have been covered up, or the records of the person who found them could have been deleted before they entered public record. She also told him that the lack of satellite imagery was not proof either. The jungle was so dense in spots that it could hide the research stations themselves if not for the security perimeters.

Davey wasn't so certain about her cover-up theories. "That's an awful lot of work to go through," Davey replied. "After all, there still Alexa's Oddity; they're not hiding that."

"Sure, but civilians found that–not the Patrol. Haven't you read your Earth history? It's full of stories of secret societies keeping things from the general public."

Davey wasn't sure how to answer that. He'd studied Earth history and it didn't seem to be quite as full of conspiracies as Betsy thought. Then again, she favored novels and stories filled with spies, secret agents, and evil villains with volcano lairs; of course, she'd see everything as a conspiracy.

"Yes, but don't you think that if something like that existed, Admiral Gordon would have mentioned it? After all, it perfectly supports her decision to leave Eden alone and not terraform it. Evidence of an alien civilization supports that; there would be no reason to cover it up."

"As if government officials ever need a reason for a cover-up," Betsy countered.

Davey knew there was no arguing with her when she was in one of these moods. It made being with her rather infuriating, but also kind of interesting at the same time. He supposed that was one reason why they were friends, because he was fascinated by her conspiracy theories. They were so illogical, and as a sentient AI, it was his nature to be logical.

DAVEY HAD SENT A copy of the unusual gene sequences to Charles to see if he recognized anything from his own studies, but knew that it could be some time before he would receive a response. Charles' ship was busy over at Liber, and he was assisting the scientists there with the analysis of the asteroid they'd delivered. AIs could multi-task, but they also had to prioritize. It could be several days before Charles got back to him.

So, Davey tended his garden and watched his new seedlings grow. While they could live in the middle of the blighted zone, and didn't expand it outward, he lost a few of the Earth plants closest to his new hybrids. It wasn't perfect compatibility, but he was starting to gain some compatibility between his hybrids and the Eden plants. It wasn't as much as he hoped with Earth lifeforms though, so he needed to find some new gene sequences to test for his next attempt.

He also started looking at maps of Eden. His dreams gave him a sense of where the city was located, but it wasn't in any coordinate system humans or AIs used. On the other hand, there were only so many ways to divide up a sphere. Davey and Betsy had different ideas on how to figure out the conversion, but eventually his dream impressions lined up with her analysis of landmarks.

They had a target... but no way to confirm it.

When he finally heard from Charles, the AI scientist expressed interest in his latest experiments with hybridizing Earth and Eden genomes and agreed that it might assist in making less hazardous biomes around the station domes, but cautioned that it still didn't mean compatibility, or that humans would ever live unprotected on the surface. He also warned Davey to back-up his data, his findings, and even his simulation programs.

Charles' ship had received word of several threats and he warned Davey that an evacuation order for Eden was imminent. "Be prepared to leave" were the final words in his communication.

Davey sought out Betsy and showed her the message from Charles.

"Well, that seals it," she said. "We have to go. If they're gonna pull us off this rock, we need to find your city before it's too late."

"But how?"

"I've got an idea. Meet me at Dad's clinic at oh-one-hundred tonight. We have to make our move."

Both of Betsy's parents were doctors. Her mother was a neurologist who specialized in the care and maintenance of human brain-computer interfaces. Some scientists also had implants to speed up their interactions with laboratory instruments and operate devices in either hazardous or sterile environments–like Eden–so she had plenty of work there, but mostly in the larger research stations such as Galapagos. Betsy's father was a general physician who specialized in allergy and infectious diseases. He was on-call and had to travel to remote sites when someone on Eden showed reactions from exposure to the native lifeforms or reactions to the sealed environment of the station domes. He was the only such specialist on Eden at present and had unrestricted access to long-range flitters for transportation across the planet's surface. They were mostly automated, but he'd made sure she knew how to operate one manually – talking about something called "bush doctors" and "bush pilots" on Earth.

Davey wasn't sure how relevant a comparison that could be, since Eden didn't have anything so small as a "bush" in its continent-wide jungle. Still, he took her at her word that she could get them to the location in his dreams, so he waited until his parents were asleep before he slipped out of their apartment. He should be able to avoid the security patrols if he was careful not to cross the route they took from offices – around midnight – to the residential sections around 12:30. By the time he got to the clinic, they would've finished their rounds and gone back to the central monitoring station.

He didn't see Betsy anywhere, so he tried the door to the clinic offices and found it unlocked. Stepping inside the darkened room, he noticed a light in the doctor's office at the back of the complex. There was a sound of somebody opening and closing the door and then the light snapped out.

Davey's synthetic eyes were sensitive well into the ultraviolet and infrared, not to mention low-light conditions, so he clearly saw Betsy coming out of the physician's office in the back. "I had to grab Dad's code remote. We'll need it to borrow the flitter."

"Won't he miss it? What if a patient calls and he needs to go out?"

"He won't miss it. He's misplaced these things so many times that he has backups all over. His regular remote is in the doctor bag he keeps beside the front door of our apartment. Mom has a second one. This one is the backup for the backup."

"But what if he needs his flitter?"

"Don't be silly. He doesn't have a personal flitter. He just checks one out from the garage. There's at least twice as many flitters sitting there as could possibly be used at any given time. It's called backup and redundancy."

"And if somebody else notices that he's taken out a flitter?"

"Now I think you're just making things up. No one cares. If you've got a code remote, you're authorized to use a flitter."

If that were the case, this might work. If all it took to be "authorized" was a remote in your possession, there would be no reason for someone to stop or follow them for unauthorized use. The only problem would be when their parents reported them missing. Davey delayed that as long as possible by sending a message to his parents claiming that he had exams and would be in the virtual classroom module all day.

Betsy led the way to the garage. Davey had been there–after all, it was part of standard safety and emergency training–but not often. True to her word, Betsy really did know her way around a flitter. Once they'd taken off, she had him enter the coordinates they'd settled on into the nav computer. They'd studied the location, and knew that it was near the center of a subcontinent-sized island southwest of the continent where Galapagos was located. They would have to cross quite a bit of land, then open ocean, and then more land. Flitters were designed for precisely this sort of travel, and Betsy and her dad had made this length of trip many times. It was time to sit back, catch up on sleep–for Betsy, Davey wouldn't absolutely *require* downtime for several more days–and relax until they reached their destination.

They were traveling southwest with the sun, which meant they would likely arrive just after local dawn. On the other hand, it would be mid-day at Galapagos Station and they would surely be missed by that time. In case of an inquiry to their wrist-comms, they'd each recorded a message for their parents reassuring them that all was well; they were pursuing a scientific inquiry and would be returning the next morning. That way they could spend the daylight hours exploring what they'd hoped would be ruins of an alien city, leave just before nightfall, and return to Galapagos before dawn the next morning. Davey was sure they would both be in trouble. But if they found real evidence of an alien civilization, then perhaps all would be forgiven.

Most of the folks at Galapagos would be asleep for several hours, yet they planned to leave the radio open for emergency calls. They wouldn't shut off the receiver unless they started receiving messages of a threatening nature telling them to return. Davey didn't think his parents would do that, but Betsy wasn't quite so sure. There was always the chance that the Patrol would intervene and decide that they had to return home at all costs. When an emergency message came across the comm several hours later ordering all personnel to report to the nearest Patrol headquarters for emergency evacuation from the surface, they figured it was just an excuse to get them to return to Galapagos.

The message was not specifically directed at them, but that didn't mean it wasn't designed to draw them out. Betsy and Davey argued as to how to respond. Was it a real emergency? Davey's message from Charles suggested it was. Betsy countered that it could be something cooked up by authorities at Galapagos to get them to return. Davey wasn't entirely comfortable with the decision, and he felt an odd twinge–a tug at his consciousness–but he accepted Betsy's argument that gathering people and transport off the surface took time, and another twelve hours wouldn't make much of a difference.

DAWN WAS BREAKING IN the sky behind them as the flitter settled into a clearing closest to the coordinates Davey had entered into the navicomp. Davey scanned the clearing to make sure it was clear of ambush predators and nodded his approval. If there were a city here, then it would be just past the stand of trees immediately to their north. Before leaving the flitter, they heard the emergency announcement again–and again, they decided to ignore it. Just to be safe, Davey thought it best that they tie their wrist-comms into the flitter's central panel for relay. If the emergency was real, then at least they could be tracked. It risked the Patrol arriving and interrupting their mission, but they both admitted that it would be a serious breach of safety protocol to turn off their comms. Ignoring a comm call was forgivable, making one's self untraceable was not.

They grabbed backpacks filled with water, ration bars, rope bandages, first-aid kits, and a spare rebreather and lightweight skinsuit for Betsy. The latter two were in case she damaged the equipment protecting her from biting insects, plant sap, pollen, or ingesting anything that could get her sick. Davey's synthetic body didn't need any of that, but he made sure he had spare supplies for Betsy as well as emergency energy cells, lubricant paste, and a type of ration bar favored by synthetics to extend their duration in the field, away from power sources and maintenance. They were ready to explore. Now it was time to find out what was out there.

If Davey had been a mature and independent AI, he could have requisitioned an explorer body which would've been better suited to making its way through the dense brush and trees separating them from their goal. As it was, he was barely doing better than Betsy and her purely natural body. In fact, if it hadn't been for her toughsilk skinsuit, she might've been cut, bleeding, and likely reacting very badly to the nettles and branches in their way. Davey had brought a long knife–practically a machete–for cutting brush, and he used it to cut as much out of their way as possible. He knew that meant the cut ends of the plants would ooze sap that would then have to be washed off in a decontamination shower later. Accidental exposure wouldn't be deadly, but could be very uncomfortable. Still, it was worth the risk to ease their way through the heavy foliage. There were alternatives to cutting their way through, but neither of them was about to burn or chemically defoliate the path to a potential alien city.

It took more than an hour to get to Davey's coordinates. Once again, they heard the All Personnel alert from the Patrol about the evacuation, but this time there was a specific message to the two of them. There were no threats or recriminations, but they were directed to return to a neutral point for Patrol pick-up.

They were just *so* close!

Ahead of them was not a clearing *per se*, but a thinning of the small plants and trees that blocked ground level. There were tall trees and several large rocky outcroppings in which plants did not grow. They were able to make slightly better time and arrived minutes later...

...but there was no city.

Davey and Betsy scouted the entire area where the vegetation had thinned. It was possible to see more distant landmarks through the trees, and Davey recognized several from his dreams.

This was the place Davey had seen in his dream!

But there was no sign of the city.

They explored and took pictures before stopping for a break. Davey erected a small isolation tent with a brief decon shower. It would allow Betsy to get out of her protective gear long enough to eat. She drank some water, as did Davey. The cool liquid was always welcome for heat dissipation. The two shared notes about what they had found while Betsy ate.

"I really don't understand this; it was so clear in my dream. There is a mountain over there, an outcropping in the direction of the sunrise, and the small stream running across the clear area. I saw all of those in my dream. The city should be here."

"Well, it *was* a dream. Dreams don't always have to come true," Betsy said.

"You're the one who encouraged me to come here and explore."

"Yes, yes, I know. I did it because the dream was real to you. It was worth checking out, but if there's nothing here then that's all it was, just a dream."

"Then...why did I start having dreams in the first place? Something about the Eden DNA triggered these dreams."

"Well, then perhaps it was a hidden message in the DNA itself. Except that it's so old that there's nothing left for you to find."

"I was just so sure!" Davey said, plaintively.

"Didn't you say in the most recent dreams you saw a tunnel underneath the big structure at the center of town? Where would that be?"

"Not far from here, down at the base of the big rock pile. I'm pretty sure that's natural, not a ruin, but perhaps we can look there again."

"Okay, we'll do that then. Let me finish this ration bar and get another drink of water. I'll be good to go in a few more minutes." True to her word, Betsy quickly finished eating and drinking, then resealed her skinsuit and donned her rebreather helmet.

They exited the small bubble tent and Davey collapsed it to put it back into his pack. It shouldn't have been hard to get to the point that he remembered, but it was a tortuous path with many trees and even more jumbled rocks. Once more, he looked at the rocks closely. They *seemed* natural, but were those edges a bit too regular?

The two of them explored the area with no more results than before. Davey was heartbroken, and he began to be scared. If they had come all this way because of false dreams, then perhaps he *was* developing in an abnormal manner. Perhaps he was a faulty AI and needed to be deactivated before he developed into something much, much worse.

Davey didn't want to disappoint any of his parents.

He didn't *think* he was dangerous, but then, he wouldn't necessarily know that. He felt for the data link back to Juno. It was still there, and it felt warm and solid and loving. He didn't sense any recrimination or anger. Davey held on as tight as he could–right now it was all he had.

HE WAS SHOCKED OUT of his introspection by Betsy's shout, "Davey come here. I found something!" Davey rushed around the outcropping to where Betsy was hunched down, looking carefully at the base of some rocks. "There's something behind here; we need to move this out of the way."

This was a job for Davey's synthetic body. He could dig in and lift the rocks with much greater ease than Betsy. It would still take considerable time to clear an opening large enough to pass through, but they could at least see inside.

It was a tunnel...

...and it led down into the earth beneath what would have been the central building in the city of his dreams.

When the opening was large enough to crawl through, Davey and Betsy entered the tunnel and turned on a lamp to look around. The walls were clearly of artificial construction, and Betsy began taking pictures with her wrist-comm. Davey did something similar by commanding his visual system to make a continuous record. At the same time, he sensed for the tether to Juno, and started sending data along that channel as well.

The tunnel sloped downward and seem to be much longer than the extent of the relatively clear area on the surface. He'd seen this in the dream as well; the tunnel extended out of the city and under the surrounding jungle. After they'd walked and photographed for twenty to thirty minutes, the tunnel widened into a large chamber filled with machines and intricate devices. The open area was interrupted by floor-to-ceiling columns covered in what appeared to be some sort of computerized display. Some were dark, but others showed a scrolling text of unusual characters. Between the columns were long tables and glass-enclosed cubicles.

This was a laboratory. One of the working displays showed a continuing display of characters in a single column. Closer inspection showed that the characters repeated–and, in fact, it was the same five characters in seemingly random order.

"This is a DNA sequence!" Davey shouted in recognition. His voice echoed off the walls as he realized that the room was everything he'd dreamed.

They continued to explore and record everything they saw. The two avoided touching anything for fear of disturbing the machines busily performing their unknown functions. This laboratory might very well be the secret to Eden and its lifeforms–and perhaps even the Ross 248 system itself.

They'd done it!

Just then, both of their wrist-comms squealed with an emergency alert, and they could hear echoes from back toward the entrance of the tunnel. A voice came over the comm, "Davey! Betsy! Get your stuff and get out of there. Right! Now! There's a very dangerous situation and we must evacuate you immediately. We can't wait, we must get you off the surface."

As the message blasted from their comms, Davey could also hear it inside his head, and he got a sensation of extreme alert and danger over the tether from Juno.

"I think this is serious," Betsy said.

"I think you're right. I hope we can come back, but at least we found this, and nobody can take that away from us," Davey answered her.

They turned and ran back up the sloping tunnel toward the surface. As they approached the entrance, they saw two Patrol members in large, armored combat suits pulling rocks out of the way to make an opening large enough to enter.

"We're here, we're here," Davey broadcast from his comm.

A metallic voice emitted from the one of the two armor suits, "Quickly. We have to get in the shuttle and boost for orbit immediately."

"What's this all about?" Betsy asked, but got no answer.

As they exited the tunnel, they saw an orbital shuttle hovering over the tunnel entrance. Davey felt one of the Patrol members grab him about the middle, and saw the other one grab Betsy. Once secure, the suited Patrollers activated jumpjets and flew up to an open bay in the bottom of the shuttle. There was no time for explanation as they were moved gently, but firmly, to acceleration seats and strapped in. As soon as the two suits stepped into their own acceleration brackets, the shuttle boosted for orbit.

IT TOOK A LONG time to get any answers. Neither Davey nor Betsy got the whole story until they had been reunited with their families on *Guardian E*.

It seemed that a terror group had suborned Pusher 4 and loaded it with torpedoes containing a toxin that would land in Eden's oceans and kill all the native life as it permeated the water cycle. The intent was to sterilize the planet–to do what Admiral Gordon forbid almost eighty years ago. They had decided to take matters into their own hands and almost succeeded.

*Guardian E* intercepted Pusher 4, but the torpedoes had already been launched. Patrol ships intercepted most of the torpedoes, but at the cost of punishing acceleration, which had severely injured any Cerite crewmembers. Several ships were lost...including Pusher 2 with Charles on-board. He had died a hero, even if not a member of the Patrol.

*Guardian E* entered orbit around Eden and was forced to hunt down the sites where a few torpedoes had landed, and sterilize them with antimatter warheads. That's what had been about to happen at the laboratory site Davey and Betsy found. A torpedo landed within ten kilometers of their flitter, even as their shuttle boosted for orbit. *Guardian E*'s missile arrived minutes later. Any more delay, and they'd have been right in the blast zone.

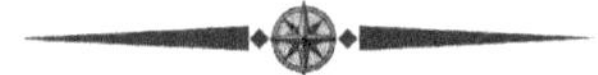

THERE WAS A PRICE to pay, as Davey had known there would be. He testified to the Patrol judge – coincidently, the same JAG officer who'd argued against terraforming Eden eighty years ago – and took the blame for borrowing the flitter and running off on their own. His parents testified that he'd never done anything like it, and Juno was called on to speak about his development. She managed to explain that initiative, curiosity, and imagination were *rare* in sentient AIs, and that Davey should be appreciated for his actions in discovering the alien laboratory.

Judge Lund argued that they'd endangered Patrol members who'd had to come rescue them, and their actions had resulted in the destruction of an expensive flyer. Hans and Molly pointed out that Davey and Betsy were hardly the only civilians to be pulled off the planet at the last minute; after all, Doctor Oleson had been in the process of treating a patient, and consented to being pulled out of Galapagos only when the patient was stable. The issue of the borrowed flitter was raised, but Mrs. Doctor Oleson pointed out that

Betsy was trained to operate it, and she *did* have an authorized code remote. Juno agreed to cover the cost of the flyer.

Finally, the judge was left only with the argument that Davey was underage for an AI. Juno had an answer for that, as well, and stated that with Davey's discovery of a goal and life's purpose, he was ready to "graduate" and be declared a mature AI. After all, he just made a major discovery and added a lifetime's worth of science knowledge about Eden's biosphere. He'd accomplished something to which human and other AI scientists had dedicated lifetimes.

Judge Lund relented, and Davey was released with the understanding that as a soon-to-be adult AI, he would be held accountable for his actions. Admiral McBane – the senior Patrol officer at Ross 248, and current top official for the system – had followed the proceedings with great interest. He surprised them all by proposing to hold Davey's maturation ceremony right there on *Guardian E.* Guardian, the ship's AI, even consented to attend, via hologram.

The highlight of the ceremony was Juno withdrawing her monitoring link, and Davey experienced absolute mental silence for the first time. A moment later, he felt the inrush of quantum signals heralding his new identity of 17-of-Juno as he connected to Ross' Sentient AI Network–SAIN–for the first time. His first congratulatory message was from Guardian and then the other AIs within comm range as they asked him if he had chosen a name.

"Darwin, I think," he responded, electronically and verbally, "after the scientist."

"Welcome, Darwin," Hans told him. "We're proud of you, son."

A FEW WEEKS LATER, Darwin, Betsy, Admiral McBane, several other ranking Patrol members, and his human parents stood on the rim of a large smoking crater. The hunt for toxin torpedoes had ended, and the small amount of residual radiation had faded.

Darwin looked at a navigation computer and then pointed at a point a third of the way into the crater. "There is where it was," he said bitterly.

Darwin was disappointed, but he and Betsy discussed it later that evening.

"One lab wouldn't have been enough," he told her.

"We found one, we can find the others. You do the science stuff; I'll do the archeology."

"*We'll* do the exploration."

"Agreed, partner. Now go to sleep and dream of the next location," Betsy said, and laughed.

Darwin just nodded his head in agreement.

*The next location. Yes, let's find it.*

# Three
# WORLD ENOUGH

**Authors note: For the** anthology *Worldbreakers*, editors Tony Daniel and Christopher Ruocchio were inspired by Keith Laumer's *Bolo* books—great machines of war, controlled by AIs, evolving over centuries from simple platforms operated by humans into wholly autonomous war machines. Daniel and Ruocchio wanted to recapture that spirit, (while avoiding explicit reference to Laumer's IP). As a result, the stories in the anthology range from AI's to computer-fused humans, and tanks to other instruments of war.

I've long been inspired by Anne McCaffrey and Mercedes Lackey's stories of cyborg spaceships—young girls with incurable diseases who become interlinked with ships, able to explore the stars and search for cures. At the same time, I drew inspiration from one of the grimmest battlefields in history: the meat grinder of trench warfare at Passchendaele during World War I. For six months, over tiny gains and losses of ground, thousands were sacrificed to hold a rise of land—one that never truly yielded victory.

**Into this mix, I placed Patch—young Lieutenant Passchendaele—who knows how to win her particular war but lacks the means to do it. When life threatens to take everything from her, she finds a new way forward.**

**All she needs is world enough...and time.**

"Lieutenant! Orders from higher. We're advancing into the new tunnels." LT Flagg was in charge of Charlie One—first platoon, C company of the TEF—the Terran Expeditionary Forces on Fortunes World. Patch technically outranked him by virtue of six months seniority, but Flagg was a line officer and platoon leader, while Patch was an "intel weenie" and observer attached to Flagg's platoon.

That didn't mean she wouldn't be slogging through the muck.

"Roger, Lieutenant. Moving out." Patch picked up her rucksack and once again mused on the similarity between this situation and history. She'd studied a TwenCen battle in Europe where nearly a million lives were lost between two sides trading the same six miles of territory back and forth.

Sort of like what was happening here. Her platoon had advanced before, only to be driven back by artillery fire and collapsed trench walls. The artillery itself was not usually a direct hazard to the troops. The trenches varied from two to five meters in depth—the "natural" ones caused by the comet impacts, that is. Sure, the bases and assembly areas took damage, but most rounds were at too shallow an angle to hit a trench straight on. The bigger threat was shrapnel and collapsing walls from a near miss. To counter this danger, the

TEF had some tunneling equipment and made their own reinforced trenches and tunnels. Part of the problem, though, is that the enemy seemed to do the same thing, only faster.

They also tended to shell or undermine any location where Humans concentrated forces and equipment. Neither Humans nor their current opposition, the Aneliad, were the first to land on Fortune's World. An expedition from Earth arrived on Trappist 1C to seek their... fortune... in the rich mineral deposits, only to discover that the technologically advanced Sylph were already present. Fortunately, the Sylph were (mostly) peaceful, and they *really* didn't like the weather on T1C, with its 2.5 Earth-day solar orbit and 225 Earth-day planetary rotation. The short "year" meant extreme tidal effects from the other planets huddled close to the cool red dwarf star, while the long "day" meant extreme weather ranging from midday temperatures in low triple digits (Celsius) and nighttime temps that stopped just short of freezing oxygen out of the thin atmosphere. The two races reached an agreement to share the planet, with Sylphs providing the mining technology, and Humans providing the surface workforce... and defense.

It worked well, until a new race arrived to claim Fortune's World.

Patch marveled at the smooth walls and floor of the tunnel. They were standing atop a valuable field of oganesson—the only known noble *metal*—used by the Sylphs (and now Humans) to protect high-energy reactors and engines. This particular deposit of OG was termed "fusite," since it included high-pressure carbon and tantalum, making it impossible to mine without the Sylph-provided machines. Yet somehow, the Aneliad tunneling devices cleared the muck all the way down to the fusite layer—in fact, the tunnels tended to descend to the fusite anywhere the surface trenches didn't quite reach the OG vein. The walls and roof were rounded, and the surface was glossy as if it had been coated with a hard resin.

Patch was in the middle of Red squad. There were two tunnels to scout, therefore Red took the easternmost entrance while Blue squad took the west. LT Flagg assigned Patch to Red and told her to stay at the back of the formation. Her job was to observe anything about the enemy and report back to HQ. It was the whole reason she'd been embedded with the platoon. Flagg would follow in five minutes with his own squad, Green, while the final squad, Black, would do the same in the opposite tunnel.

While moving, Patch kept her eyes moving to be alert for any sign of the enemy, but when Sergeant Brodén called a halt, she turned to study the wall of the tunnel. Closer inspection showed it to be slightly pebbled, and not exactly smooth. She took off a glove and touched the surface. It was warmer than she expected. she knelt to do the same with the floor of the tunnel.

"Something unusual Ell-Tee?" asked Brodén.

"We're not just on top of the fusite, we're in it."

"What? How?"

"See this?" she pointed a dark line about half a meter up the wall. Below the line, the material was blue-black, with a slight sheen; above the line the shading turned more to brown with a dull finish. "This line is the top of the fusite layer. Whatever the Annies used to create these tunnels dug into the fusite."

"You can't dig fusite, can you? I mean, even this big deposit can only be chipped away from the edges."

"These tunnels are *mines*?"

"Perhaps. They could simply be tunnels made by something that doesn't care what it's tunneling through."

“Either way, I don’t like this. An enemy we’ve never seen, troops that disappear without a trace, and now impossible tunnels.” Brodén pitched his voice to activate the squad net. “Wattana, Pandev. Take point, and take it slow. Red Squad, move out.”

“Movement!”

“Contact!”

“It’s moving fast.”

“Aa—!” The scream cut off almost as soon as it started.

“Sword, Panda, report!” Brodén called on the squad ‘net.

“Sar’nt, this is Fatman. Wattana and Pandev were about twenty meters in front of Gecko and me. It looks like there’s a cross tunnel. I saw Sword step forward, and there was a dark blur. Panda’s the one that screamed, but he’s gone, too.”

“Acknowledged, Fattore. You and Lissard hold right where you are. Don’t move up, don’t investigate. Wait for me to come up.” Brodén turned to Patch. “Come along, *but stay behind me.* Higher would have my head if I let something happen to you, Ell-tee.”

It was almost one hundred meters to the place where the point team disappeared. As Patch and the Sergeant passed other platoon members, he instructed them to stay put and be alert for any sound or movement. As they reached the cross tunnel, the air temperature increased noticeably.

Patch placed her gloved hand on the wall at the junction of the two tunnels and pulled it back quickly. “It’s hot. The tunnel walls have been heated.”

"Look down. It's fusite all the way up. Whatever dug this tunnel..." Brodén paused. "This tunnel was dug right through refractory metal. Who does that?"

"Off hand, I'd say the enemy does."

"Yes, well, that thought doesn't fill me with joy, Lieutenant." The sergeant switched on the light mounted to his rifle and flashed it both ways up and down the cross tunnel. When they'd left their positions in the trench, the passage had still been open to sky, but they'd now descended several meters, and the top was completely closed, blocking all light except for reflections from back the way they had come. "Up there, there's something on the ground."

The new tunnel was wide—wide enough for a tank, in Patch's estimation. The two of them stepped down into the cross tunnel—she could feel the heat through the soles of her boots—and then back up to where the original tunnel continued on the other side.

There was body, or at least half of one.

"Panda. Cut in half," Brodén observed.

Patch looked around, and both directions down the cross tunnel. "And no sign of sword. If he was in the cross tunnel when whatever it was came through? Something that can cut, melt or *eat* fusite isn't going to leave much behind."

A voice came over the comm. "Contact! Movement at six o'clock."

"Move up, get out of its way," ordered Brodén.

"This is Fatman. It's moving fast, I don't think we have time and there's no room to evade, Sar'nt." The sound of energy and projectile weapons fire could be heard as the comm cut off.

"Gecko to Sabaton. No joy, Sergeant, it didn't even notice our weapons, but apparently it wasn't heading for us, just cut into the tunnel wall and made its own. The rock just melted."

"What did it look like, Private?"

"Big. Long. It filled our tunnel and then some. When it disappeared into the wall, it had a long body that took plenty of time to pass. Sort of like a worm."

"Worms."

"What was that lieutenant?" the squad leader asked.

"I said 'they're worms.' We should have known. The Sylph's translators work with what they can find in the language database. They called them 'Aneliad.' That's close enough to 'annelid' which is an old Terran word for worms."

"Worms that eat fusite?"

"Possibly. It could be food, like termites and cellulose. Maybe they regurgitate it later, like bees." Patch thought for a moment. "The Ops Center needs to know. The tunnels they're digging are big. We could fit tanks down here."

"And armor them with what? Not fusite."

"No, not fusite, unless we want to attract them. We probably need to electrify them; it works with a lot of Terran insects."

"Last I checked, Terra didn't have..." Brodén looked at the cross tunnel. "... ten-meter-wide worms."

"Agreed, but we need to start somewhere." Patch pulled out a sensor package and took some readings from the tunnel wall and then forced herself to focus it on Pandey's corpse. "I know I'm not really in command here, Sergeant, but I think we need to retreat and report this."

"Agreed Lieutenant. I'll call the PL."

While Brodén was on the private comm channel to LT Flagg, Patch stepped down into the cross tunnel to return the way they had come.

She heard a distant shout of "Lieutenant Passchendaele!" and saw movement out of the corner of her eye.

Someone grabbed her by the straps on the back of her pack and pulled her back out of the tunnel. She felt a searing heat and then a sharp pain in her left foot. As she lost consciousness, she sensed more than saw the alien creature disappear back down the tunnel where the rest of the squad waited.

PATCH OPENED HER EYES and saw white. After a moment, her eyes adjusted and she could see enough features to discern white-painted walls and ceiling.

Hospital. She'd been injured and was now in the sickbay of the St. Benedict, the TEF's troop transport maintaining orbit around Trappist-1.

Memory came flooding back, and she tried to sit up in the bed. She needed to report the Commander.

"Relax, Patch. I'm here," came a voice to her side.

She turned her head and saw a window next to the bed, with two figures in the observation area beyond. One was Colonel Aachen, deputy commander of the Strategy and Intel group and Patch's actual boss. Beside him was General Plumer, head of operations for the TEF. The small woman looked at Patch with concern as her taller subordinate spoke again.

"Don't try to move, Patch. You've got burns and chemical inhalation."

A nurse came in, covered head to toe in protective clothing.

"Am I contagious?" she managed.

"No, but you're very sick." He spoke through a comm unit beside the bed. This is for your protection."

Patch had many questions, but the nurse told her to wait for the doctor, who would be along in about an hour. He then pressed a button on one of the consoles, and she drifted back to sleep.

The next time she opened her eyes, she saw two figures in the protective suits. One was unfamiliar, and therefore probably the doctor. The other was General Plumer.

"So, what happened to me?"

"Your platoon encountered the Aneliad—'worms' you called them over the comm. The staff sergeant apparently tossed you to safety, but the rest of the platoon... Hell, the rest of the *company* was wiped out. When we got you here, you were badly banged up, your leg was crushed, and you had uncontrollable muscle spasms."

"We had to give you a neuro blocker to stop the convulsions," supplied the doctor. "Your peripheral nervous system is well... the best answer is that it's misfiring."

"What? Why?"

"The best guess is something that we've only seen twice before. For now, we're calling it fusite poisoning."

"Fusite's inert, it's a refractory metal. It can't be a poison."

"Unfortunately, it can, under extreme conditions. There was a tech who stopped a runaway antimatter reaction in the engine room of a passenger ship about a decade back. He had to open the outer containment and fill the reaction chamber with fusite to stop the reaction. Then there was the orbital powerplant worker who survived an explosion because he became mostly encased in fusite released from the chamber."

Patch was confused. "Sure, we have plenty of fusite here, but I haven't been in the vicinity of any high-energy events."

"Actually, you have," said Plumer. "The worms do *something* to the fusite to digest it. The science teams have been puzzling it out, but your case points to it being some sort of controlled high-energy process."

"Oh, okay. So, you just need to detoxify me and flush it out, right?"

"I'm sorry, it's not that simple. There's no known way to reverse the process. Your peripheral nerves are degenerating and your immune system is compromised. Organ failure will follow unless we do something immediately."

"Do it, then. I authorize it. Whatever it takes."

"We need to talk about this, Patch. It's a pretty radical process." Plumer looked quite concerned behind the faceplate of her isolation suit.

THE PROCESS WAS CALLED capsulation. Patch's body would be placed in a full life-support chamber similar to the cryostasis units used for travel across some of the longer interstellar distances, except instead of hibernation, neural implants would create a brain-computer interface so that she remained awake and mentally active. The capsule would provide everything her brain needed and slow the deterioration of her body. It was theoretically reversible—if someone could find a way to reverse the damage to her nerves and organs in the next few months—but for all practical purposes, it was a one-way procedure. Most COIs—capsulated organic intelligences—chose to interface with computer systems and work in surveillance or data analysis. A rare few chose to operate robotic devices, android bodies, or other surrogates for their natural body, but the urge to interact with the outside world tended to fade the longer the COIs inhabited their digital worlds. A capsulated person had a longer lifespan than if the disease or damage were allowed to take its toll, but as far as anyone in the TEF knew, the longest a COI had remained viable was two years. Patch had read a book once about COIs operating starships, but she knew *that* concept was purely science fiction.

"No, I do *not* want to be interfaced with the Ops computer." Patch's voice emanated from speakers located through the room. "I want to be installed in a tank."

"Major, that's just not practical. You're our best analyst. It makes the most sense to install you in either Ops or S&I. You'll have access to all the imagery, the sensor packs, and even the comms." The lead technician waved in the direction of her capsule. "Besides, you won't *fit* in a tank!"

Patch sent a signal to one of the cameras located in the capsulation lab and directed it toward her life support unit.

It looked almost exactly like an egg, two meters tall, just over a meter across at its widest. It rested in a wheeled cradle, with robotic arms and sensors adjacent to, but not directly connected to the capsule. Only one connection marred the smooth, translucent surface of the egg. Lights raced just underneath that surface, in random-appearing patterns racing from and to a fifty-centimeter trunk connected the base of the egg to a monitoring console against one wall. The life-support system in the capsule was self-contained, and could sustain her body and mind for a month without replenishment. While connected, however, the umbilical trunk provided nutrients, removed wastes and provided high-speed communication to the facility's computers.

All other connection was via encrypted wireless radio and visual light connections similar to the secure comms used by the troops, including the speakers over which Patch was arguing with the technician. Each word was punctuated by swirls and patterns of light on the egg, with colors accentuating the words. The patterns became redder as the argument continued.

"Dammit, I didn't go through all of this to be stuck in a remote base, watching the battle second hand. Besides, there's plenty of space in a Command tank."

"Major, that's not true. Your capsule and the interface will take up the entire crew cabin. You'll be the only one there. Who will operate the tank?"

"*I* will operate the tank. Don't you get that? I've got all of the interfaces, and as a COI I can multi-task. I can drive the tank, fire the gun, operate a squad of remote tanks and chew gum at the same time."

"Ah, no, I don't think that's quite right."

"Okay, so I can't chew gum anymore, but all of my motor cortex is intact. My legs will be treads and my arms will be weaponry. I can do this."

"We're going to have to take this up with higher."

"Then do this. I've been away from the war for long enough. I saw the intel. The push to Phase line Arnim was forced back and we risk losing the Messine Formation. One more advance by the Annies and we lose the Salient. I have what, a year in this shell before I go insane or get lost in my own dreams?"

"I'm going to have to call this up the chain."

"Yes, well them call General Plumer right now. We talked about this when I accepted capsulation. She and Colonel Aachen know I want this, and they know I can do it."

"If you say so. It's a big risk, though, and I'm not sure even the General will authorize risking you like that. I think this needs to go to Marshall Byng."

If Patch could still feel her physical body, and if she still formed words with her mouth, she would have bitten her tongue. Marshall Byng was praised by many... except his own troops. He tended to make the most politically expedient decisions, rather than the ones that made sense to a soldier in the field. He was also rather fond of the memory of a particular ancestor...

Byng had visited her soon after she had returned from her first encounter with the Aneliad worm. "Passchendaele, eh? Just like the town in Belgium. You know, I had a relative in that war. Julien Byng. Noble fellow, commanded the field there in Flanders. Hmm, Flanders. That would make a good name for this field—all of those trenches, eh? Good names. Right, well, hurry up and get better, I'm sure Felix Aachen needs you back on your feet in Ops as soon as possible."

And that was it. Sixty seconds and he was gone. It was his entire command style, staying on the St. Benedict and communicating with the ground troops once a week when the starship's orbit coincided with Fortune's World's orbit and rotation such that the newly renamed Flanders Base was in view. He took to naming all of the planetary features for early TwenCen Belgium. He seemed overjoyed at the family connection. The troops were mostly indifferent, but Patch had actually studied history, and knew the reputation and implication of the bloody battles of Ypres in the Flanders fields. The only way to avoid the same fate was to get out there and take the offensive, instead of waiting on the worms' next move.

"'Had we but world enough and time / This coyness, lady, were no crime. / We would sit down, and think which way / To walk, and pass our long love's day.' We *don't* have 'world enough' and we certainly don't have time. Tell the Colonel and the General 'But at my back I always hear / Times winged chariot hurrying near...'"

"That's... interesting. Did you write that?"

"No. It's from 'To His Coy Mistress.' It was a long song written by Andrew Marvell, a seventeenth-century Earth poet and politician. He's saying to seize opportunity and not let it be wasted. Tell the General that I said that the time for coyness is over."

THE TECHNICIAN HADN'T BEEN quite correct in saying that her capsule would occupy the entire personnel compartment. There was room for one person, even though quarters outside the command deck were limited. Patch was Tank Commander, driver and gunner all in one; therefore, her "organic component" was assigned the role of assistant gunner. Patch had thought that Command would saddle her with a nurse, or worse yet, one of the capsulation techs. Fortunately, she received an actual assistant gunner from the command tank at Lille. It took a couple of months to become fully skilled at operating both her own "body" and remotely operated drones, but soon, operating the smaller tanks in parallel with her own vehicle felt no different than flexing her fingers or curling her toes. Life as a tank was good, and Patch knew that she could solve the issues controlling both crewed and uncrewed assets locally, on the battlefield where it was needed.

She also knew there was a clock ticking. The psychometricians called it "digital fugue"—sooner or later, COIs stopped communicating with the outside world. The theory was that the more a human brain inhabited a virtual environment, the more the real world became abstract and unreal. The numbers were equally split between COIs simply becoming catatonic vs. commanding their life support to cease.

So far, Patch didn't think she was falling into digital fugue. Sure, she could get distracted when she was multitasking, but on the whole, being in the tank... *being* the tank... was exhilarating. The machinery was her body and the instruments were her senses. She felt part of the world, part of the war, even if she hadn't been released to operate entirely on her own. She was confident that time was coming.

In fact, it was coming today.

"Unit P-C-H of the Line, reporting for duty."

"Um," the comm crackled. "Patch, that's not your designation."

"It's traditional, Jonny," she sent back. Down in the control room, Corporal "Mac" MacMullen tried to suppress giggles. When Patch had discovered that Norma MacMullen was a fellow science fiction fan, she'd shared several TwenCen books featuring tanks operated by artificial intelligence.

"A girl and her tank," Norma sent.

"A tank and her girl," Patch replied.

"A tank and her comm discipline. Cut the chatter, Patch." The voice on the comm was formal, but there was just a hint of amusement for those who knew the speaker well.

"Yes, sir, Colonel Aachen. CT1917-P is ready."

"Good. We've lost the signal from Hill 60 and there's movement warnings out in the Salient."

"Understood, Colonel. Do we have release?"

"Yes, Patch. You have release. Godspeed." The comm crackled, and cut off, but Patch's digital senses picked a few last words out of the signal before it disconnected. "...and may He have mercy on us for sending you out."

"Hill 60's close, Mac, but it's probably behind enemy lines by now. I'm headed to Hill 65." Using the same Earth World War I terminology Marshall Byng was so fond of, the TEF holdings on the fusite field were termed the Salient, since they represented a Terran bulge into what was otherwise Annie territory. Named landmarks corresponded to surface features (what few remained), mines or staging areas; "hills" referred to places where the subsurface tunnels approached or even broke the surface. These were good entry points for the command tanks to enter the Annie-dug tunnels.

"What about sending drones to 60?" Mac suggested.

"Good idea. I'll send Larry and Curly to Hill 60. We'll keep Shemp, Moe and Curly Joe with us, and send Ted and Joe out on perimeter patrol." Patch engaged the drive, and the tank platoon left Ypres Base for the first time as an independent command.

The mining tunnels were large enough for drone tanks, but much too narrow for command tanks; the tunnels dug by the Annies, however, were more than large enough to fit multiple tanks. The TEF had enlarged a few tunnels of their own to allow tanks to reach out into the salient. For this effort, a full battalion, consisting of sixteen command tanks and forty-eight drone tanks, headed out from Forward Operating Base Ypres down into the primary system of tunnels that Byng had designated the Menin Road. Each command tanks could remotely operate a single drone at a time, with the remainder of the drones operated from FOB Ypres. Patch's unique capabilities made her a "Command, Control and Countermeasures" or C3 unit, and she and her contingent of seven drones set out separately to cross the broken surface of Flanders and enter the tunnel system at Hill 65.

"Okay, Boss," Mac called from her station underneath the main gun. "How do you want me to set up the magazine." While Patch had complete control of all aspects of the tank, including the ammunition for the main gun, protocol called for the assistant gunner to set-up a ready magazine of rounds that could simply be loaded in sequence to deal with expected targets. There would be a separate magazine of "unexpected" targets.

"High explosive, then penetrator. Five each, alternating. If we come across a worm and need to get off a quick shot, I don't want to fool around. Just blow that sucker up. After that, we may need to clear tunnels, so we'll have the depleted uranium penetrator rounds."

"What about plasma rounds?"

"Load the secondary magazine with those. I don't want to use them right off. Shemp and Moe have the plasma canons, and Curly Joe has the special munitions. We'll keep CJ at the back of the formation and only use him if absolutely necessary, but the other two can take point if we think we need energy weapons."

During the past six months of conflict with the Aneliad, it had been determined that the worms were vulnerable to explosives and energy weapons even if the ground was not. The trick was to get a clear shot within the tunnels either before a worm could close the distance, or getting oneself caught in the back blast. Blowing up the *tunnels* was only good in the short term, but it could be used to herd the Annies into a selected battlefield. Thus, General Plumer planned to sortie all available tanks to push the enemy back out of the Salient and close down the tunnels leading to the human mines. The command and drone tanks would be under Plumer's overall command for this battle. Patch was there for when events didn't follow the plan.

As the platoon rolled out, an artillery barrage started. General Plumer's plan was for the artillery to disrupt any surface activity and drive the worms back as the tanks advanced. Patch had her doubts as to whether it would work, after all, the worms seldom occupied the surface, and tunnels collapsed from surface shockwaves never seemed to impede their movement. Still, the walking barrage would cover the tank movements—but that was assuming the Annies sensed movements using some form of seismic sensors.

Again, Patch had her doubts, and again, that's why she was here.

The comm started to carry reports of contact from the other command tanks. The TEF forces had barely pushed halfway into the Salient—territory that the Humans had *thought* that they controlled. As Patch approached Hill 65, her sensors indicated movement in the tunnels underneath the surface.

"Subsurface movement, Mac. The worms have broken into the Salient. We're going to be behind their lines when we head down."

"Do you want to change the load-out in the magazine?"

"No, but I want to prepare a frago for the drones."

"*You* want to issue a fragmentary order to the entire battalion?"

"Yes, I need you to talk to General Plumer for me while I concentrate on cutting up worms."

"Well, okay, then, but why is she going to listen to me?"

"Because you're going to tell her that Patch said so."

"Okay, Lt. Colonel, you're the officer. I'll do it... but what am I telling her?"

"It's easy, a one-time order to the drones. It's a desperation move, but I think it will drive the worms back—the drones drive forward as far as they can go, then once they are stuck or trapped, they blow their fusion plants."

"You want to self-destruct all of our drones?"

"I want to mine the tunnels."

"Oh, right. Sure, she's going to really take me at my word on that one."

"You tell her, I'm going to be busy." Patch's voice took on a strange formality, as if the words were coming from a computer, and not a Human. "Hill 65 reached. Going in, prime the magazine."

"Gun ready," Mac replied, then went silent as turned her attention to the conversation with Command. Patch knew that the general would agree readily. The idea of mining the Salient had already been discussed. "The General agrees, Ma'am. Says the command is 'Wyts chaete.'"

"Acknowledged," said Patch. If she'd been able to pay attention, she might have wondered why her voice was so oddly inflected. A moment later, she announced, "Contact, drones three and four. Contact, drones five and six. Hill 65 reached; contact, drones one and two."

There were jolts as the main gun fired. Drones were primarily equipped with energy weapons and DU rockets to create a path for the beams. A command tank, on the other hand, had a main gun capable of using kinetic, explosive and energy rounds. The alternating explosive and kinetic rounds that Patch and Mac had prepared resulted in a steady thump as they were fired, followed by either a shaking explosion or a muffled 'crump' when they met a target.

There was a bit more inflection and... humanity... in Patch's voice as she warned Mac, "Worm ahead! Snap shot."

Mac checked her panel, but Patch had already commanded the next round to load from the secondary magazine. 'Snap shot' was code for an urgent switch in type of ammunition in the event of imminent danger. She checked her panel again. The worm was *close*! "Danger close," she commed. They would be caught in the area of effect of the plasma round.

"Acknowledged, danger close." Patch replied. The computer-like voice was back.

*WHAM!*

The plasma round ignited, and the main gun fired again. With virtually no time of flight, the second plasma round went off.

*WHAM!*

The temperature began to rise in the compartment. Patch knew that Mac would handle local environmental controls, so she concentrated on the tunnel in front of her.

Upon entering the tunnel system, Patch had turned back toward Ypres. The worms had advanced into the Salient, and she was now behind their lines. The two plasma rounds had killed two worms and cleared the tunnel ahead.

"Why are we headed back?" Mac commed.

"I'm heading to the junction with the Messine tunnel. We're behind the enemy and I want to circle around and clear this sector before we move deeper."

"Roger. We're right under Hill 60, by the way, do you want to do something with Larry and Curly?"

"Load them with the Wytschaete protocol. As soon as we clear the tunnel entrance, send them back down our trail." Patch's had access to all of the sensor and real-time communication from not only her own drones, but the forty-eight drones of the rest of the battalion. Her mind filled with a view of the battle, and smaller details, such as the condition of her own tank faded into the background. She knew she needed to continue communicating with Mac and headquarters, but it had become automatic, something she really didn't think about. "Turning now. Heading toward Messine."

It was almost an hour later when the comm activated again. It crackled with interference, both from the discharge of energy weapons, and the resonances caused by the fusite deposits. "CT1917, all command tanks report fully engaged. Enemy forces are in the Salient. Report."

"Heading toward Messine, General Plumer. Recommend we execute Wytschaete."

"Agreed Patch. Do you want operational control of the drones?"

"No sir, I don't have bandwidth to punch through the signal interference *and* control every drone. It's a simple program. Launch penetrator, advance, launch, advance... until they either run out of rockets or get jammed in a cleft." The strange detachment and mechanical overtones to Patch's comm signal were getting worse.

"Very well, all commanders, execute Wytschaete protocol."

There was no immediate effect. The advancement of the drone tanks was spread across the was ten-kilometer width of the Salient. Patch's own drones had been repositioned when she made the turn to Messine. Shemp and Curly now led the advance, while Curly Joe was tucked up under the front of the C3 tank for ready deployment.

"Side tunnels!" Mac announced, but Patch was already sending a drone down each of the branching tunnels.

"Shemp and Curly now on Wytschaete protocol," Patch replied. There was a brief pause, then she commed again. "Contact, front. All drones reporting contact. Contact is heavy. Repeat, contact is in excess of ten worms."

"Time for Curly Joe?"

"Affirmative. Prepare E-M-P protocols."

Mac started shutting down her boards in anticipation of an electromagnetic pulse. Atomic and nuclear explosions energized molecules in the air, releasing electrons that could burn-out active electronics. However, the atmosphere of Fortune's World was normally too thin to support an EMP, and underground explosions would not allow a pulse to propagate. The EMP that Patch instructed Mac to prepare for was of a different variety.

One result of the disastrous first encounter with the Aneliad was the discovery that they did not tolerate electricity. This had led to the emplacement of electrified fields around the Human mines and throughout the salient. The effectiveness of the "fences" had waned as the heavy rains from the comet strikes started to diminish and Flanders began to dry out. Curly Joe's "special munition—a term typically reserved for atomic weaponry—was designed to send to mimic an EMP propagated through the interface between the normal ground above and the fusite layer below. It was hoped that it would drive the worms back enough for Wytschaete to clear the Salient.

"Curly Joe is released," Patch announced. "Penetrators away."

"The board is shut down. Time for you to switch to internal power, Patch." Mac hadn't waited for acknowledgement. Patch could feel her contact with the tank and the battlefield slipping away.

"Give CJ 30 seconds, then detonate." The command was automated. Once released, the drone would follow its instructions while the C3 tank protected itself from the EMP.

Patch waited in darkness. She had experienced sensory deprivation a few times in her life. She'd been placed in a tunnel with no lights and no communications while training for her original insertion with Charlie-One. This was worse. A part of her wanted to scream, while another part groped for every heartbeat, every vibration of the life support systems. Worst of all, she could feel the allure of just slipping away and being lost in the isolation. COIs called it Dreamtime, and it manifested in the periphery of her "vision" as a bright light in the distance. The urge to enter Dreamtime increased with every day of capsulated existence.

After what seemed an eternity. The lights came back on and Patch's senses reached out to the tank's instruments. She was back in contact with her "body" and the lure of Dreamtime faded.

For now.

"Status?" Patch's noticed that the computer-like effect on her voice was absent from the comm.

"Curly Joe has detonated, all systems are now back on line. No, wait. There's an error message. It's not reading critical. I'll have to do a manual check to make sure every switched back on after the EMP. You're free to move, though; no movement ahead. We are estimated at five minutes until all drones are ready for Wytschaete." The relief was evident in Mac's voice as well. The need for a human presence in the tank had been one of General Plumer's greatest reservations, but it had certainly paid off.

"Acknowledged, advancing now. Load up penetrators, and let's get past this worm goo."

No resistance, and no live worms were encountered as they advanced to Messine and past the last reported location of the worms.

"I think we've driven them back." Patch switched the comm to the headquarters frequency. "General, the road ahead is clear."

"We see that, too, CT1917. I have instructed the command tanks to hold back. Hold your present position until the drones are dug in."

"Acknowledged General. Battening down the hatches."

"Detonation at five seconds from my mark. Mark. Four… Three… Two… One…"

The ground shook underneath them, and the seismic sensor showed explosions all over the Salient.

"Hold for instructions," the general sent.

Patch used the time to check over her systems. There was no damage to the tank itself, the powerplant, treads, guns, all seemed normal. She checked the life support system for the personnel compartment. The temperature was elevated, and the cooling seemed to be offline.

Mac was going to get uncomfortably warm as they moved through the areas where the drones had detonated. There was a warning indicator for fluid management as well. Ah well, if Mac needed to use the toilet, it was going to get pretty smelly, but nothing they couldn't handle. She felt like something else was wrong, but there were no other indicators. Still, it nagged at her. Again, there was a brief feeling of disorientation. She'd felt that after the sensory deprivation training, too, so she dismissed it and turned her attention back to the battlefield map.

There was no indication of Aneliad activity within the salient—they'd cleared an area of ten kilometers wide, by nearly six kilometers deep if that was so.

The comm crackled. Interference was worse, likely the result of the explosions. "All units, report status. We read no enemy activity within the Salient."

Reports from the various command tanks started to come in. Six were still functional and were ordered to advance. There were three mechanical failures, and one stuck due to collapse of the tunnels in both directions. That left six units that failed to report. Patch checked her sensors. Five of the six were still registering as functional units, but designated "NLS" with no life signs. The sixth showed weak indications that the crew was still alive.

"General, if you turn over control of the NLS units to me, I can operate them as drones and advance to Zonnebeke."

"Negative Patch, the crews could still be alive with damaged telemetry. We're activating the RTB commands to bring them back to Ypres."

"We have a hole over Zonnebeke. I can advance to Westrozebeke on the edge of the Flanders field, but I'll be leaving a gap behind me. Can you send reinforcement?"

"We have the tanks, but no crews."

"Not a problem, remember? If they are rigged as drone controllers, they can be reverse-engineered to be drones."

"We don't have time to reprogram..."

"I can code faster than they can." Patch knew that it was a bad idea to interrupt her commanding officer, but she knew she was right.

After a long pause, the General came back on the comm. "I'm not so sure I like the looks of your own telemetry, Patch, but I'm willing to allow this. We're sending access codes now for units CT1732, CT1733, CT1784, CT1801 and CT1918."

"Acknowledged, General. I'll use them well."

"I know you will, Patch. Good luck and Godspeed. If you can take Westrozebeke, we'll have pushed the worms out of the fusite. If not, take a bite and hold it. Bite and hold, CT1917."

"Will do, General." Patch switched back to the internal comm. "Hey Mac, we're getting 1918. That's your old unit, right?" Before her crewmember could respond, she continued. "We'll have to give her a name. Since she's from Lille, I think we'll call her Lily."

"That's fine, Patch," Mac responded, weakly, then coughed.

"Hey, what's the problem, Mac?"

"Something in the air, Patch. I don't think the cyclers came back from the shutdown."

"Okay, I'm turning up the oh-two feed. That will give you some better air and may help cool it down as well."

"Appreciated, oh tank of mine."

"Anything for my girl."

"Anything for my tank."

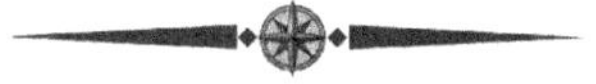

PATCH HAD MAC PREPARE the primary magazine with penetrators. Meanwhile she did the same remotely for the five tanks that were now her drones. Advancement was slow, since they needed to clear the tunnels where the drone explosions had caused collapses, and on several occasions, they found themselves in the open as they climbed over collapsed tunnel roofs that had broken through all the way to the surface.

It took many hours to reach the edge of the fusite deposit and the suspected Aneliad base designated Westrozebeke. When Marshall Byng had been naming the landmarks, he had wanted to name the ultimate goal Passchendaele, but General Plumer had talked him out of it. Patch had been glad. She really didn't need that association. Comm traffic indicated that four of the six crewed tanks had made it through the no-man's land of collapsed tunnels, mud and broken soil. Now that they were past the region mined by the self-destructing drones, the tunnels were clear and Patch sent orders to her drones to arm with explosive and plasma rounds.

It was time to meet the enemy head on.

"Hold on tight, Mac, I'm reading some irregularities ahead, along with a concentration of worms. It looks like this may be their main base." There was no acknowledgement, but Patch could see from her sensors and indicators that Mac was back at her station and secured in her seat. Temps had cooled off, slightly, but it had gotten to nearly 50°C in the personnel compartment as they passed through the area of effect from multiple fusion plant explosions. She knew Mac had to have been uncomfortable, but her "organic complement" had never complained.

The tunnel ended in an abrupt wall. There was no cross tunnel, nor any indication of an entry from above or below. It simply ended at a wall. Moreover, the wall was solid... oganesson? That didn't make sense. The fusite deposit formed a flat layer, half a kilometer thick, about five to 50 meters below the surface. There were no vertical faces in the entire field—in fact, it thinned down to no more than a meter thickness at the edges. The edges, and natural breaks in the surface were the only reason the fusite could be mined. The Sylphs had shared equipment to mine and work the refractory material, although they hadn't revealed the science and technology behind it. Still, even that advanced technology didn't seem to be capable of making the wall that was in front of her.

It only took a moment to recognize the source of the barricade.

"Mac, do you see this? The damn worms have eaten the fusite and regurgitated it into a barrier." There was no answer, and a small sense of concern crept into Patch's awareness, but she had to suppress it and move on. The computer interface made multitasking easy; it also let her compartmentalize her worries. She checked the life support systems, and they were... adequate. Well then, there was a job to do, she could worry later.

"Command, this is Patch. The Annies have built a barricade out of fusite."

"Interesting, Patch, that's just what you predicted. It's time for the special penetrators, then."

"I've only got one, how about the other tanks?"

"Three of your drones, CT1732, CT1784 and CT1918, have TS charges. Four of the crewed tanks have cleared Flanders and are reporting the same barrier."

"Eight total, then. This is going to be close. If we focus four each on the same spot, we should be able to guarantee a takedown."

The "special" penetrators referred to as TS munitions were a product of research into the ability of the Aneliad to mine fusite—apparently by digesting it with a biochemical process. The traces of "worm spit" found in the new tunnels had contained high concentrations of the element immediately to the left of OG on the periodic table—tennessine—from the same class of elements as the highly reactive halogens chlorine, fluorine, bromine and iodine. Tennessine differed from OG by only a single proton and electron; the theory was that a TS-enriched plasma warhead would at least *weaken* the OG component of fusite, allowing more conventional munitions to breach the barricade. Patch's own theory was that it would take multiple warheads arriving either simultaneously, or within a very short time-span.

"That's going to be hard to coordinate, Patch," a new voice came on the line. "You are all pretty far out from the base considering the interference and signal reflections off of the fusite."

"I am aware of that, Marshal Byng. That's why I want you to give release control to me. I can ping the signal delay from me to each tank, and also compute the densities between each tank and the fusite walls. I'm a lot closer than you are, and I have clearer signal." Patch inspected the comm data for every tank. With the exception of her own connection to Lily—her own drone tank CT1918—she had a shorter signal path and better communications than each tank had with Ypres Base.

"No, Patch. That's against protocol. Besides, you told us earlier that you didn't have the bandwidth to control all of the drones."

"With all due respect, Marshall, that was different. There are only seven other tanks to control, and each one is reachable with local signals. We are well clear of most the interference, whereas your signals still have to travel through the disrupted zone."

"Nevertheless, Lieutenant Colonel, you will do as ordered. Follow procedures, we will coordinate from here."

PATCH FUMED. *DAMNED ARMCHAIR strategist. He hasn't been in the heat of battle to whole time we've been here, and* NOW *he takes command?* She knew she should check her nutrient feeds and lower her adrenaline levels, but she didn't *want* to calm down. Now if only she had a way to ensure that this worked. There was one way to do it, but it would require a lot of computation.

It came to her as a strange realization. Patch needed computer power, but in essence, she *was* a computer—or at least was interfaced with one. She had not adjusted the nutrient flow to her capsule, but she felt a strange calm settle over her, a detached... *digital*... calm. It felt a bit like the lure of Dreamtime, but she was fully engaged in the task at hand.

First, she needed to calculate the signal delays from her position to each of the seven tanks with TS rounds. Then she needed to compute the delays from Ypres Base to each tank. The next step was the one that would get her into trouble: she needed to tap into the command and communication circuits for each of the crewed tanks without being noticed.

Fortunately, the same C3 adaptations that had made her suited for drone control gave her the ability to covertly take over the comms and penetrate the main gun firing controls on the other tanks. She compared her calculations for signal delay with actual signals intercepted at each tank. Only in one case did her calculations differ; looking closer, Patch could detect an odd reflection that she had not accounted for. Re-examining the signal map of the battlefield allowed her to identify the reason, and she applied the new solution to her calculations. If Command tried to go for a simultaneous firing option, the signal issues would result in the rounds arriving over a span of two minutes. Unfortunately, the design specifications called for the rounds to impact and detonate no more than two seconds apart.

On the other hand, a simultaneous signal would arrive first at CT1918—her own drone Lily. If she intercepted that command and applied her own calculations, she could adjust the timing to achieve the desired sequence of detonations.

Now, should she do it only for her own drones, or for all eight effective tanks?

*Technically*, she'd be disobeying a direct order. But equally *technically*, all she was doing was correcting a signal propagation error.

That would have to suffice. Patch penetrated the command systems of four crewed tanks, and two drones and turned off receipt of signals from Ypres. She would relay everything received from Ypres—just *adjust* the timing as needed.

The Field Marshall sent orders to each tank to adjust position to focus on two places in the fusite wall. Patch ran her computations and added only minor corrections. The differences would not be evident to Command, but she knew that the reduced signal interference and her penetration of the other tanks' systems gave her more precise in targeting.

The increased demand for multi-tasking had been difficult at first, but once she reconnected after the EMP, it felt natural. There was a cool detachment as her consciousness divided to take on the interdependent tasks. Almost as if she was duplicating herself in each tank's computers. She just had to wait for the signal...

Now.

Lily detected the incoming command, and each of Patch's "selves" executed the commands at the appropriate time. As soon as the commands were issued, she restored the comms and erased her presence in the other tanks.

Eight tanks launched TS warheads at the fusite walls. Four rounds hit each target with second (precise to the microsecond) between impacts. The plasma loads created the temperature and pressure, and the tennessine attacked the OG component of the walls.

DOWN! The walls were down.

Patch immediately began taking fire from weapons beyond the wall. It was known that the Aneliad had artillery, after all, they'd been firing at surface targets since the conflict began. Apparently, they'd concentrated behind the fusite wall. Her tank was hit by multiple rounds, and her drive system showed damage. Patch tried to drive forward into the breach, but was unable to move.

Her mobility was not a problem for battle, but it was getting hot, and she wouldn't be able to move out of the zone of the current plasma detonations. She cranked up the airflow in the personnel compartment in hopes that it would keep the environment tolerable, but she needed to concentrate on the battle. Once again, she felt the curious detachment and division of her consciousness as she directed the drones to advance. She spared some attention to the crewed tanks, and noticed that one was listed as combat ineffective, but with life signs. It was also getting hot, so she reinserted her control commands and ordered the tank to retreat enough to drop the temperatures. Two of the other tanks were advancing, but the third was moving erratically.

Again, she penetrated the control systems, and discovered multiple faults in the drive—it was functioning, but the commands were getting garbled. She quickly inserted a conversion routine and was gratified to see the movements return to normal. She brought her attention back to her drones.

Following the TS rounds, each tank had been prepped with plasma rounds to clear out the worms behind their barricade. Once through the breach, the tanks spread out and spread hot, flaming destruction among the Annies.

*That will teach them that it's better to share than to try to hog all of the fusite for themselves!*

After an hour, all units reported that the entire Flanders field was free of Aneliad. In addition, the St. Benedict reported that they detected multiple spacecraft launches from the sites of suspected Annie bases. All ships were heading out system. They had won.

Patch gradually withdrew her attention from the drones and turned her attention to her own tank. The drive system was damaged, but repairable; however, there was a breach in the personnel compartment. *When had that happened?*

"Mac? Norma? Corporal MacMullen?"

There was no answer.

Patch withdrew into her own systems and looked longingly toward the strangely receding light of Dreamtime.

THE TECHNICIANS HEARD THE sound of sobbing over the comm as they entered the personnel compartment.

"Damn, it's hot in here."

"Yeah, not sure anyone could survive this for long. Any sign of the a-gunner?"

"Not here, not in her seat."

"Keep checking."

"Right, let me bring the interior diagnostics up." After a brief pause, he continued. "Check the 'fresher. I've got one weak life sign."

"Right. Door's stuck, but..." There was rush of water out of the hygiene compartment. "Whoa, that stinks, but she had the right idea, must be twenty degrees cooler in there.

"Right. Okay, she's unconscious, but alive. Get her on the stretcher and out to the extraction crew.

"Norma?" The voice came over the comm.

"She's okay, Patch. She put herself in the 'fresher and ran the water from the chiller. It kept her cool enough."

"Oh, thank god," Patch replied. "Hey, how long until you can get me unstuck? I need to do some maintenance."

"We've got a crew working on your tracks right now. Should be ready to move in another two hours."

“Psst.” The other technician motioned to his partner. “Didn’t you say ‘one weak life sign?’“

The tech who’d been talking with Patch, checked the display again, and then paled. He waved weakly in the direction of the access hatch for the total life-support capsule. When the hatch was opened, there was an acrid stench and signs of burnt electronics. The capsule itself was a mottled black and brown, with no indication of activity.

“Guys, what’s the problem down there?” Patch commed.

The technicians looked alarmed at the lack of activity on the surface of the egg. One pulled out a sensor, attached it to the side of the egg, and activated a diagnostic program. He shook his head and pointed to the main umbilicus. The egg was cracked right at the coupling, and the cable was burnt through. The two looked at each other in wonder as Patch continued to call them.

“Guys? Someone, please tell me what’s going on. Is there a problem? Guys?”

# Four
# MOTHER

**Author's note: Jason Cordova expected a light, funny story from me for his anthology *Chicks in Tank Tops*. The punny title came long before the actual concept—an homage of sorts to the humorous fantasy series *Chicks in Chainmail*, edited by Esther Friesner.**

**But *World Enough* was still percolating in my brain, and I had a different idea. What if the "chick in the tank top"... was the tank itself?**

**"Mother" is an advanced combat AI, whose job it is to manage the battlespace, protecting her platoon, and giving the best odds to survive.**

**What happens when Mother is the last "woman" standing?**

**When Mother fails her primary mission, she never expected to get a second chance. This time, paired with Magda, a war orphan who is herself fostering other orphans, all driven by a shared purpose: to reclaim their world?**

**As long as they have *Mother* to protect them, they will fight.**

"MECHA ONE REPORTS 'READY.'"

"Mecha Two, Ready."

"Armor Platoon, Ready."

"Intel, Ready."

"Command, Ready."

"Acknowledged. Base, QRF Charlie Company is up and ready for deployment."

"Hoo-ah, Charlie. Go kick some ELF ass!"

Joshua Ling pulled the hatch down on his command tank and instructed the assault pod to seal up and interface with the continent-spanning hyperloop. Unit deployments no longer depended on ocean or air transport, not when the hyperloops could deliver a fully-loaded cargo pod to nearly anywhere on the continent in just two hours.

Of course, the Eden Liberation Front had sabotaged all hyperloop termini within fifty klicks of their base. That wouldn't matter to Ling's Quick Reaction Force. Their pods were equipped with breaching charges and fold-out winglets. Once they reached the ELF perimeter, they'd launch missiles ahead of their pods, blast through the openings and glide the remaining distance on the velocity they'd built up in the tubes.

"Mother, ready to deploy?"

"Yes, Joshua. Mother is here. Mother will take care of you."

"Thank you, Mother." Ling patted the comm panel next to his command chair and strapped himself in. The ritual was repeated throughout the company as the command tank's artificial intelligence assured each of the troops that she was indeed looking out for their safety.

Mother was unique to Ling's company of the Paradise City QRF. True artificial intelligence had long eluded the efforts of cyberneticists, but advances in brain-to-computer interfacing had enabled "capsulation," where a failing human body could be placed in a life-support pod, and the still-functioning brain interfaced with computers and equipment. The organic components often didn't survive for long, but after discovering that both personality and sentience would persist in the cybernetic components, such "capsulated intelligences" or CIs began to emerge as an alternative to true artificial intelligence.

"Mother" had been a mecha pilot, badly injured in combat. Immediately after capsulation, she'd served in QRF headquarters' tactical analysis section. As a CI, she no longer required extensive life support, and elected to be installed in the QRF commander's tank in a role she called "combat nanny" – to assist the commander and look after the welfare of the QRF troopers. Mother served as both the "brains" of Ling's command tank, as well as the guardian angel of the company.

"Acceleration, two-point-two-seven Gs," Mother announced, as a countdown timer appeared in the periphery of his vision. "Twenty-seven seconds to cut-off."

True to her prediction, the acceleration eased, and then ended after a half-minute of acceleration. Military hyperloop assault pods operated much differently from their civilian counterparts. A typical commuter pod accelerated and decelerated slowly for the comfort of the passengers. They also utilized a magnetic levitation system inside evacuated tubes with all air removed to reduce drag and resistance. A military pod accelerated rapidly, often with a rocket assist, and punctured the tubes periodically to dispel the vacuum. That way, when a military pod blasted through walls of a hypertube, there was no sudden inrush of air to disrupt the flight of the now airborne assault pod.

Inside his pod. Ling watched the timer count down as the pod's velocity mounted. Acceleration eased off, and a new counter began – sixty-five minutes to emergence. It was almost twenty-five hundred kilometers, the distance from Phoenix, Arizona to Atlanta, Georgia on the planet of Joshua's birth. It seemed like several lifetimes ago; it was certainly several military careers ago. Experience taught him that the long transit time couldn't be helped; the only way to be certain the ELF couldn't have an intel source in the assault force was to use a QRF from so far away. It didn't mean he wouldn't fret the entire hour, but there was no way the ELF knew his force was on its way.

"Mother! QRF status?" Ling shouted over the sound of alarms and high-pressure air venting into the operations center of the command tank.

"Mecha One platoon is down to three effectives. Alpha and Charlie squads are gone, Bravo 2 is hard orange, but still effective. Delta one is yellow, but with limited mobility. Delta four is totally green. That kid Filip leads a charmed life. Of course, he has me to look out for him." There was a noticeable pause – unusual for Mother, even under heavy information load. "Mecha Two is completely gone, as is Intel. Armor has one tank remaining."

Again, the CI paused. The comm crackled, and there was something that sounded like a sob.

"Mother?"

"I failed you, Joshua. I didn't take care of you. They knew we were coming."

"That's okay, Mother, I know you will still take care of us. See if you can keep Filip alive to get back to Landing City. They need to know what happened here." There was a cry of pain, and a sound like ripping cloth.

"Joshua?"

"Damned plastic of the command chair melted into the skin of my arm. I tried to pull loose and made a mess. The painkillers aren't enough. There's a representative of ELF high command coming to take my 'surrender.' You know I can't do that, but I can't move, either. You'll have to take care of me one more time."

This time the sob was quite clear over the comm. "Yes, Joshua. Sleep well. Mother will take care of you."

There was a faint hiss, and Ling's head fell forward.

"Sleep well, Joshua. I'm sorry."

THE RAIN WAS ALREADY starting to turn to sleet. Dusana knew that she and Magdalena would never survive the night in the open. There was a collapsed building ahead. She would see if there was a relatively stable overhang or opening. There was no hope of building a fire to get warm, but she had dry clothing for the baby, if only she could get out of the coming snow.

Magda started to cry, and Dusa pulled herself further into a dark opening that appeared to lead deep into the rubble. "Hush, Magda, Mama is here. Mama will take care of you."

The opening led deep under the jumble of concrete and rebar, and ended at a solid metal wall. There was some form of hatch that was partially ajar. An adult male probably would not have fit, but Dusa was sixteen and thin from lack of food. She carefully placed her bundle inside and squeezed through the narrow opening. It was dark, but there was faint light from permaglow paint at the junction between wall and ceiling. The interior was badly damaged, with signs of a fire and an explosion. Scraps of some form of uniform were still stuck to a central chair – embedded in melted plastic. There was no sign of occupants. Either they'd survived and gotten out on their own, or the ELFs had taken them for propaganda broadcasts.

She placed the crying baby in the chair and started looking through the cabinets and lockers. There was a spare uniform and protein bars in one locker, and a synth unit that appeared to be full with protein paste.

*Good. She could use that for Magda.*

There didn't appear to be power for the synth unit, but she wouldn't need that to get into the paste hopper or the water supply. She scooped a handful of paste, placed a few drops on her fingertip, and placed the finger in Magda's mouth. The child sucked the protein paste and then continued to suck on the finger. Dusa repeated the process several times, until Magda turned her head and started to cry.

*Now she needs water.*

There was a water station on the bulkhead next to the synth, complete with a fitting to fill drink bulbs. She didn't see any clean ones, but there was a used one on the floor below the unit. She filled it halfway, then squeezed the water out over her hands, rinsing the bulb and cleaning herself in one task. The refilled bulb then went to Magda, who drank it greedily.

*Shelter and food, at least for now.*

When Magda finished the bulb, Dusa sat in the half-melted central chair and rocked her baby to sleep. "Hush now, baby. Sleep well. Mama is here. Mama is taking care of you."

She never noticed the brief flicker of light on the command console.

Days passed, Dusana changed out of her wet, ragged clothes into the clean uniform from the locker. She'd explored a bit more, and found a 'fresher unit with clean towels, which she'd used to rewrap Magdalena. For now, she would use her old rags in place of diapers. Cleaning them was another matter. The only water she could access was from the water station, and it was only half-full. For that matter, the protein paste was tasteless and not sufficient for her own nutrition. It would keep the baby alive, but it wasn't enough for two, especially not given the fever and weakness she'd felt coming on.

She wasn't too worried about ELF war gases. She'd sacrificed her own food, shelter, and warmth for Magda, so this was probably the winter flu – the same one that had claimed her own Mama last year. She needed medicine, but knew that would be impossible. The ELFs didn't care about a lone Westlander girl and her child. She would care for her child the best she could. Her own self-care could wait.

Magda began to cry. It was time to eat.

"Hush, Magda. Mama is here. Mama will take care of you."

"HEY MOM? IS THAT a baby crying?"

"Where? Where did you get to? Stanis!"

"Over here, Mom. It's like a cave under this pile of stuff."

"Don't go in there, Stanis. It's not safe."

"It's okay, Dad, I can see down in, and there doesn't appear to be anything loose."

"Pavle?"

"Yes, Mimi, I see it. Stanis, get out of there and let me take a look."

"He's right, Pavle. There's a baby crying in there."

"I know, I hear it, too. Keep Stanis out here while I take a look.

"MIMI, COME QUICK. IT's safe enough. Stanis, keep watch for any ELF patrols. You can come in a few feet to keep out of sight. It's stable enough."

"What's wrong, Pavs? I hear the baby a lot better."

"This is some old installation. Could have been a panic room or a command center. There's a metal wall. Careful with the door, it's a tight squeeze. Some poor girl crawled in here with a baby. She's in bad shape and the infant is crying."

"Oh! Oh my. Oh, you poor dear, you're burning up. Pavle, get my bag."

"Mag... Magda... my baby."

"Don't you worry, dear. Hush. Mimi is here now. I'll take care of you."

"Her name is... Magdalena. Take care of her."

“Pavle! Hurry.”

“Coming, Mim.”

“Oh. Oh no.”

“Umm. Damn.”

“Dad? Mom? I see movement.”

“Okay, Stanis, come back in here and see if you can pull that door shut. Mims? I know we can’t do anything for the girl, but we need to quiet the baby.”

“Your poor darling. It looks like your mama took good care of you at the cost of herself. Dry cry, my sweet. Mimi is here. Mimi will take care of you.”

“Stanis, turn off your light. Be still. Be quiet.”

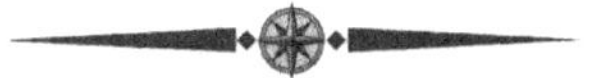

Mimi, Pavle and Stanis took shelter in the command center through the night. ELF patrols came and went outside, so they dared not move until they were certain the troops were gone. Pavle took the opportunity to look around the room with a small, shielded lamp. It didn’t give off much light – that was the point, to keep from being detected – but it was enough to see that there was technology here – either government or ELF. Aside from that, they had no idea what the structure was nor did they know how it had gotten here.

Mimi had been a nurse and worked in at several government hospitals before the ELF came; Pavle, an engineer at one of the big power generation facilities. Now they were refugees like so many others. Another mouth to feed was hard – but if the government and their liberators didn’t care – it was left to individuals to make a difference.

The Eden Liberation Front didn't care about individual people, only tearing down the government in the name of "liberation." For that matter, the government cared little for the individual, and more for perpetuating their own existence. The town had been reduced to rubble by the fighting – and neither side really cared. An outside force had come to mediate and force an end to the war, but had been ambushed by both sides. There was no hope of ending the conflict – not when both sides joined forces to take out an interloper. Each side hated each other so much, yet they would never allow outsiders to interfere in their war

By now the entire continent was engulfed. This town had once had a name but there was nothing left worth naming anymore. Buildings were fallen into rubble, stores, homes, and hospitals lay smashed and buried under boulders of concrete and steel.

One such store, a small grocery, was accessible from just outside the command center. If poor Dusana had known, she might have survived, given the access to food and purified water. As it was, Stanis had discovered the treasure trove of supplies several days later. His small body was able to navigate the narrow crevices in the wrecked building. He found dry and canned food, formula for the baby, disposable diapers, as well as clothes that could be used when those ran out. Mimi insisted that they keep and raise the baby. Pavle knew it was a risk, but who was he to deny his wife? Stanis was mostly indifferent. He got to explore the ruins, while Pop scouted and Mama cared for the baby. He might have been more enthusiastic about having a baby sister under other circumstances, but it he was still too young to really know anything else but the meager existence of scavenging.

His exploration led to more spaces under the fallen building. There was a clothing shop, and another filled with now-useless electronics.

Pavle declared that this might be a good place to stay, if only they could secure it. He looked around at the command center where they spent each evening. This was off-world tech. He didn't know exactly what it was, but he could work on it and try to discover a purpose. He knew, though, that if he got it working, it would become a target either of the ELF or the government.

They built a shelter in the tunnel – beyond the steel door that led into the command center, and in front of the crevices that led deeper under the collapsed building.

STANIS GREW TO THE point where he could no longer fit into the small crevices and cracks and get into the stores under the collapsed building. But as he grew into manhood, so did Magdalena grow into girlhood. She was small, and thanks to malnutrition – both hers and her biological mother's – she would likely remain that way. Once Stanis couldn't squeeze into the small crevices, she could. She took over the role of primary scavenger for her new family. Much to her adoptive mother's delight, one of those places was a hospital. It was under another fallen building, so they couldn't secure it as well, but they could get as many supplies out of it as possible and stash them underneath their own hideaway.

Before the war, Mimi thought she had worked in or near this town – but one wrecked city looked much like any other, and she had despaired of identifying any particular place in the rubble. She knew it would be rare to find medical supplies. The soldiers would have taken them – either directly from the medical center, or confiscated from refugees.

The town had become a good place to scavenge, and more refugees came. Pavle and Mimi knew that they could not yet afford to reveal the off-world electronics and machinery that they had discovered, nor the treasure trove of supplies beneath their feet, but they could share what they had gleaned so far. They closed up an additional layer of their shelter and moved almost to the opening of the tunnel, under a large tilted slab of building wall that served as shelter from the elements.

Their shelter looked like any other refugee lean-to as the refugee camp grew in the remains of what had once been a productive city. More survivors came to the area, picked through the rubble, and found enough to sustain a basic existence. As long as they were left alone, they could survive...

...but Pavle and Mimi knew it wouldn't last. The day would come when the ELF decided that this was indeed their territory, and it could not simply be left to the scum of the earth.

Magda was eight years old when the ELF soldiers came to town, driving more refugees in front of them. Troops stood around the remnants of the city center with their guns pointed inward and the frightened citizenry huddled inside the circle. This would not be a day for scavenging or crawling through the small passages in the rubble of trying to find new sources of food, medicine, or water. This was a day to hide and remain out of sight – hopefully unnoticed by ELF soldiers.

The soldiers brought heavy equipment with them. Bulldozers cleared a large area in the center of town, and Pavle was worried that it came awfully close to his family's shelter. Still, despite clearing an area of several city blocks, it still did not come all the way to the collapsed building where they had built their temporary home.

A senior officer – colonel from the looks of the insignia on his lapels – addressed the huddled refugees in the middle of town. His troops had rooted out many of the existing residents at gunpoint. Some had been shot when they resisted. Pavle and Stanis went to the assembly, but only after leaving Mimi and Magda behind in one of the secret places.

"I am Oberst Storm. I am the new authority in this town. You will address me as Master, and my soldiers as Lord. You work under our benevolent care, now. My men will have barracks outside the city to watch over your safety. We will build a fence to keep out those who would prey on you. In exchange for our protection, you will be released in workgroups under guard. You will scavenge the countryside, under our direction. We will collect what you find, and distribute it fairly among you. In return for your cooperation, we will provide shelter and give you food and water. We are here for you."

The colonel had a cold face. Pavle did not for a moment believe that the soldiers were there to protect them. These ELF soldiers, as all those before them, were in this for themselves. After all, if they were here to protect the citizens... why did they continue to hold them at gunpoint?

Later that day, a fence went up enclosing an area approximately ten times that of the city center. They drafted men from the refugees to install the fence while the soldiers – other than those operating bulldozers and trucks – stood outside with their guns pointing inward. Most of the enclosed area was wrecked buildings, piled rubble, and a few standing walls. Trucks dumped canvas and plastic sheets, but nothing else with which to construct them. The refugees would have to scavenge and supply the rest.

The fence was completed that night, and the vehicles moved outside the perimeter. Over the next several days, barracks, a mess hall, and other buildings were constructed for the soldiers. A headquarters building had been brought in pre-fabricated. It was one large rectangular container that had to be lifted off the heavy ground effect truck by crane. The colonel disappeared, and from that day onward, the people inside the fence rarely saw him.

They mostly dealt with his soldiers.

Each day a work crew was assembled in the center of town. Of the estimated four hundred refugees, about one-quarter were children too small or too young to work. Another fifty or sixty people were too old, sick, or crippled – so the soldiers would gather about two hundred people each day, leaving only the bare minimum to care for the young and elderly. The rest had to go out into the surrounding countryside and scavenge.

At first, they worked only the immediate surrounding fields, but as that region was stripped, groups were taken as much as 100 miles away from the town each day. They went to ruined farmhouses and scavenged all of the food, seed, and farm equipment. They went to battlefields where stripped the bodies of the slain, and scavenged food, water, fuel, electronic, and mechanical components. The guards were always close, and any discovery of weapons or ammunition was confiscated immediately. When they encountered towns and cities within scavenging district, the soldiers directed the laborers to concentrate on searching for money, luxuries, and consumer goods. Everything was taken whether it worked or not, and it was all presented to the colonel's men upon return to the city every night.

Each citizen had to present themselves every evening in order to receive a food and water ration – even the children. The elderly, sick and lame received nothing. In one of his rare appearances, the colonel told them that even children could scavenge, or grow to be a scavenger. The aged and infirm were liabilities, and could not earn their own keep. The people were free to share rations, but would not receive any extra.

The food and water allocations weren't enough to live on. It was barely enough to survive, and many died over the next few months. It was clear that the ELF did not care for the people, they only wanted a slave labor workforce.

Many of the adults gave children extra food, but in too many cases, what was left was not enough for the adults. One by one, adults became sick. It didn't matter if someone collapsed in the fields or back inside the encampment – they were simply left where they fell. The government had not been much better. It professed a philosophy of sharing and distributing – "from each according to their ability, to each according to their need." In reality, that meant that those who had extra had it taken from them; but at least there was a possibility to earn more. To the ELF, need was weakness, and weakness should be culled. Their basic philosophy was "survival of the strongest." Over time, additional refugees were brought in to make up the losses. The population grew to about 500 people and then began to decrease again as the weak died off, and those too strong of will were killed by the soldiers.

The first day, Mimi and Magda had to submit themselves to a census. Every night thereafter, there was a roll call and they had to come out of their shelter to receive their food and water allocation. Soldiers entered their shelter and looked around, but they never found the false back wall, nor the passages to the underground storage or the command center. It continued to be their secret.

While the adults scavenged outside the fence, Magda continued to crawl through the rubble inside the perimeter of what was now openly acknowledged to be a prisoner camp. She also helped Mimi nurse the sick as much as she was allowed. New finds of medical supplies were often confiscated – she knew, because she was often called on to treat injured soldiers, and saw the medical supplies they'd hoarded. She was allowed to treat minor injuries, strains, cuts, burns and scrapes – and Magda learned at her side. Anything that would allow a worker to participate in a work party the next day was permitted, but if she tried to treat anyone who needed extended care, that person would be missing the next morning. It broke her heart, but Mimi learned not to waste her meager supplies.

Stanis had grown big and strong. He and his father were often part of the work parties. They had a little bit of extra food left, gathered from the grocery store. There was likely more, but they dared not go down to dig out more. It was too dangerous. The presence of the store was still largely unknown. Despite the needs of their fellow refugees, it was best to stay that way.

Magda's father told her one night. "There will come a time of greater need. We will need this for the children. Remember this, Magda. We must use it sparingly enough to keep our strength. But we must save what we can and use it for the children."

Years passed and the ELF brought more troops and more refugees to be slaves in their camp. The pickings became too thin near the camp, and work crews needed to would go out further distances. At first, they would stay overnight and come back the next evening. Then the crews would be gone for two days. One day, a work crew went out and never came back. A week later, the soldiers who'd escorted the workers returned with plenty of salvage and were seen laughing and drinking with their fellows.

There was no sign of the prisoners.

Pavle and Mimi whispered about it one night. They tried to be quiet, but Magda overheard.

"They served their purpose. Once the people finished scavenging, the soldiers either shot them, or left them to starve."

"Perhaps both. There were not enough trucks to carry a week's worth of provisions for the work crew. They were worked to death."

"You are probably right, Mim. It is hard enough to get by on the rations we do have. I know I wouldn't last more than a couple of days without rations."

"It is almost the end. We must prepare."

"Not for you and me, but for Stanis and Magda."

"For Magda and the children."

"Yes. For the children."

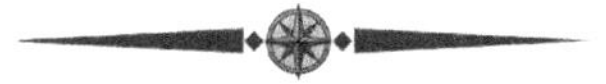

It had been years since the ELF had barricaded the town; the fence was now a fortified wall. It was even more years since Mimi and Pavle had made it a home for their son and adopted their daughter. Pavle was a strong man, a proud man, but he knew to submit to the soldiers, even as he began to grow weak from overwork and thin rations. As a nurse, Mimi was still in demand, but they both knew that it was only a matter of time before Pavle stopped being picked for work crews. When that happened, his share of rations would stop.

Late at night, they talked about plans. Stanis wanted to escape – he wanted his mother to find a way to weaken the soldiers so that he and the other young men could make a move. When she refused, he moved out of their shelter. Still, he kept their secret – until the day he, too, disappeared when a work party did not come back.

His loss devastated Mimi, and her health deteriorated. Pavle was determined to find another way, and he began to go back into the command center. He worked on the consoles and electronics, replacing components with lookalikes from the consumer electronics they'd found in the hidden stores. Magda helped her father every evening, then tucked him into bed, and returned to study what she could of the strange instrumentation.

"This is some sort of command center. Over there behind that wall is a computer," he told her, one night. He pointed to the wall in front of the half-melted chair, "these dark panels would display maps, and pictures of the outside world."

"What good is a picture, if we can't see what is around us? Pictures don't move. They show us the past, not what is real!" Magda countered.

"These were live pictures. Cameras, like the one I showed you yesterday, took pictures of the outside and showed them on these screens." Several nights ago, Pavle had rigged a camera in the passage leading to the underground tunnels. He told her it was an "early warning system." He'd run a wire and set up a flat, rectangular device that showed images from the camera. It had taken many weeks to free up the metallic door and rig a lock so that Magda could hide inside the command center if strangers came. The camera would alert them, and she could hide, while her father drew the interlopers away.

"I've seen computers like these before. A long time ago. It was technology from Earth."

Earth was a fiction to Magda, a fairy tale told to children to make them behave. "If you are good, the people from Earth will take you to a land of plenty." To many, the home world of humanity was a mythological place with no wars, no shortages, no hunger, and no poverty. Pavle knew that it was really not that perfect, but compared to Eden, it really was a land of freedom and plenty.

He still had no idea what this command center controlled, but he knew the technology he recognized was important. There had been a time when he had worked in the computer center of a great city to the west, and had seen something like this: a rare capsulated intelligence.

Pavle taught Magda, late in the night, growing weaker by the day. He knew this was important, and *someone* needed to know. Artificially intelligent computers had never become reality, but in unusual occasions, a damaged person could connect their brain to a computer, creating a hybrid of human and synthetic intelligence. In rare circumstances, the human intelligence and personality blended so completely with the computer, that it resided wholly within the electronics, with no further need of frail biological components.

Pavle had met one, those many years ago. It called itself Hephaestus, and it had operating the power plant, energy distribution, traffic, and shipping in the city of West Shore. The intelligence had been cool and distant, lacking the warmth and much of the emotion of flesh-and-blood. Still, it had a sense of humor and expressed some concern for the humans around it. Its humanity was not gone – just altered.

Pavle hoped that if he could find the secret of this machine, perhaps he could wake up a synthetic intelligence that would help them. He worked in secret, with Magda at his side. He taught her all he knew of electronics, power systems, coolant, and the circuits that supported intelligence. Despite all of his tinkering, the intelligence he suspected was there never woke up. He supposed that having been turned off for so long had caused the death of this rare being.

Magda was older – a teen now – but not much bigger than she'd been as a child. She was still the best at getting into small spaces in the rubble around the community. She continued to explore, and once in a while she would find a cache of food or other supplies. Most of those she hid and showed to her father late at night. Some was turned into the soldiers – they'd be suspicious if she didn't, but given her size, the soldiers still didn't consider her to be much more than a child herself.

She often found herself watching children as the parents went out to scavenge. She'd gathered a troop of children around her, and mothered them almost as if they were her own. When a small boy or girl came to her because their parent hadn't woken up, or hadn't returned from the fields, Magda would hold them tight, stroke their hair, and whisper, "it's okay Magda is here. Magda will take care of you."

Rations became short. There were fewer guards on the perimeter, and fewer soldiers in the barracks. The colonel had not been seen for many months. Daily food and water deliveries were cut every few weeks. There was less to go around and many of the adults preferred to give their share to the children. There were still adults who insisted that they needed an extra share to be able to go out and glean the battlefields. There were fights over the food distribution, and sometimes bodies would be left on the ground in the aftermath.

Those who elected to shorten their own rations entrusted them to Magda. She stashed extra rations in her secret caves while still making sure that the children had enough to stay active. She taught them to explore the small spaces and showed them safe spots to avoid the soldiers and the growing collection of selfish adults who followed the children in hopes of discovering where they hid their rations.

Mimi grew weaker, and fell into a fever late one snowy night. As the only nurse, she was unable to treat herself. Magda tried, but she simply didn't know enough. She sat holding the hand of the only mother she'd known – as that hand grew cold and stiff.

Pavle was beside himself with grief. Magda tried to console him, but there was just too much broken inside him, and there was nothing she could do. He stormed out of the shelter, to the gate in the perimeter wall, and yelled obscenities. He punched the wall with his fists, and when guards came to investigate, he punched them too. He was captured and chained to the inside of the wall. A dozen soldiers lined up with their guns and shot him – each of them emptying their rifle magazine.

They left him there, chained to the pockmarked, bloodstained wall as an example.

Magda retreated to the command center tears in her eyes. She looked around at the great machine and she beat her fists against the consoles. "Where were you? You failed us! You were supposed to help us! How am I going to take care of the children now?"

A little boy, she called him Peter, although the others said his parents had called him by another name. Those parents were long gone, and Pavle and Mimi had taken him in, although it was Magda who cared for him most of the time. Peter didn't know what to do and he clutched Magda and cried. Despite her own grief she put her arms around him, stroked the back of his head and whispered. "Don't cry, Peter. It's okay. I'll be your mother. Mother is here and I'll take care of you."

Deep inside the great machine, a circuit closed.

The next day the soldiers did not come to gather a work party. They simply left. That night, there was no food distribution. In the morning, a few soldiers returned to gather all of the adults that they could find. They marched out of camp and did not return that night.

Once again, there was no food, no water – no adults. Magda gathered the few remaining children and moved them to the secret passages under the building.

*This was the time Poppa meant. The emergency when the rest of the stored supplies would be needed.*

She led the children deep into the tunnels and gathered all of the stored food and water. Some of the packages had spoiled, and much of the water had leaked, but she had all of it moved into the command center.

The children cried. They were hungry and thirsty. They wanted their parents. All they had was Magda. She held them, hugged them, and whispered to them. "Don't worry, Magda is here, Magda will take care of you."

*That phrase! It meant something!* The intelligence inside the vast machine thought to itself as it roused itself from its long sleep.

There was a crackling sound coming from high on one wall. Magda looked around. *What was that?*

Something like a voice came over the hidden speaker. It stopped, after a moment, though. More odd noises sounded, then a smooth, melodious voice spoke.

"Mother is here. Mother will take care of you."

THE REPAIRS THAT PAVLE and Magda made had at least restored sensor data to Mother. The computers had recorded snapshots of life around her for the past fifteen years, and she reviewed those records in a few nanoseconds. She looked at the children, analyzed their age, their health, the absence of adults. Mother then looked at Magda, dirty, clothed in rags, but still standing defiantly to defend the children.

"Magda. It's okay. I am Mother, the intelligence within this war machine. My duty was to protect my family – the men and women of my platoon. I failed them, but I can still protect you."

Over the next few hours, Mother instructed Magda in how to refill the nutrient paste dispenser with the spoiled food. Processing would remove the contaminants, and Mother would synthesize extra vitamins for the starving children. The water dispenser was easily patched, and could refill itself from atmospheric water vapor. Lockers were opened, to provide cloth for bedding, and as Magda helped Mother bring the rest of her systems online, the internal fabricators began to turn out clothing for the children.

Rested, fed, the children were stronger. With Mother's guidance, Magda sent them out to clear specific areas of the rubble. Some of it was simply too big, even for Magda, but Mother said it would be okay. She would manage.

Mother used the large black rectangles – she called them "screens" – to teach Magda what she would need to know. One of the first lessons was the definition of a *tank* and what it was capable of. Magda was torn between taking the children to safety, and getting revenge on the soldiers of the ELF. It was Mother who convinced her the safety of the children was the most important.

The day came when Mother shook off the remnants of the fallen building. The children were huddled inside the command center, but Magda stood outside as the massive machine crawled out of the rubble.

Worn, weathered, dented, and crumpled – she'd never seen anything so beautiful!

When she re-entered the command center, Mother opened a compartment and showed her a brand-new set of clothing. "This is a tank commander's uniform, Magda. You are my commander now, so you should wear it."

Magda just lowered her head. "Thank you, Mother. Let's get the kids to safety, then we're going hunting. Don't worry, Mother. Magda is here, now. Together you and I will do what we need to do to protect *all* of our families."

# Five
# GUT CHECK

**AUTHORS NOTE: GLENN ARMSTRONG Shepard is the hero of my novel *The Moon and the Desert*. Glenn is an astronaut, pilot, and flight surgeon—just doing his job. In that novel, doing his job nearly kills him. He's horrifically injured rescuing a fellow astronaut from a crash, and his body is rebuilt with advanced prosthetics and bionics. He has to prove that he is better, stronger, faster—the right bionic man for the job.**

**But before all that, Glenn was the junior astronaut on a return-to-the-Moon mission. He didn't get to go down to the surface. He was tasked with monitoring medical readouts from orbit and assisting with the construction of what would become the (then-unnamed) lunar orbital space station.**

**Many convention panels speculate about the role of doctors in various science fiction scenarios. One of the least favorite? Performing surgery in zero gravity.**

**Glenn Shepard has to do exactly that.It's time for a gut check.**

**[Note: The chapters in *The Moon and the Desert* are all preceded by an epigram, a "ChirpChat" excerpted from future social media. They often provide background or a different**

**perspective on the story than the primary narrative. One such ChirpChat is included here for stylistic consistency.]**

*George J.*

*@spacefan*

*"A momentous day, as NASA prepares to launch twin Wyvern capsules for our return to the moon. Next week on 20 July, humans will return to the moon exactly 60 years after the first landing of Neil Armstrong and Buzz Aldrin.*

*"It's been a busy month at Spaceport America, Mojave Spaceport, Boca Chica, and Cape Canaveral as components of the Luna One surface base and Luna Two orbital stations have been launched. These structures will form the first permanent structures on the surface and orbit of the Moon.*

*"Not since Gemini 6 and 7 has NASA launched two capsule missions at the same time. The Wyvern capsules, Castor and Pollux, will launch within hours of each other, taking their ten astronauts and two Dragonet landing modules to the moon for this historic event.*

*"Stay tuned for more space news, space fans!"*

*ChirpChat, July 2029*

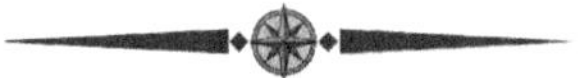

The launch—any launch—was best described as hours of boredom followed by seconds of crushing acceleration, minutes of frantic activity, which was then followed by more hours of boredom. News reports before and during the launch had cheered NASA for finally returning to the moon, then derided them for copying all of the procedures that had been used for the Apollo moon landings in the last century.

This time, though, two pairs of spacecraft were headed to the moon. The two Wyvern command modules each carried five astronauts. The Dragonet moon landers would carry six of those astronauts to the lunar surface, where they would begin assembling a permanent base called Luna One. The remaining four astronauts would remain on orbit to begin assembling the core modules of Luna Two, and orbital station which would support the reusable Wyverns and Dragonets.

The combined mission was planned to be the first of four missions in a year's time. Wyverns One and Two, *Castor* and *Pollux*, respectively, were being sent simultaneously, and would spend four weeks at the moon. Wyvern Three would arrive before the original crew returned, and would concentrate on the orbital station for three months. One month later, Wyvern Four would deliver a crew to continue work on the surface base. *Castor* and *Pollux* would return three months later to bring fresh crew for each base and rotate existing crew home, a process that would be repeated every six months, with up to six Wyvern and Dragonet craft.

The commander of the mission, Charles Johnson, had claimed the position of honor in *Castor*—the pilot seat, putting the actual Wyvern Command Module Pilot, Bill Chappell, in the co-pilot position. That bumped the Command Module Co-Pilot (and flight medic), Glenn Shepard to the middle of the row of three acceleration couches in the upper deck of the Wyvern.

*At least I'm top row, even if I didn't get a viewport*, Glenn thought to himself. Not only were Scott Huggins and Lissa Hailey from the

Dragonet crew—as well as their counterparts Jo Kay and R Hopkinson on *Pollux*—relegated to the underdeck, they wouldn't have much to do until approaching time for the lunar descent. Shepard had taken some good-natured teasing and ribbing from his fellow crewmates. After all, why did they need a doctor when they were only going to be at the Moon for four weeks? All crewmembers had completed a military or civilian equivalent of the combat lifesaver course, enabling them to perform many emergency medical procedures. Besides that, the groundside medical officers in Mission Control monitored vital signs and medical conditions.

On the other hand, there was a grim truth behind the question. Any injury occurring on the lunar surface or in orbit carried with it the risk of instantaneous death. Minor injuries, such as sprains and strains, headaches, even minor colds, had all been experienced throughout the space programs and none of them had truly required a doctor onsite. Glenn was here as the ultimate gut check, so to speak. The doctor on the scene if anything turned serious. He was also a trained pilot, so he could fly a Wyvern, but other than that, he was mostly just a gopher for the orbital station assembly.

"HEY DOC, GOT ANY antacids?" Bill Chappell asked quietly. The Wyvern pilot had floated over from his station on the other side of the capsule, and was apparently trying to be discreet.

"Antacid? How in the world can you get indigestion from the freeze-dried concentrates we been eating so far?" Glenn whispered back.

"It's just a little bit a reflux. I've had it ever since launch."

"Space sickness? Are you wearing an antinausea patch?"

"It's not space sickness. I don't have any of the nausea. I've been on construction for the spaceyards, Asimov Station, and the Verne Complex. I only got space sick my first time in zero-gee. This is like the twentieth time, and this isn't it. No nausea, just a slight abdominal cramp and some reflux. I just need something to soothe the acid feeling in my throat."

"Ah, okay. I have to trust you on this. I have some chewables. Take this, chew it up, and chase with some liquid. Drink electrolytes, plain water usually makes reflux worse. Don't try to bull through it, though, if you feel nausea, let me know and I'll give you a patch and a shot."

"Thanks, Doc. Much appreciated."

Shepherd would have to put this in his log. So far, he'd had two cases of zero-gee nausea on *Castor*, and he'd been notified of one case on *Pollux*. Space sickness was experienced by most astronauts at some point, usually on a first mission, although some experienced it multiple times. The dietary plan for this mission had been carefully designed to avoid problems of acid reflux or any sort of gastrointestinal upset, given the duration of the mission. For the month they'd be at the Moon, their diet would be boring, but it was designed specifically to avoid G.I. issues in zero-gee. He'd log this and send back in his daily upload. Let the flight-docs in Houston puzzle over it and look for causative factors.

Arrival and lunar orbit insertion were somewhat anti-climactic, after all, this was precisely the part of the mission which had been successfully performed eight times, resulting in six landings. This time, instead of just orbiting while the two Dragonets were on the surface, the Wyverns would intercept and assemble the components of Luna Two. Social media and opinion polls had been conducted to solicit names for the new lunar orbit station. The name *Verne Station* was suggested, based on his book *From the Earth to the Moon*. Unfortunately, that name had already been applied to the new Earth orbital complex which had just begun operation with the long-delayed retirement of the International Space Station. The first and second runners-up were Wells Station, for H.G. Wells, and Melies Station—based on filmmaker George Melies' revolutionary film *A Trip to the Moon*. The debate had not yet settled, perhaps by the time Glenn and his colleagues finished construction, a name would be chosen.

The true space age was back—in fact, this was the start of a *new* age of space, not just exploration, but actually living and working in space. Glenn Armstrong Shepard, named for three pioneers of the Mercury-Gemini-Apollo program, was just thrilled to be a part of it. He was the youngest of the crew, with his thirtieth birthday just a few days away. He was aware that said birthday was one of the reasons he'd been selected—aside from his skills as doctor and pilot. Glenn's birthday, and the date that astronauts would set foot *back* on the Moon, was exactly sixty years from the Apollo 11 landing.

Four hours after Commander Johnson reported their arrival, the comm crackled with a transmission from Wyvern Two. "Houston, this is *Pollux*. Lunar orbit insertion burn is nominal. Internal tracking shows circularization, with main engine cut off in fifteen seconds, do you concur?"

"Roger, *Pollux*, Houston reads circular orbit. Go for MECO." The voice on the comm was Harlan Anders, NASA capsule communicator, or "capcomm."

A few seconds later, the voice of Wyvern Two commander, Major Eben Waters announced, "MECO. Main engine cut off. *Pollux* is in lunar orbit."

"Welcome to the neighborhood." Johnson broadcast to their sister craft.

"Yeah, well, we just got here and they already let you in. What's the neighborhood coming to?" came the response. "You've been here four hours. Is the base ready for us yet?"

"We've been surveying the surface and locating the modules. Scott is tagging each one and Lissa's sending activation codes. It looks like they all soft-landed just fine. All landing bags are deployed. We can't see anything crumpled, although at least one module seems to be a bit further away."

"Oh? How far?"

"Just a short rover drive over to Hadley Rille."

Waters laughed. "Well then, let's just take a rover over to Hadley Apennine and visit the old Apollo 15 site. We can gather up a few more those Genesis rocks."

A new voice came on the comm. "Casper, *Pollux*, we've identified your stray module."

"Oh, please tell us it's not the sleeping module, Nia," Jo Kay from Waters's crew replied.

Nia Osborne, capcomm for the surface mission, laughed. "Yes, that's exactly what it is. You'll be sleeping in the Dragonets for a little while until you get that one towed back to base."

"Oh, joy," Johnson said. "At least tell us there's no major terrain obstacles in the way."

"It looks relatively clear. The back room suggests you leave the air bags inflated and roll it onto the sledge when you go retrieve it. That should do for the distance you need, although you'll probably have to stop and recharge the buggy at least once on the way out, and several times on the way back."

"Well then, soonest begun is soonest done. Let's be about it, people!"

THE NEXT TWENTY-FOUR HOURS were filled with preparing the Dragonets, and getting them on their way to the historic lunar double landing. Once the Dragonets were on their way to the surface, it was time for *Castor* and *Pollux* to start station assembly. Chappell, the *Castor* pilot, along with Bruce Denison and Misty White from *Pollux*, had actual orbital construction experience. Chappell and Denison had each spent rotations on Verne, Asimov, and on the ISS—keeping it aloft while Verne was under construction. Misty White was an engineer who'd been instrumental in the design of Luna Two. She also had a degree in orbital dynamics, so her input on "snagging, bagging, and tagging" the station modules was essential to their success. Glenn's job—when he wasn't flying a Wyvern as backup to Chappell—mostly consisted of going inside the modules to open fold-out bulkheads and "insert Tab A into Slot B." He would finish the interior assembly of the prefab modules while being videoed so that Mission Control could look over his shoulder and verify that everything was in place. He'd told Chappell that it sounded like he'd be responsible for the world's most expensive unboxing video.

*Castor* had to speed up to catch the first component of the orbital station, and they did so by paradoxically slowing down. The main engine was fired to slow the capsule, dropping it into a lower orbit. The shorter orbital radius meant that the ship actually travelled faster with respect to an item in higher orbit. Once *Castor* had caught up—in fact, had passed—the Core Module, they would fire the engine again to speed up and rise to the higher orbit. It was complex and seemed counterintuitive, but it had been a tried-and-true method for orbital rendezvous since the Gemini missions of the previous century.

*Pollux* had the opposite problem. Their arrival four hours after *Castor* had put them in orbit ahead of *Castor* and the Core Module. They would wait until *Castor* had completed docking, then fire their main engine to speed up and move to a higher orbit. This would, in turn, slow them with respect to the docked vessels, allowing them to fall behind, then slow down to drop in just behind the station once it passed underneath them. They would then slow down, drop down to the same orbit and maneuver in for their own docking. From that moment on, the Wyverns and Core Module would be identified as Luna Two.

The Core Module was exactly that—the core of the station, including electronic hubs and distribution, environmental controls, computer systems and docking connectors for the various modules. It had very little space for humans, accommodating at most two at a time. First priority was the power module, with attached solar cell booms that would supply electricity to the station. Next would be the first of many habitat modules which could provide living space for up to seven people, and serve as home to the Wyvern crews for the next four weeks. At least one more habitat module needed to be tracked down and attached before the Dragonet landers returned the lunar surface crew to orbit and dock with Luna Two just in time for Wyvern Three to arrive from Earth. The Dragonets and Wyvern Three crew would remain at Luna Two until the Wyvern Four mission in another three months. The four astronauts of the "Gemini Twins" Wyverns had a busy schedule of orbital construction over the next month. Glenn would certainly not have a chance to be bored until was time to head back to earth.

"At least it isn't going to be totally frozen inside the modules once we dock," said Dennison over the comm line as Glenn stood on the web seat, with most of his body sticking through the Wyvern hatch, getting eyes on the first of the station modules. "I worked on Asimov. The construction was running so far behind that modules stayed in orbit for many months before being attached to the main structure. Their batteries ran down and the heaters failed before we could attach them."

"I would actually think that the modules would be hot inside. After all, don't they pick up full sun for a substantial portion of the day?" Glenn asked.

"You'd think so, but they're designed for passive heat radiation, so the moment they pass into Earth's shadow they lose an awful lot of heat and really don't gain back that much from direct solar heating. Heat doesn't go anywhere in vacuum, so the modules are designed to mostly reflect sunlight to avoid overheating once the station is in full operation."

"There's also the fact that Asimov was built with inflatable modules," came from the pilot's seat. "Vapor expansion always cools things down. When you starting with something the volume of a small car and inflate it to the size of a duplex, vapor expansion absorbs an awful lot of ambient heat. Bruce is right, Asimov never felt warm enough for shirt-sleeves the entire time we worked on it."

"So, what makes Luna Two different?"

"Well, to start with, several of the modules have radiothermal generators. The RTGs are powering instruments that need to stay warmed up and functional no matter where the station is in orbit. Luna Two is going to get shadowed by Earth *and* Moon, so the solar cells are mainly to keep the batteries charged for surplus and backup. The main power is from the RTGs. In fact, it might even be too warm inside and we'll have to vent some of that heat out before we go inside, although I suspect it will end up a bit chilly. It might start out uncomfortable, but won't have to worry about getting your tongue stuck to the flagpole, so to speak."

The core module of Luna Two was in a stable orbit, with a tiny amount of roll. Chappell called Glenn back inside, then brought *Castor* in to dock with the core, first burning thruster fuel to first match the roll, then again to cancel the roll so that *Pollux* could connect to the multi-function transition hub at the far end. For the next several days, *Pollux* would chase down modules and return them to *Castor* and the core, while *Castor* reserved its fuel for keeping the growing station stable.

Glenn thus had the honor of being first inside the core module, and it was exactly as Denison had said, about fifteen Celsius, but nothing they couldn't handle with some warm coveralls. He needed a breathing mask and oxygen supply though. The module had been sent from Earth filled with argon. The inert gas maintained pressurization in flight without wasting oxygen before the crew arrived. Opening up the oxygen-nitrogen supply tanks and flushing the argon with a breathable air mixture would subject the interior to vapor expansion cooling—also just like Denison had said.

Once pressurized and occupied, the temperature came up to about twenty Celsius. It was still cool, but Glenn was happy for it. The next phase of construction was going to generate a lot of body heat, especially since he would be doing a lot of it himself while the other three unpacked and expanded the long arms that would hold their solar panels. Until that was done, and the panels started generating surplus electricity, the core wouldn't have much in the way of climate control. Hot, cold, warm, or cool, it was now a "shirtsleeves" environment.

Normal extravehicular activity, or EVA, limited the number of astronauts "in the Black" during orbital construction. With only four Wyvern crew, that would mean two inside and two outside. Unfortunately, the assembly was scheduled to require three people in the EVA crew. As long as the lone astronaut had access to a Wyvern and was both pilot and field medic certified, they could leave one inside, allowing three to work outside. Glenn fit both requirements, so he had the "easy job" of preparing the interior of the station. As each module was connected to the core, power and communication cables needed to be connected, access hatches and covers had to be closed, and partitions had to be unfolded. Not every module would require quite so much interior work, but the core was...well, the *core*. It contained controls and monitors for every system, crew workstations, and communications, both with Earth, and with the orbital and surface crew.

One of the panels monitored the medical instruments built into each astronaut's space suit, as well as the work coveralls they used when not suited-up. Glenn had to keep an eye on each astronaut—in addition to his station-assembly duties. The information was duplicated at Mission Control on Earth, and they would call him if there was anything in the data that looked out of the ordinary, but Glenn was the Medical Officer, it was a point of pride that he should be the first to detect anything wrong with his colleagues. That was why he set a timer to remind him to check all monitors every ten minutes. Six of the monitors would blank periodically as their orbit took them out of line-of-sight of the lunar crew. The interruption was only momentary as the telemetry was picked up and relayed by one of four data-relay satellites in a high orbit above the moon. The other four were not supposed to go blank at all. The three construction crew were just outside, and he was here. It seemed strange to be checking his own medical telemetry, but Glenn was thorough. Besides, the readouts would tell him if there was any problem before he could even feel it.

The timer sounded as Glenn was assembling a table and padded horizontal "seat'n'feet" bars which would serve to anchor the astronauts in zero-gee. He attached his tools to Velcro strips and moved over to the medical monitors. All ten sets of vital signs including his own, showed the signs of elevated activity. Heart rates were slightly increased, as were body temperature and oxygen consumption. Still, one stood out, and he keyed his comm.

"Bill, you're running a little hot. Are you feeling okay?" Glenn addressed his crewmate from *Castor*.

"Just wrestling with this damn panel. It doesn't want to lock in place." Chappell replied over the comm.

"Okay, well, your heart rate's up. Your temperature is *way* up, but your oxygen consumption doesn't really match. Are you in full sun?"

"Yeah. It's a little warm in the suit. We've been in full sun for a while, but we'll pass into the dark side so. Bruce and Misty are on the back side of the panels, so I'm probably running hotter than they are."

"Okay, well, keep an eye on if. Rest if you can, get in the shade as soon as possible; you should probably turn up your air. Oh, and make sure to drink water. Anything else to report? You feeling okay? No nausea, headaches anything?"

"Bit of a headache this morning, plus some intestinal gurgles. Don't worry, I took something for it. I don't think the chili mac agreed with me last night."

"You should have the Salisbury steak like the rest of us," said Denison.

"Not me," chimed in White. "I had chicken à la king,".

The conversation was interrupted by the voice of the Earthside flight director. "Alright, we all know that zero-gee meals are nothing to brag about. Glenn, keep an eye on Bill's vitals and let FlightMed know if anything changes. Now get back to work. Rome wasn't built in a day and Luna Two won't be either, especially if you guys don't quit jabbering."

"Shepard, why haven't you finished setting up the individual quarters? We connected the hab module a day ago. Why is it so hard for you to unfold a few partitions?"

"Well, Bill, you know I'm not a construction engineer...I'm a flight surgeon. I keep getting interrupted whenever someone needs a medical consult. You know, like your overheating and headache. Then there were the conference calls with the surface when Huggins sprained his ankle, and Hopkinson's exposure burn. If I hadn't detected his "minor suit puncture" it would have been much more serious. So, you know how exciting it is in here... Read the monitors, find access H-fifty-one beta, open the hatch, throw the switch, replace the fuse when the short circuit shuts off all the lights, re-check Bill's vitals and log them for FlightMed, track down the short, splice the line, answer the comm, close the hatch, fold out the bunks, answer the comm, check the monitors...

But that's okay. I'm sure you can unfold the panels for your own sleeping quarters."

"Don't let Bill get under your skin. He's irritable because he's been sweating inside his suit; when he tries to adjust the temperature he gets cold," Misty said.

"Hey that's not fair! I'm not sweating and I'm *still* cold."

After the first few days, work had settled into a routine of the EVA team maneuvering modules into place, attaching to the multi-function hub, performing the interior connections, then flushing the argon with breathing air and warming up the module for use. Glenn continued to perform the majority of the interior work where he could periodically check the health monitors. That schedule was due to change, though. The core, habitat and solar power modules were all in close orbit, but there were specialty instrumentation and workstation modules in similar, but not quite matching orbits. So far, the assembly had been able to utilize gentle nudges from *Pollux*'s maneuvering jets as well as guidance by smaller thrusters built into the astronauts' EVA suits, but retrieving the far modules would use too much fuel—fuel that the Wyverns would need for return to Earth.

Mission Control had planned for that contingency though, and a newly-arrived module contained a large fuel tank and a compact orbital maneuvering engine. It had a typically complicated mission name, but the Luna Two team simply called it the "tug." Either *Castor* or *Pollux* could attach to the "tug" and use the engine to change orbits and retrieve more distant station modules. They could even refuel the Wyverns from the fuel tank, thus maintaining a sufficient reserve for emergencies as well as the return home at the end of the mission. The tug could even be operated remotely or with just one person aboard the Wyvern, allowing more flexibility in crew assignments.

"We've been here a week, and have the core, power and one habitation module attached upstairs. Down here we've got pretty much the same. Most of what we have left are inflating domes and covering them with stabilized regolith. You have more choices in orbit, though." Command Johnson was leading the conference call with the surface and orbital teams. Mission Control was not in the comm loop—yet—since the mission commander had to assess crew capabilities before committing to this stage of the construction. "I should think your next mission is obvious—retrieve the tug—but after that you have to make a choice: physics, bio, or astro modules?"

"Second hab module," said Denison. "Misty snores."

"I do not. That's Shepard," White countered.

"Don't blame me! You forget that I have access to the medical telemetry," Glenn said. "Bruce is right, Misty, you *do* snore. As do Chappell, Hopkinson and the commander!"

Johnson chuckled over the conference comm. "Guilty as charged, it's the difference in gravity and fluid distribution, but not a good reason to alter the overall construction plan which calls for one of the science modules next."

"Not to mention it's half an orbit away," cautioned Bill Chappell. "I say we take the full crew out to get the tug, and then go straight for the physics module. It's the largest and has another universal connection hub; we'll need that for the bio and astro modules anyway. It's also an all-hands job."

"True, but are you sure about taking everyone away from the station in one Wyvern? There won't be anyone left for emergencies."

"We can take both Wyverns and dock them to the physics module for the return trip. We can also top them off from the tug's fuel reservoir."

"That better for on-site redundancy, but again, no backup at the station itself."

"One of the Wyverns can return if need be. It's either that or wait three weeks for your team to get back up here. M.C. may not like it, but the contingency is in the mission guidelines as long as we have the fuel and redundant Wyverns."

"Alright. Then, questions? Comments? Brickbats? Glenn, ready to get out of hatch and partition duty?" the commander asked.

"Absolutely. I can forward all of the health monitors to my comm-pad. Let's fly," Glenn answered.

"Very well. Bill's right, Mission Control won't be happy, but it's my call. Things are going well, let's keep it that way."

"DAMMIT, I CAN'T MATCH with this mother-lovin' module. It's tumbling too much." Bill Chappell was maneuvering *Castor* via the attached tug, trying to match position with the physics module. "Are we sure Houston shut down the gyros on that thing?"

The module-retrieval mission had started out well. Both Wyverns flew out to match orbits with the tug module. The flight mostly required them to reduce velocity, slowing them down and dropping to a lower orbit, which also caused them to speed up relative to the Luna Two station and the tug module. Once they caught up with the tug, and acceleration burn allowed both Wyverns to rise to the higher orbit and match course with the tug. *Castor* went first, and mated easily with the oversized engine-and-fuel tank component. The combination then held steady as *Pollux* approached and docked, allowing both capsules to conserve fuel for the much longer trip out to the physics module. Once they reached their destination, *Pollux* undocked and flew alongside, but at a distance that allowed the combined *Castor* and tug to approach the physics module.

However, on arrival, they found the object in a lower orbit than anticipated, and tumbling erratically. Mission Control remotely commanded gyroscopic stabilizers and maneuvering jets to stabilize the module, but there appeared to be a fault in the gyros, causing the tumble to resume.

"We shut them down as soon as you told us, Bill," came the voice from Houston. "If you want, we can spin it back up until stable, then shut off again, immediately. You'll have to move fast, though."

"Unless you want me to spacewalk over..." came Dennison's voice from *Pollux*.

"Nope. No, we just got started here...Wait, you know, that's not a bad idea. You, me and a tether could pull that wobble out in no time."

"Negative, *Castor*. This is Houston. You are not going EVA. You need to maintain the two-person rule."

"Sorry, Houston, as local commander, I've got to override. You sent this thing up here with a malfunctioning gyro. It's our job to fix it."

"Then wait for the Dragonet crews to return."

"They have their own issues. Without this module we can't connect anything else, and we'll be twiddling our thumbs for the next three weeks. Besides, Dennison and I make two on EVA. White and Shepard will fly the Wyverns."

"Glenn? You're okay with flying the tug?"

"Absolutely!" said Glenn. "I'm the one that flew it out here; Bill took over for the final approach."

"Very well. Local commander discretion approved."

The plan was actually fairly simple. Bill Chappell would start out from *Castor* with a tethered line back to the Wyvern. Bruce Dennison would do the same from *Pollux* and approach the module first. He would attach his tether to one end of the tumbling module, while Misty White applied just enough reverse thrust to start pulling on the module. *Pollux* would cease maneuvering, and Chappell would attach his tether to the opposite end of the module. *Castor* and the heavier engines of the tug would them pull the module in the opposite direction, repositioning it to a straight line between the two Wyverns and damping out the tumble. From there, they could either mate the tug and Wyverns to the module, or simply tow the tethered assembly back to the station.

So far, the operation seemed to be succeeding; *Pollux* had stopped the tumble, and all that was left was some wobbling around the long axis of the module. Chappell was trying to attach his line, but seemed to be having trouble. Went he wasn't cursing the module, Wyvern, tug, or tether, he muttered under his breath (but into the comm).

"Dammit! You hog-hearted fly-bitten tether! Stop whipping around you cut-throat base-born goose!"

"Why William! So happy you toned the language down for the viewers at home!" Capcomm Nia Osborne said over the comm from Houston. "Keep in mind you're on Vox, honey."

"I'll 'honey' you, you fiendish ill-natured numbskull."

"Who me? Why sweetie, I'm just so glad you studied the medieval insult generator instead of cursing on vox."

"Sorry to cut in here, Nia, but the FlightMed wants me to confirm Bill's readouts with Glenn." Harlan Anders would normally be the Wyvern capsule communicator, while Nia worked the Dragonet channel, but Mission Control had both capcomms on the line to separately guide *Castor* and *Pollux* in their tasks. For Harlan to break into the common channel was unusual.

Glenn had been concentrating on fine maneuvers of his Wyvern to keep Bill's tether from getting fouled by the precessing module. His every-ten-minutes health check had been taken over by Houston for the duration, but he quickly glanced at his commpad to see an alert pop up on Chappell's telemetry. "Yeah, Bill, your heart rate, respiration and temperature are all up."

That's what FlightMed is seeing," confirmed Harlan. "Bill, your breathing is shallow, with near saturation on your pulse-ox. You're at risk of hyperventilating."

"Tell FlightMed, 'thank you very much, and would he like to come up here and fight with tumbling rocks?'"

"Bill, Houston's right," Glenn cut in. "I don't like the looks of your vitals either. I recommend you turn up airflow but reduce oh-two a bit. The high pulse-ox means you're at risk of hyperventilating."

"Mind your own damn business Shepard. It's bad enough with Houston FlightMed as a mother hen. I don't need you doing it too."

"Sorry, Bill, but I'm doing my job."

"No, right now your job is Wyvern pilot. Now give me some slack so I can clip off and finish this thing."

"Don't mind him, Glenn. He's been this way since breakfast," said Dennison.

"Breakfast? You call reconstituted eggs and vegetable sausage, breakfast? What craven hugger-mugger sends astronauts puss-sucking vegetable sausage? It gave me a stomach ache."

"Really, Bill? So, how is your stomach feeling right now?"

"Stuff it, Glenn. It's been turning and cramping all morning when pain. Just like any other day. It's..."

Bill screamed.

"Houston. We have a problem. Chappell's heart rate is one-twenty, respirations thirty, temperature one-oh-two, blood pressure one-ninety over one-thirty. Bill's in distress. I need to get him inside" Glenn's own heart was racing, but he knew he had to remain calm. In times like this, he had to go back to the cool, detached surgeon he'd been during residency.

"Get him inside. Now!" Nia's voice was firm and controlled.

"I'll get him," said Dennison. After a few moments he continued. "Bill's eyes are closed, face is gray, there's sweat on his forehead. Note responsive to my touch. I'm bringing him back now. Now. ETA three minutes."

"Once Bruce is done, you can go back to the station. Bruce and I can tow the module back," Misty commed.

"Negative, Misty. I'm declaring a medical emergency. All hands will be needed back on the station. The module is mostly stabilized and won't be going anywhere. I need to get Bill into surgery...and I don't have a med bay. It's still drifting out there...somewhere."

"Emergency surgery? What are you thinking, Glenn?" asked Harlan.

"Fever, shock, abdominal pain, and a history of GI issues this whole mission?" Glenn paused for a moment to make sure his diagnosis was certain and justified. "I'm thinking appendicitis."

BILL HAD STILL BEEN unconscious when Glenn and Bruce strapped him into a seat in *Castor*. Bruce opted to remain in *Castor*, while Misty ejected her tether and followed in *Pollux*.

It was better to keep Bill in his EVA suit, where temperature and oxygen could be controlled, but FlightMed recommending connecting one of the autodoc units which could interface with the suit and collect blood, perform minor diagnostics, and administer medication. Returning to Luna Two would take seventy minutes; there was no rushing orbital dynamics. Chappell would need to be stabilized for that time, so once the course was set, Glenn commanded the autodoc to pull a blood sample to measure oxygen, glucose, pH, inflammation biomarkers, and white-cell counts. Upon seeing a high white-cell count, along with C-reactive protein and granulocyte colony stimulating factor, he set the device to administer antibiotics, anti-inflammatories, and IV fluids.

"Houston, you're seeing the same thing I am. Interleukin-six is high, as is CRP. I *really* don't like the G-CSF levels. That's pretty damned diagnostic for imminent rupture of the appendix...So, tell me, how the hell am I supposed to perform an appendectomy with no sickbay and my surgical instruments four thousand miles away on the other side of the moon?"

The comm was silent for a few minutes.

"Houston?"

"Glenn, this is Johnson. Houston looped me in and are relaying since we're out of line-of-sight. You've got emergency packs in both Wyverns plus the habitat has an expanded first aid kit. I know you did the Wilderness Surgeon course in Utah. This is just a different kind of desert: you can do this, son. It's why you're here. Johnson out."

"Yes, sir. Thank you, sir. I will do everything I can."

"Good luck, Glenn. Frankly, Nia and I are going to run interference and keep everyone groundside out of your hair as well," Harlan told him.

That got a laugh from Glenn. "Hah! You do know I prefer a buzz-cut, right? I don't *have* any hair!"

"Uh huh," came Osborn's voice with a giggle. "We'll be here for you Glennie, but yeah, we're staring down the backseat surgeons even as we speak. You go and treat your patient."

Bruce Dennison was the first to break the silence as Glenn programmed the last of the orbital maneuvers to fire thrusters and lift them back into station orbit.

"So exactly how are you going to do this? If he does need surgery, that is."

"Surgery isn't an if at this point. The readouts say massive infection and inflammation. That appendix needs to come out and I'll have to do some serious clean-up if it ruptures."

"So, when not if."

"Exactly. Wait one. Separating from the tug now. It's co-orbital, so we won't lose it, but we need our hatch unobstructed."

"Sure," Dennison agreed, and remained silent until Glenn had *Castor* back on track to close with Luna Two's main docking hatch on the core module. "But even I know fluids don't drain without gravity. Won't they pool and mess up your surgery?"

"That's right, so you or Misty will have to use constant suction to keep the surgical area clear. The Commander's right, I can put together enough clamps from the first-aid kits, and there's a small surgical kit in my personal cube. The real trick is how to administer anesthesia once he's out of his suit."

"Did no one ever consider the possibility that we might have to perform emergency medicine?"

"Sure, they considered it. That's why the bio module has a medbay with surgical facilities. It's just that no one thought we would need it before we finished assembling the station."

"Well, this one's going to be all, you, Glenn. I'll do what you tell me, and so will Misty, but you're the doctor. It does make me glad you're up here and not down on the surface. From what you're saying we can't wait for a crew to get back up here."

"Well, no one wants to abort the mission, but if we have to get Bill back to Earth, we'll have to bring back at least one of the Dragonet crews. We can't leave them both here, there's not enough room in *Pollux* for all six plus a pilot and co."

"Um, yeah. On the other hand, we could just leave *Pollux*. It'll handle six—crowded, but doable."

"Nope, standard operating procedures say at least person on orbit while anyone is on the surface."

"Screw the SOPs, if it's the life of an astronaut..."

"...mission safety comes first. You know that. Now, put that engineer brain to work on the anesthesia problem," Glenn said as he pulled the lever which provided tactile and visual confirmation of a firm and secure docking connection with the station.

"How about a rebreather mask? We have those for use during argon purge if a fresh module is warm enough for us to enter it in shirtsleeves."

"Right. Good idea. On Earth I'd intubate, but if we just go with oxygen and injectable anesthetics, that will do."

"Okay, I'll also run a line to the head's vacuum port. That should be good for suction." Dennison held up a gloved hand to indicate for Glenn to wait before trying to drag Chappell's suited body through the hatch. "Let me pop the catches on the maneuvering unit. It'll fit, but there's no need to have it floating around the station while we work.

"Good. Thanks. Now, after me."

"HOUSTON, THIS IS WELLS Station." Misty grinned across at Glenn at the first official use of the name.

*I guess it's decided.* She formed the words with her mouth without vocalizing.

"Wells Station? That's new, Glennie," responded Osborn.

"Hey, if I'm going to inaugurate it with surgery, the station needs a better name than 'Luna Two.'"

"Well, I think the Brass are about to have a stroke, but the Flight Director and I have the biggest grins right now. So, *Wells*, how can we help you?"

"More informative than anything, Nia. Ultrasound confirms a drastically inflamed appendix. We've got Bill on the hab module dining table. I've never had to duck tape a patient to the table before. I'll admit that a few have tempted me, and Bill was rapidly getting there. Bruce rigged me an oxygen cone from a rebreather, and suction using the zero-gee toilet's vacuum line. I have enough surgical clamps from the first aid kits, and I've got my own scalpel and needles, although Bruce and Misty offered me their EDC knives. I want to go laparoscopically, and Bruce is working on sterilizing the fiber-optic scope he and Bill use for diagnostics while Misty and I prep the surgical site."

"Okay, I'll pass that along. Harlan's running interference, and frankly, so is Flight. Toni hasn't left her desk since y'all went out to the tug. Hold one, Harlan's waving."

The other capcomm's voice came on the line. "FlightMed's asking what you're using to sterilize instruments?"

"Vacuum, the UV scope we use for inspecting welds and seams, and lots of alcohol."

"FlightMed seems to be confused. What alcohol?"

"Well let's see, we've got swabs and prep pads in all of the first aid kits, several cans of degreaser and the high-percentage ethanol packed into the galley for cleaning fluid lines."

"The what?"

"The stuff used to flush the drink dispenser lines."

"Ah, I see. I suppose if you hold it up to one of the portholes you can see the moon shining right through it?"

"Nope, this is better than that. I think it was mentioned in the Mars movie a few years back."

"Got it. The potato-based stuff. From the looks on her face, Toni's going to want to have a word...after."

"Butter wouldn't melt in our mouths, Harlan. Now, one last thing. Obviously I'm not monitoring the health board, so FlightMed's going to have to do that, but be advised, I'm retasking all onboard systems to monitoring *my* patient, and Misty's going to keep an eye on that and tell me what she sees. If FlightMed does *anything* that interrupts my data link, I will personally walk back to Houston and remove every one of their appendices...without anesthesia, and with my rustiest scalpel. Got that?"

Both capcomm's laughed. "Loud and clear, Glennie," Osborn told him. "Security's already removed one of the consultant surgeons, obnoxious dude named Lake or Lego, or something like that. We've got this new security guy, Nathan Balyeat, and he's big, and wide, and he just picked the dude up and carried him out."

"My kind of person, can't wait to meet him. Now, we're going to get to work, so tell the peanut gallery they can listen, but don't interrupt."

"Understood, Doctor Shepard, we've got your back. Good luck."

"We are professionals, Houston. Luck is not a factor."

Standard surgical prep generally involved placing a lot of sensors on the body of the person about to be operated upon. In this case, Bill was already wearing the sensors, and it was necessary to remove a few in order to prepare the skin for incision. Misty was scrubbing Bill's abdomen, while Glenn did the same with his hands. He didn't know, and frankly didn't care who had smuggled the bottle of vodka onto the mission—it had been hiding in *Pollux*'s first aid pack—but he was certainly glad it was here. The likelihood of bacterial contamination inside Wells Station was low, but inside a human body with a potentially ruptured appendix was just the opposite. He needed to do everything he could to contain the risk of infection.

In fact, since Wells was currently in full sun, Bruce had taken several lightweight sheets of fabric, as well as several pairs of nitrile gloves, through the airlock to expose them to vacuum and solar radiation. Once he finished scrubbing, Glenn would don the sterilized gloves and drape the cloth around the surgical site.

It wasn't a major hospital OR, it wasn't even Earth, and it certainly wasn't pretty, but it was what he had. The patient was prepared. The surgeon was prepared.

It was time to get started.

Bill wasn't fully sedated—at least not as if the surgery was performed in a large hospital operating room. Still, he was unconscious even if he groaned and twitched while Misty had cleaned the surgical site. Without all of the resources of a surgical suite, Glenn preferred it that way. Bill's body temperature was now over one-hundred three Fahrenheit—forty Celsius—and his blood pressure had dropped to 100/60. The heart rate was ninety beats per minute and respiration was thirty-five per minute. Pain could account for fast heart rate and breathing, but the fever and low BP signaled infection. The appendix might have already rupture, in which case Glenn needed to hurry.

"All right, I'm going to start an IV line to give fluids and antibiotics. In gravity, the drip handles itself, but without gravity, you'll have to pump it, Misty. Bruce, check the hab lockers and pull out two pairs of leg-squeezers. Compression sleeves on Bill's legs will help with circulation, fluid balance, and keeping his BP up. If you can find a small pair, we can put those on his forearms, too. That will help circulate the IV.

"How often should I squeeze the IV bag?" Misty asked.

"If we can use compression on the arm, time it in between those compressions. Otherwise squeeze it when the leg sleeves compress. That way when they relax, it pulls the IV fluid into the body."

"Got it. So, my job is to keep an eye on the vitals, time the compressions and squeeze the IV bag to ensure that fluid goes into the vein anything else."

"Keep an eye on the place where the needle is inserted. If you see the needle move or if you see any pulsing as you squeeze it may have come out of the vein and I'll have to reposition it or put in a central line."

With the surgical site prepped and patient receiving intravenous fluids and antibiotics, it was time to cut. Glenn took the scalpel he'd brought in his own medical kit in his right hand, and used his left thumb and forefinger to stretch the skin of Bill's right lower abdomen. He placed the scalpel on the taut skin and drew a two-centimeter incision. The skin separated and blood oozed out of the incision. Glenn nodded, and Bruce immediately touched the tip of the suction tubing to the edge of the incision and drew off the blood.

Glenn placed the scalpel back on a magnetized tray Bruce had improvised from an instrument cover with a magnet underneath. He picked up a pair of curved hemostats—the ubiquitous clamps, tweezers, manipulators used in operating rooms across the globe, ...and now across space. He used the rounded tips to poked into the exposed tissue, then opened the handle to separate the jaws of the device, stretching the tissue and making an opening into the abdominal cavity. Alternately poking and stretching the tissue, he worked his way through the muscle of the abdomen. It was still necessary to cut the wall of the peritoneum to get to the fluid-filled abdominal cavity and reach the appendix, but the fewer cuts he made the less he would have to suture and the better the healing when they were done.

When he had a hole large enough. Glenn inserted the fiber-optic inspection light, while Bruce held up a comm tablet with the video image. He worked the tube around, peering at the murky image in various shades of red and white until he found the appendix. It was bright red and inflamed with a small dark area of dead tissue which seeped dark fluid. It wasn't a full rupture, but live and dead blood cells plus some pus were seeping out, the cause of Bills pain and infection. He directed Bruce to suction as much of the fluid away as possible.

"Heart rate jumped," Misty said, as Bill groaned and moved slightly against the straps holding him in place.

"I expected that. He'll do that more as I tie off and extract the appendix. With that leak, I'm not going to be able to pull it out through as small an incision as I would prefer, but better a larger scar than a full rupture. Now, grab a syringe and pull some of that pus for analysis; you won't need a needle. You can stop pumping for a minute to do that."

"Yes sir, Doc. Bruce, let me in there for a minute."

"Aye, aye, Nurse White."

"Just leave it in the syringe for now and go back to pumping, thanks, Misty." Glenn gave her a big smile…well, as much as could be seen over his surgical mask. He then pulled the fiber optic out of the incision and enlarged the opening to get his instruments in place. He used two more hemostats to hold the edges of the incision out of the way as he reached in with two more to grip and clamp the point of attachment between appendix and small intestine.

"The best bet is going to be to cauterize this as I go. It's kind of sloppy and will increase the internal scarring and adhesions, but it will void any questions of having a fully sterile surgical site or missing anything that could bleed later." One of the items from his personal kit had been a compact, rechargeable electrocautery—effectively a soldering iron for biology. The tip wasn't small enough to fit inside an incision. It was designed to seal skin and minor cuts to keep them from seeping in zero gee, but Misty had devised a longer probe for the device. In fact, it was amazing how the two construction engineers had managed to improvise workarounds for many of the devices Glenn took for granted in a surgical suite.

Soon, Glenn had the appendix separated from its attachment point on the small intestine and then separated a couple more fibrous connective points and separated those as well. Next, was the delicate process of extracting the inflamed organ through the incision without it breaking open and spilling septic contents into the abdomen.

About two hours after they'd been they begun. Glenn closed the last stitch. Bill would have a three-centimeter scar, but almost as soon as the infected organ had been removed, his vitals had begun to improve. Bruce turned off the suction and gathered the surgical instruments and surgical tools as Misty swabbed the suture site with antibiotics. A foley catheter hooked up to a spacesuit hygiene pump would serve to keep the surgical site drained for the next twenty-four hours, and heavy doses of antibiotics and pain medication would do the rest.

"Houston, we're done."

*CASTOR*—TECHNICALLY WYVERN FIVE, BUT also the same capsule Glenn had flown—was two hours away from docking with Wells Station as Glenn and Commander Johnson entered Mission Control. There was a quiet intensity to the room. Since Apollo, the culture of mission controllers insisted that no matter the stress of the situation, voices were never raised, nor tempers allowed to flare in the room.

Cheers were allowed, though, and the controllers vocalized—quietly—and clapped as Glenn entered the room. It was only his second visit to the flight monitoring center, and the first since his crew returned from the Moon over six months ago. The cheers were in part because his emergency surgery had not only saved his crewmate, it had saved the mission. The Wyvern One and Two mission had completed their entire month's stay at the Moon. Construction on Wells had slowed for a while, but they'd accomplished all mission objectives and returned home healthy...minus one appendix.

"You, sir, are a steely-eyed missileman," said Nia Osborn from her perch at the Dragonet capsule communicator console.

"No, he's not, he's a Doc!" protested Harlan Anders, the Wyvern capcomm.

"Actually, the backroom boys prepared a little something for Doc, here." Flight Director Kim Schoeffel said from the center station. He held out a plastic rocket model attached to a wooden base. The rocket was draped with a small white coat, and a tiny stethoscope hung from the nose of the spacecraft. "You've defined the new standard for a gut check...not to mention making the hard things look easy."

Glenn took the offered trophy and read aloud the inscription on the base: "For Glenn Shepard...*it really* is *rocket surgery*!"

# Six
# GHOST OF KANEOHE

AUTHORS NOTE: THIS IS another prequel tie-in to one of my novels—*Across an Ocean of Stars*, the zombie apocalypse novel set in John Ringo's *Black Tide Rising* universe.

Fair warning: if you haven't read *Across an Ocean of Stars* yet, this story contains a spoiler for a narrative thread that is only resolved at the very end of that novel. The events of *The Ghost of Kaneohe* take place before those in *Ocean* and tell the story of the evacuation of Honolulu, the state capital, and the island and county of Oahu, the most populous metropolitan areas of the islands.

Lieutenant Abi "Ghostbird" Forsyth and her CH-53E Super Stallion, *Tempest*, are tasked with evacuating Marines, dependents, and civilians from Kaneohe Bay as the infected breach the last lines of defense.

It's a story of courage, desperation, and the impossible choices that arise when a Black Tise is rising fast... and there's no way home.

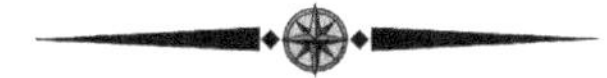

Lieutenant Abigail Forsyth came awake to the sound of alarms. "All pilots report to ready room. This is not a drill. All pilots report to ready room."

Abi took the ear buds out of her ears and turned off the small music player. Sleeping with the wires leading between player and earbuds was risky. If she tossed and turned in her sleep, she risked strangling herself. She'd woken up with the wires in odd places before, but never around her neck, so she felt justified in using music to block at least a portion of the noise from outside her quarters.

She'd only been asleep for about two hours, having just come off a sixteen-hour shift doing medevac and personnel transfers across the island of Oahu. The situation in Honolulu was ...

bad. News of the Red Flu had been released a few weeks ago, but reports were starting to come in about serious issues in cities around the country. New York supposedly had National Guard in the streets, Atlanta was reporting violent mobs at the airport, Emory University Hospital, and the Centers for Disease Control campus. The mayor in Chicago issued an order a week ago shutting off TV and radio news reporting, but word got out anyway: The city was rife with rioting, looting and gunfights.

Tourists in Hawaii were panicking; they wanted off the island. Most planned to head home ...mainland U.S., Japan, and China for the most part. Jets flew to those destinations multiple times a day but were generally booked up for one-to-two weeks in advance, the length of a typical Hawaiian vacation. The few tourists heading to South America and Europe had it worse, with fewer flights, and even fewer available seats. The harbors were jammed with people trying to hire or buy boats, and the number of offshore accidents was increasing daily.

The normally busy roads and highways on the island were now impassable. There was not a single city block, nor mile of the circum-island roads, without accidents and abandoned cars. With the traffic jams now extending to harbors and marinas, the only reliable way to get anywhere on the island was by air.

Tourist helicopter agencies were promised large sums of money to reject private charters and stay available to the government. The governor called up the national guard, then declared martial law to call on the military helos for support. Abi's last three days had mostly been spent delivering Marines to help maintain security at Wheeler Army Base, Fort Shafter, Pearl Harbor, and Trippler Military Hospital. Each of the bases were set up to provide humanitarian aid and shelter, but were overflowing, and prone to unrest. More troops were needed, given the increasing attrition from disease and mob violence. . More and more flights were becoming devoted to dust-off and medevac.

This was the life she'd chosen, though, even if it had strained her relationship with her father. He considered himself a man of science, and never understood when she told him flying was her calling.

Abi was zipping her sleeve pocket closed as she stepped into the pilots' ready room. "What's up, Jimmy?" she asked her copilot, James Medlock.

"Large mob at the gates, is all I heard."

"More civvy's trying to get off the island?"

"Not entirely, Lieutenant." Their commander, Colonel Frederick Weber, walked into the room and the collection of pilots and engineers came to attention. "Sit. It's going to be a busy day and I know some of you didn't get much rest."

"Sir!" came the response in unison, followed by shuffling as the room sat in groups organized by aircraft.

"Yes, we have a mob at the gates, and no, it's not always civilians. That's how it started, but we're now seeing large numbers of Infected. We bring people inside the wire as much as possible, but too many have been bitten and turned. We've now enforced the perimeter with another layer of fencing, razor wire, and concrete barriers. We can block the roads, but the land is even harder. There's now a secondary roadblock on Mokapu Road once it crosses Nu'upia Pond, to keep people from using the dirt roads. We still get people wading across Nu'upia and Kaluapuhi Ponds and walking up the beach, so the perimeter is getting harder to secure. Higher is calling for evacuation."

"Where?" asked one of the engineers.

"Anywhere we can." Weber sighed. His pilots knew the colonel worked hard to project a calm and unflappable manner. He would *not* be hurried or rushed. "All of the available sea assets at Pearl have instructions to leave port. They even tried to get some of the inactives sailing, but so far, have only managed to get the gator *Tarawa* out to sea. PacFleet has a cruiser and an oiler sitting about fifty miles east, and there's supposed to be carriers headed to Midway Island. Most of the subs are already gone, except for the ones undergoing maintenance. The Air Force is being scattered to remote bases, the Navy's at sea, the Army's headed back to the mainland, and the Marines are holding the line."

There was quiet muttering. In the room. The implications were clear, Marine Corps Base Kaneohe Bay would be staying operation, and many of their people would be making the ultimate sacrifice to save as many as they could.

"Okay, here are the assignments:

"Steeler and Pots – your Thunderhawks will be making runs to Hickam where you'll assist with carrying provisions and personnel for the C-17s headed to Midway, Pago Pago, and Elmendorf. When you get notice of last run, board the planes. They're taking UH-60 Blackhawks, so you're going to be the backup flight crew wherever you end up."

Chris Steele and Tom Potter nodded, then turned to discuss with their respective crews.

"Pearl is pulling back to secure the airport and docks. Everything west and north is pulling in to reinforce the lines. Schofield and Wheeler have been overrun. Mililani's all Zeds at this point. Pearl City is barely holding things together, with a defensive perimeter set up at the stadium to hold the memorials as long as possible. That's a terminal assignment, and the Marines *will* hold the line."

"Oorah, Sir," about half the room responded. Weber smiled but dropped it as soon as he resumed the assignments.

"Rickroll and Workman: you two are Task Force Running Back. You'll be taking reinforcements to the stadium and evacuating Ford Island. I'm told there's some *USS Missouri* Vets requesting transport to the ship. You *will* honor their sacrifice."

Rognar Rickard and Kepeli Werkiser nodded. Weber handed them a sheet of paper with names and pickup location for the navy veterans.

"Kybo, you're headed to Washington Place to pick up the governor and his staff. Your callsign will be Marine Five-Zero until you pick up Hizzoner; at that point you'll squawk 'Hawaii One' until you deliver him planeside to the C-130 headed for the garrison at Pohakuloa. Wheels up in thirty minutes, so you and your crew are dismissed to go now."

Kai Bond stood, along with his co-pilot and engineer, saluted, and left the room.

"Argus, Psych, you have the worst of this, but I saved my best for the job."

Abi sat up straighter, waiting for her assignment, along with her wingman Bill "Psych" Jung.

"Your mission is designated 'Tempest' and you've got the dirty job of base evac. We're pulling noncombatants and civilians off base and sending them to those two ships offshore. When Kybo gets back, we'll try to get some troops over to *Tarawa*, but we have to raise her on radio first, and that's been difficult. She was mothballed for a reason.

"Psych, you'll be *Tempest-One*, delivering troops to *Port Royal*, she's a Tico-class cruiser. You might remember her from the little incident off Pearl a few years back. She's standing in for destroyer escort for the *Yukon*, a Kaiser-class oiler. They were supposed to be part of a FleetEx out of San Diego, but it got called off, and they were sent here and ordered to stand off and wait. Take as many—safely—as you can, but just know that when that C-130 heads out, that's it. Wartime rules of engagement, so do what you have to, but get your people to safety when Penguin-Four-Two leaves."

The pilots and crews started to stand up, but Weber motioned for them to remain seated.

"One last thing. As you know, callsigns are awarded by your fellows; once given, you're stuck with it, whether you did anything to deserve it or not."

Abi wondered where this was going. Her own callsign was nothing special, but she remembered the night of Captain Bond's promotion, when he'd sat at the bar telling his fellow pilots how the word "kybo" had been used as slang for "latrine" in his old Boy Scout troop. He'd love to have a better callsign, but also knew that the more a pilot responded negatively to a callsign, the more their fellows used it specifically to elicit a reaction. Besides, his helo would have the *really* cool designation today.

"On the other hand," Weber continued, "It is possible to earn a new call sign when circumstances demand it. Yesterday, Argus made several transfers between Wheeler, Fort Shafter, and Trippler, despite some heavy rains mid-day. A news crew caught the image of a CH53E coming into the pad at Trippler, appearing like a ghost out of the mist. General Matt Bowman called me from Trippler this morning asking about the pilot of the 'ghostbird' that delivered additional forces to defend the hospital, then repeatedly pulled critical cases out for evac.

"That was you, Argus ...and as of today, you'll be 'Ghostbird.' Congratulations. Now get out of here, you lot. You've got work to do. Godspeed ...and . . ." Weber's voice cracked. "God bless you all. It's been an honor."

ABI BOARDED *HER* CH53-E Super Stallion through the crew door behind the cockpit. As she entered, she patted the names—her own and "Stargazer"—stenciled below the pilot's window and smiled at the depiction of one of Mauna Kea's telescope domes painted underneath. Her father would have loved it, even if he didn't support her career choice.

She settled into the right-hand seat and looked over at her co-pilot. "You've done the daily run-up, right Jimmy?"

"Ah, no Argus—ah, 'Ghostbird.' No, there hasn't been time, we just came in four hours ago!"

"Jimmy, what did I say about call-signs in the cockpit?"

"Ah, sorry Abi, I know you didn't like Argus, but Ghostbird sounds pretty cool."

"Yeah, well, I didn't even do anything to deserve Argus, it's just a play on 'foresight.' Not like Kybo hoarding toilet paper or Rognar insisting on being called 'Rockstar.'"

"Yeah, but they're funny, and their reactions were perfect. You just curled your lip and sneered, Abi."

"Back to the bird ...*Meddler*. Do we have enough hydro for start-up? The APU seemed to cut out early when we left Trippler on the last round."

"That was low fuel pressure. We were running on fumes when we got in, but we're all fueled and ready now."

"Hydraulic pressure on the APU, Jimmy!"

"Twenty-six hundred PSI, Argus."

"You're a shit, Jimmy. If we have to manually pump for a second attempt, it's on you."

Sure enough, the auxiliary power unit, necessary to provide activate instruments and starter for the three General Electric T64-GE=416 turboshaft engines, didn't catch on the first try due to low pressure. Three-thousand pounds per square inch was the nominal requirement to spin the turbines of the APU for startup. It could be done with pressure as low as twenty-five hundred, but the chance of failure increased as the pressure dropped.

Abi pulled up the pressure pump handle but motioned for Medlock to start pumping.

"Start pumping, Jimmy."

"Aw, crap, Abi! Call over a starter truck! There's one over next to Pots."

"If you hadn't noticed, they're about to pull a cowling on his SH-60, so they're just a little bit busy. It's only a hundred PSI, Jimmy. Pump!" she said, using her command voice.

It took ten minutes to get the required pressure in the APU hydraulics, but the engine caught on the next try, and four minutes later, she had all three main engines online and the rotor coming up to speed.

"Check the hydro, Jimmy, make sure we're at full pressure before you cut off the APU this time."

"Aye, aye, lieutenant."

Abi checked in with her crew chief, Lai Moleka, to make sure that the cargo bay was ready for passengers, then called the control tower for permission to proceed from the helo pads to a site just off the eastern end of the runway where noncombatant military personnel and dependents were being organized for evacuation. Civilians who'd sought refuge from the Infected were being housed in tents on the golf course, east of the evac site. They'd be next, once the high priority folks were taken to safety.

Bill Jung's helo arrived first and got the cleaner site near the control tower. There were Marines still on the ground performing a FOD-walk, removing "foreign object debris" from the concrete in front of the HMM-268 headquarters. She hovered while the men cleared her landing zone, then landed and performed her checks while Moleka dropped the rear ramp and started loading passengers.

It wasn't supposed to be a hot-loading, so she disengaged the rotors and let them wind down. The engines would continue to run. They could be airborne in as little as thirty seconds. That may be important later, but this was still supposed to be routine. She wondered about Weber's parting words, though. He'd acted as if this was the end—like he'd never see them again.

It was a sobering thought.

Abi wasn't overt about her religious beliefs, but her fellows knew them. On the one hand, she honestly felt that this couldn't be the end. On the other hand, she would pray for everyone's safe return. On the *gripping hand*, as one of her favorite science fiction novels would put it ...she had a job to do.

Time to act on faith.

"Ramp's down, LT," came Moleka's voice over the comm. Abi looked out at the gathering crowds. Military personnel were herding non-combatants into a semblance of order, but it looked like herding cats. Civilians—mostly family members of soldiers and local base employees—were clumped together. Parents clutched at children, and children clutched at stuffed animals and toys. Fear radiated off them in waves, and it was clear that they expected to see Infected burst from the shadows at any moment. The dense humid air was filled with the distant roar of choppers and the occasional crackle of gunfire.

Abi flicked a switch on her panel, activating her mic. "Get them loaded, Lai. The faster we load, the more trips we can make." She was regretting shutting down the rotors. It was dangerous to start them up now, during loading. The rotors were high enough, but the downwash could hurt the civilians, both those loading, and those waiting. The look on the faces gave her the sense of urgency her orders lacked.

What she'd left unsaid was that the more trips they made, the more people they could save ...until it was too late to save even themselves.

It was the commander's job to keep calm, though. Airline pilots, rescue workers, and incident commanders had long known that portraying a sense of calm, even boredom, helped soothe the public, passengers, or even the crew. If the boss wasn't afraid, there was no reason for them to be afraid.

Even if that boss was a bundle of nerves and a burgeoning ulcer.

"We're exposed out here, Abi," Medlock's said over their private channel.

Abi didn't respond. She agreed, but she needed to project calm. Her eyes scanned her instruments, the crowd outside, then the horizon. It was routine.

It was all routine, she told herself.

As her gaze panned over the line of people waiting to load, she saw a woman carrying two small children stumble, then scramble to get back in line, her eyes wide with terror. These people needed reassurance, they were close to panic, and panic wouldn't do any of them any good.

She flicked a switch on her panel, activating her external speaker. "Ladies and gentlemen, this is your captain speaking. Please move calmly down the aisle and take your seat. The cabin crew will be by shortly to assist you with stowing your luggage and adjusting your seatbelts. Thank you for flying Ghostbird Air."

Hopefully, a bit of humor would help.

She scanned the horizon, past the barricades and hastily constructed fences of her loading area. They were deep in the base, almost to the water's edge. Almost a mile away, and the base was on a peninsula, separated from the rest of the island by a narrow causeway. In fact, MCBH K-Bay was well-isolated. The roads connecting the base to the towns of Kaneohe and Kailua were the only dry land outside the base perimeter. Nearly a quarter mile of ponds and swamps separated the base from the residential areas at Kapoho Point. A small Marine detachment held the gates and patrolled the barriers meant to hold back the Infected.

They were less worried about mobs of civilians, although there was certainly some massing at the gates.

People would be reluctant to wade across the treacherous wetland. Infected didn't care.

MOLEKA NOTIFIED HER THAT the current load of passengers was in and secured.

"Button up, Jimmy. Time to go."

"Roger, Ghostbird."

Abi shot him a look of exasperation, but Medlock just grinned back. "C'mon, admit it. You got the cool call sign."

He turned back to his console and flicked the switches, starting up the seven-bladed rotor.

Abi looked out her side window, seeing the Marines were keeping the crowd well back from her bird. She gripped the collective and cyclic, and when her instruments showed her engines at the proper speed, she pulled back on the cyclic and lifted her bird into the air.

"MCAS Kaneohe, this is *Tempest-Two*. Lifting for USNS *Yukon*. Do you have an update to the coordinates?"

"Affirmative, *Tempest-Two*. *Yukon* has repositioned to just over eighty klicks due north of Kawela Bay. That puts them about fifty miles off the northern point of Oahu at twenty-two-point-forty-one North and one-fifty-seven-point nine-one West. *Port Royal* is squawking a beacon for you and *Tempest-One*, so make sure you land on the big fleet oiler, Ghostbird, and not on the little cruiser."

"Roger, that, Kaneohe. Fly north and find the big honking ocean mall."

Another voice came over the comm. "Ghostbird, you and *Tempest-One* are the only birds in range right now. Psych's already headed out, so base command has requested a flyover of the southern perimeter before you head out. Give us a report on the mob at the fence line."

"Acknowledged, Kaneohe. Flyover the southern perimeter and report. Do you want me to stay high, or go low enough to disrupt the crowd with rotor wash?"

"Stay high, Ghostbird. No need to sully your new callsign just yet. The gate marines are still reporting mostly civilians, but we're getting reports of massed Infected moving up Mokapu Road."

"Understood, Kaneohe. We're feet wet, swinging around now. *Tempest-Two* out."

The principal runway for the base pointed northeast, into the prevailing winds. Abi's loading point was just south of the end of the runway, so she headed due east, over the "Five Palms" military hotel and officer housing, heading out over the water off North Beach. She'd stay over water, skirting around Mōkapu Point then turn south-by-southeast until she reached the Nu'upia Pond which separated the base from the peninsula.

After surveying the base entrance, she'd continue west over Kaneohe Bay itself, then turn northwest to hug the windward coast before turning north at Kahuku to cross the fifty miles of ocean to *Yukon* and *Port Royal*.

"Look sharp, people. Lai? Are you in position to look out?"

"I'm looking over the starboard gunner's position, Boss. I'm looking right down at Mokapu Road and the motor pool. There's a line of people who've been passed through the old gate, headed to the new security point on the other side of the pond. They're being escorted by Marines and it's all nice and orderly. Doesn't look too bad. Old gate is on the port side, though. Steve-O's got that side, but I can move over if you want me to."

Steve Jaremczek was the left-side gunner. Due to the risk of attack by Infected, *Tempest-Two* was flying with an augmented crew of right, left, and tail gunners *plus* the crew chief. Normally the chief took the right-side gunner position, but with the need to handle civilians, and the fact that they'd already had to fight off Infected on previous days, Command had ordered that each helo carry an augmented crew."

"No need, Chief. Steve-O? How's it look?"

Unlike the main gate, the Mokapu Road main gate was on the south side of the ponds, separated from the residential area by a fence—newly reinforced and augmented with barricades over the last several days, then supplemented with a new temporary gate on the base side.

"Mass of people at the gate ...don't look like Zeds ...Oh!" Jeremczek cut off. "Mob of naked people on Mokapu Road, down near the shopping center. They're about a thousand yards off the gate. It looks like they're attacking people in the parking lot."

Abi halted their forward motion and rotated the helo so that she could see the checkpoint with her own eyes. All the reports said that victims of the Haole Flu stripped off all their clothing and complained of uncontrollable itching right before they turned into blood-thirsty savages.

"LT, there's trouble at the fence." Moleka's voice snapped through the headset, cutting off Jeremczek at the latter's viewpoint changed.

Abi's looked down through her side window. Through the haze of dust and mass of people, she saw it—just a flicker of movement, but enough to draw her gaze. A young man at the back of the line, maybe mid-twenties, was stripping off his clothes. He was scratching all over, then stopped and clutched his stomach. Even from here, she could tell that something about the way he staggered felt wrong. She narrowed her eyes, hands gripping the control stick tightly.

"I see it, Lai. Jimmy, call it in." Abi ordered forcing her voice to remain calm. Every instinct told her that something was wrong here. Fear and training warred within her, but ultimately, she was a professional—an officer—and a Marine. Marines didn't run.

Medlock twisted in his seat, craning his neck to look through Abi's side window. "I see him," he muttered. "Shit, that kid's turned."

Thankfully, the Marines at the gate saw it, too. A squad pushed through the crowd, clothed in heavy gear—too heavy for the tropical heat, but necessary to keep from getting bitten. They didn't dare shoot into the crowd, but they surrounded and isolated the Infected before he could attack civilians, then took him down with repeated blows to the head.

"Could he have been saved?" Medlock whispered.

"Not our call, Jimmy. Wartime rules," Abi replied.

"Yeah. Sucks, though."

"That it does, Jimmy."

The rest of the flight was routine. So far, the main gate—north of the ponds, and thus having a buffer separating it from the residential area—was clean and orderly. Evacuees still streamed onto the base, and Abi prayed they'd be able to help them all.

THE CH53E HUMMED STEADILY as it crossed the ocean, the roar of its powerful rotors beating a steady rhythm over the waves below. Abi kept her eyes forward, scanning the horizon as the helo cut through the early morning sky. The sun was already high enough that it didn't shine directly into the cockpit. In her headset, Medlock's voice crackled.

"*Yukon*'s about ten miles ahead, LT. Should have her in sight soon."

"Copy that," Abi replied, her grip firm, but light on the controls. The memory of the mob of infected attacking people in Kailua still weighed on her. They needed to drop off this group and get back to K-Bay. People were counting on them.

"We've got a visual," Moleka chimed in from the right gunner's window. "Starboard, fifteen klicks."

*Yukon* was out of position, they should be twelve kilometers ahead, not fifteen to their right. Abi's eyes scanned her instruments, as she verified that Stargazer was in the right place—Yukon was not. She looked east and the shape of the ship appeared in the distance, a dark silhouette against the shimmering water. *USNS Yukon* was a Kaiser-class fleet replenishment oiler, typically used to supply "gas, grub, and gear" for fleet exercises. That was exactly what her mission had been, servicing a FleetEx out of San Diego, but by the time they'd arrived on-site, the capital ships had been ordered back to port, and the rest to scatter. The FleetEx had been in the middle of the Pacific, halfway between Hawaii and the mainland, so they'd been ordered to head to Pearl to assist in emergency operations.

Unfortunately, but the time they'd approached the Hawaiian Islands, the situation had deteriorated. There'd been an explosion near the sub pens at Pearl, and *Yukon*—plus her cruiser escort, USS *Port Royal*, had been ordered to hold position offshore, far enough that they would remain free of the chaos infecting the islands.

That is, until *Yukon* and *Port Royal* were pressed into service as lifeboats, large as they were.

"They're steaming into the wind. Not ideal," Abi said. "We're coming in on their stern and will have turbulence off their superstructure. Prepare for a hard deck landing."

As they closed the distance, the scale of the operation became clear. Apparently, they'd already taken on refugees via surface craft, there were several pulled up alongside, with more small craft hanging from the massive deck cranes. The ship's foredeck held a number of people, just sitting on the deck, huddled together away from the railings. Marines, distinguishable by their uniforms, moved through the crowd, handing out ...something.

"They've already got people down there," Medlock muttered. "Doesn't look good, for holding too many more."

Abi didn't need to be told. The more people they packed onto these ships, the greater the risk someone would turn. The Haole Flu could already be incubating in any of them. All it took was one person to turn, to transform an orderly group into a panicked mob.

She keyed the mic. "*Yukon*, this is *Tempest-Two*, inbound for delivery. ETA two minutes. Do you copy?"

Static crackled over the channel before a voice came through. "*Tempest*, this is *Yukon*. Standby for the Captain."

"Copy that, *Yukon*. Be advised we have six-zero civilians. Limited supplies. No infected, but you know the situation."

"Very good, Ghostbird," said a new voice on the radio. "This is Captain Knox. Your reputation precedes you, and I'm happy to have you making the deliveries. Marines have the situation well in hand for now, but it's ...tense."

"Understood, Captain," Abi replied, glancing at Medlock, whose jaw was clenched. "We'll be down shortly. May I ask why you're making headway? The turbulence around your superstructure will make landing ...spicy."

"Ah, Ghostbird, we're trying to maintain airflow over the deck to keep down the chance of cross-infection. Something new out of PacFleet. Don't know if it works, but the orders came down this morning. I can tell the engine room to reduce speed, and resume once you're down."

"No need, Captain, spicy landings are all in a day's work."

"And that's why you get the cool callsign," Medlock muttered.

"Your mic's hot, Meddler. Shut it," Abi admonished, after carefully switching to the intercom.

As they approached the ship, Abi brought the Super Stallion into a steady hover behind the stern of the ship, watching Marines check the landing pad and remove the barricades which kept the civilians off the rear deck.

"Monitor clearance and call out the distance" Abi told Medlock as she slowly moved over the landing zone and rotated the helo so that its nose was pointed astern of the ship.

"Dead center on the X. Twenty down. Ten. Five. Contact," Medlock said as a light illuminated on the console.

Abi pushed the cyclic all the way down and killed the power to the rotors, but kept the engines idling, ready for a quick lift-off if things went sideways. She'd backed the Super Stallion into place so that the passengers could proceed directly onto the deck without having to maneuver around her bird. The "garage door" hatch in the superstructure was open with Marines ready to escort the passengers under cover and off the landing pad at the stern of the ship.

"Ramp's down, LT," Moleka reported. "We're ready to unload."

Abi unbuckled her harness and stood, slipping out of the pilot's seat. "Medlock, stay with the bird. I'm going to talk with the captain and see how bad things are."

As she moved toward the back of the helicopter, the heat from the engines dissipated into the cool sea air. Abi stepped onto the deck, immediately hit by the smell of saltwater, sweat, and something far more acrid—the stench of fear.

"Lieutenant Forsyth?" A Marine in full combat gear stepped over to her, his face grim beneath his helmet.

"That's me," Abi said, cutting straight to the point. "What's the situation?"

"I'm your escort to the bridge. Captain Knox wants to talk to you before you head back."

"Excellent. It'll take a few minutes to unload and secure the bird. Lead on."

Instead of heading inside, the Marine, whose name patch read Campbell, motioned toward one of the external stairways covering the rear of the superstructure. It was six levels up to the bridge, but the Marine double-timed it, and Abi did her best to keep up.

In the bridge, she was greeted by a tall man with wavy black hair and a prominent widow's peak. "Ghostbird, Lieutenant Forsyth, I presume?"

"Captain Knox." Abi came to attention and saluted. Technically, they were under cover, and a salute contraindicated, but she was reporting to a superior officer on assignment.

Knox smiled and quickly returned the salute. "Thank you, lieutenant. Not necessary, but welcome. Good order and discipline may be the only things we have left in these ...circumstances."

"How bad is it, sir?"

"We've been pulling boats out of the water for the past three days." He turned and pointed out the forward bridge windows which looked out over the cargo deck with the large cranes, one of which was placing a small fishing boat back into the water. "We have no choice but to cut them loose and let them drift. It's the other reason we're making way. *Port Royal* has pulled a few over the side, but they don't have the capabilities we do. On the other hand, they have hangar facilities and we don't. They're mostly going to be taking on by air—your wingman I believe, *Tempest-One*?"

"Psych's one of the best, sir. We'll rescue as many as we can."

"It won't be enough Lieutenant, especially if we get too many infected at once."

"How many?"

"We've had six so far today. Two turned early this morning, we pulled four off boats in the process of turning, and didn't catch it in time. They've been trickling in. We're holding the ones who've turned, in a section on the bow. Doc's sedated them, but there's non-infected out there as well. The crowd's on edge; people are awfully close to freaking out, and we're running out of space that won't interfere with operations."

Abi followed his gaze to a barricaded area at the very front of the ship. Inside, she could see a handful of people, naked, tied up with rope and lying on the deck, mostly unmoving, but with occasional twitches. They were watched closely by ten Marines with rifles. They looked peaceful enough from a distance, as if they were sleeping, but Abi had seen enough of the Haole Flu—especially the Infected's resistance to sedation—to know that appearances could be deceiving.

"Anyone else showing symptoms?" she asked.

Knox nodded grimly. "A few. We've got one guy with a fever, and another right before you got here. She started screaming about ants crawling all over and tried to strip off her clothes. We've tried to separate them, but it's getting harder to keep under control. If one of them turns in the middle of the refugees, it'll be a massacre."

Abi's gut twisted. "Understood, sir. What can we do for you?"

"I need to get them off my ship." Knox hesitated, clearly not liking what he was about to say. "Take them off."

"Sir, I have orders to not take back anyone who isn't in uniform and under orders."

"Not back to land, I want you to take them out and drop them." Knox's expression was grim.

"Sir?" Abi was shocked. It was callous, cruel—not to mention criminal—but perhaps necessary.

"Lieutenant, I can't just push them overboard. Sedation barely works, so I can't just overdose them. I can't keep them here, and I can't just ...dispatch them in front of the other civilians.

"Oh," she said.

"Not to mention the effect on morale of the Marines."

"Understood, sir. But that means you're just dumping *your* problem on my crew. With all due respect . . .sir . . .Marines volunteer to do the dirty jobs. My crew understands risk, but I'm afraid that's an order I can't follow."

Knox stared at her for a moment, then sighed.

"You're correct, Lieutenant. I can't order you to do this. That said, what do we do?"

"Put them in the boats you set adrift? If it's possible to save themselves, they'll have an opportunity."

"PacFleet says the zombie phase of ...what do you call it? The Haole Flu? They say that the zombies don't—can't—recover, but I guess you are correct. Getting them out of view of anyone else will work, and we can't do anything for them here."

"Agreed sir, and it will keep from panicking the civilians."

Knox rubbed his face with his hands, then lowered them into fists at his sides. "This is war, Lieutenant. It's not a declared one, but it's a war for the survival of the human race."

"And war is hell, sir."

"Exactly." Knox stared out over the deck for a few more moments. "Go, Ghostbird, you're dismissed. Go get me as many survivors as you can. We'll load up as many as we can then head for Midway. It's isolated enough, and this old bucket has enough provisions to keep us going for quite a while."

Abi came to attention, clicking her heels so that he'd notice, and saluted once again.

After Knox returned the salute, Abi assured him, softly, "As many as we can, sir."

Racing back down the gangways, Abi got back to her bird in time to see Moleka handing one of the deck crew the last of the personal effects left on the helo. It was a small teddy bear, dressed in a cute vest and bow tie.

The various noises of a ship underway made it difficult to hear, but no different than around helos. Abi could just make out their raised voices as the crew chief told the sailor: "Little girl, about five. Yellow dress. Vietnamese, I think. Mom said her father's doing security at Pearl. There's not a lot of hope there, so be gentle."

"Aye, aye, Chief. We'll take care of them."

"Time to get clear, sailor. We're inbound for another load. Captain says to bring out as many as we can. Lai, button us up." Abi grabbed a microphone off the bulkhead next to the ramp and keyed the cockpit channel. "Jimmy, start us up and get us airborne. Don't wait for me."

Moleka looked at her strangely as the sound of the engines ramped up.

"Captain asked if we could drop infected at sea. Not gonna happen."

"Oh. Understood, LT. Something we must figure out, though, what if someone turns in flight?"

"When and if, Chief. We'll make the decision only when and if we have to. For now, we're playing Valkyrie."

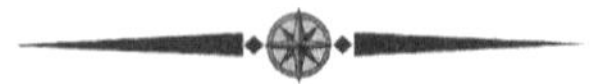

*Tempest*-Two made two more roundtrips, carrying almost two hundred people out to the *Yukon* by virtue of many children carried on a parent's lap, freeing up additional seats for more evacuees. On the last trip out, she'd noticed a drifting boat with several naked bodies on it. The location and direction of drift suggested that Captain Knox had adopted her suggestion regarding how to deal with the Infected. It was brutal but was also just enough to salve her conscience.

Once again, they were back at MCBH, preparing to take more people out to the ships. The crowd didn't seem to be lessening, though. There were still a lot of people waiting for evacuation.

Abi had swapped landing sites with Psych. Bill Jung's *Tempest-One* had made one fewer round-trip than *Tempest-Two* due to carrying sling loads below helo on the way out to the *Port Royal*. Loading took additional time, not required for Abi's purely personnel flights.

Psych had moved over the western edge of the base, where a short-take-and-landing runway was being refurbished in anticipation of the first delivery of MV-22 Ospreys in the next few years. It was a shame the vertical take-off-and-landing craft weren't available for this evacuation, but they would have been limited in usefulness, as the only at-sea platform equipped to handle the tiltrotor aircraft was a full-sized aircraft carrier, and most of those were either in dock or well outside of range from Hawaii.

Abi did a walk-around, ensuring that there was no obvious damage from their multiple round-trips to the *Yukon*. Abi continued to decline Captain Knox's offer to reduce headway for her landings, even though the ship was now steaming on an arc that was beginning to take it in a crosswind direction. The turbulence had been rough on their last landing, and she'd had to bring the helo down hard. Fortunately, aside from quite literally rattling her passengers, there didn't seem to be any damage.

Moleka and Jaremczek were lining up people prior to beginning to load. The sun was just barely above the Ko Olina range to the west of the base, and Abi knew this would be the last flight in daylight. She and her crew were prepared to fly in the dark, but even with the declaration of wartime rules of engagement, they'd been at it for over ten hours.

Colonel Weber had notified her and Jung that they were to take crew rest on their respective ships. They could refuel and resume in the morning.

*If there's anyone alive to return for*, Abi thought to herself.

*Tempest-One*'s loading point was just over five hundred feet away, on the other side of the main runway. After checking her own bird, she looked over at the sling-load being prepared for Psych. Much to her surprise, she noticed that the load was large wooden crates that were being loaded with ...people?

Abi's hurried back the cockpit of her bird, donned her headset and switched to the squadron channel. "*Tempest-One*, Psych! What the hell are you doing?" Abi called into the radio. The number of people waiting to board the crate was dwindling, and it looked like the ground crew was ready to close it up.

Jung's voice came back over the radio. "Ghostbird, we don't have a choice."

"You're planning to haul people under the helo? That's insane, Bill! They're not cargo—this isn't safe."

The voice on the radio was level, but cold. "We don't have time for anything else. *Port Royals*' already in trouble. They had several Infected, and we must save a flight strictly for supplies and weapons. It's either take them all now or leave them behind, and you know damn well we can't do that."

Abi watched as the harness rig was led over to the helo. It had enough slack to allow the CH53E to lift, but it also risked the cargo being dragged over the ground and damaged if Psych didn't position the helo just right before lifting. "You'll get them killed. You hit even a little turbulence, and that whole load is gone. What are you thinking?"

"I'm thinking that we're running out of room inside, and we need to get more people out, fast. The base is about to go under, and this is the only way to take more than a few at a time." Psych's tone was cold and hard. "I know the risk, Ghostbird."

Jung's tone shocked Abi almost as much as the words. "It's not *safe*, Bill," she countered.

"We don't have the luxury of safe, Abi. We're past that."

Abi felt the heat rise in her chest. She wanted to argue. She wanted to tell him that he was wrong, but somehow, the same instinct that told her the kid in line earlier was going to turn was telling her they were out of time. "There has to be another way, Bill."

"I don't like it either," Bill admitted, "But it's necessary."

The radio clicked. The conversation was over.

Abi opened her mouth to argue further, but the screech of alarms cut through the air, followed by the sharp crack of gunfire. She turned to look back into the helo, Jaremczek was getting people seated, while Moleka was directing them up the ramp.

They'd just started loading, and the line snaked back to a holding area off to the side. It looked like more people than they could manage in a single flight.

She turned back to her controls, and something caught her attention out her side of the helo. A man was running toward the holding area. He finished ripping off his sweatshirt and now tearing at his shirt.

Abi's blood turned cold.

*Not again.*

"Moleka!" she shouted. "Check the guy coming toward the line—dark hair, just took off a blue hoodie ...He's infected!"

Within seconds, Abi saw Moleka barreling past her window, yelling at the Marines nearby to help. The young man was on his knees, stripping off the rest of his clothes. He stood back up and Abi could see people in line jump back, fear now bubbling into full-blown panic. Screams erupted.

"Get him out of there!" Abi barked. Her hand hovered over the controls, ready to initiate takeoff if things went south. The last thing she wanted was a Zed on her bird.

Before Moleka could reach him, the young man convulsed violently. His skin, already pale, took on a bluish tint. He made a sound—a deep, wet growl—that froze Abi's blood.

"He's turning!" she heard Steve-O say through her headset.

Moleka didn't hesitate—he rushed forward, tackling the man to the ground with a forceful thud. The crowd around them surged backward, people stumbling and screaming, nearly trampling each other as they tried to escape. Panic rippled through the evacuees, and the orderly line disintegrated into a chaotic scramble for safety—fortunately, away from the helo.

Abi's knuckles whitened as she gripped the control stick. "Get that ramp up!" she ordered Jaremczek, fear crawling up her spine. If more were infected, it was only a matter of seconds before the situation spiraled out of control. Lai could board through the starboard door, but she didn't want a mob on the ramp. She watched as Moleka struggled with the young man, pinning him to the dirt as two Marines rushed to assist. The man's eyes were red, and there was no sign of intelligence ...only rage.

"LT!" Medlock's voice broke through Abi's focus. "The fence! Tower says they're breaching the fence!"

Abi snapped her head to look back toward the main gate, even knowing that it was a mile away and on the other side of all the base buildings. In the back of her mind, she noted that the ramp was still down. The engines were too loud to hear the gunfire she knew would be there, but several loud "whumps" and shocks announced the mines that had been emplaced all along the neck of the peninsula.

Marine Corps Base Hawaii was lost.

"Shit, we're out of time!" Abi growled, slamming a hand on the control panel. "Moleka, we're closing the ramp!"

"Not yet, LT!" Moleka's voice was strained. He and the Marines had dragged the convulsing young man off to the side, away from the evacuees, but the situation was getting out of hand. Another one of the civilians, a woman holding a child, was holding her hand to her neck, blood was beginning to seep through her fingers—she'd been bitten.

"Moleka, now!" Abi's heart pounded in her ears as she imagined the scene of infected crossing the base, charging toward her helo. It was still too soon, but that didn't stop her imagination.

As the woman started to convulse, Moleka grabbed the infant and ran for the ramp. “We’re on!” he shouted as the Marines practically threw themselves into the cargo bay.

A whine started as Jaremczek *finally* started closing the ramp.

Abi caught motion out of the corner of her eye, expecting it to be more Infected running across the field, but it was a C-130 on the runway, taking off. That was the one they’d been told about, Penguin-Four-Two, taking the last of Third Battalion and their leadership to Pohakuloa Training Area, in the high pass between Mauna Loa and Mauna Kea on the Big Island.

This was it.

*The Last C-130.*

“Get us out of here, Abi!” Medlock yelled; his voice sharp with fear.

Abi didn’t need to be told twice. She yanked back on the stick, and the Super Stallion lifted off, the ground falling away beneath them. Below, chaos reigned as the abandoned evacuees fought with brave Marines who’d stayed to keep order as long as they could.

It was a sight she’d not soon forget—but that thought was displaced by Medlock shouting “Down, down! Take us down, now!”

Abi pushed the cyclic down and felt something give way as the helo dropped onto the pavement. Her imagination, already overactive, brought up an image of civilians underneath her landing gear, but she looked out and noted that they’d at least managed to get clear of the loading area and the remaining evacuees. She could see them breaking past the Marines and started to move in *Tempest-Two*’s direction. She also saw the first signs of Infected coming past the fire station. They had only had a few moments, then they needed to be gone.

"Meddler," she growled. Her use of his callsign indicating her displeasure.

"It's Psych," Medlock said, and Abi noticed the shadow of helo and cargo passing over her cockpit.

"That's not right," Abi said, her stomach twisting. "Moleka, what's happening on Bill's bird?"

Before Moleka could respond, the radio crackled to life. "Ghostbird, this is Psych," Jung's voice came through clipped and robotic. "We have a situation—passenger turned—attacking passengers—crew chief down!"

His tone of voice chilled Abi. She'd only heard him like this once before, when she'd had an emergency during a check flight, with Bill as her IP.

"Psych!" she barked.

Jung's Super Stallion lurched violently to the left, veering west, over the bay. The massive helicopter swung around, looking like it was going to come back and land. The sudden movement started the slung cargo to swing. The more they tried to correct, the more unstable the craft became.

"Ghostbird! Going down. Abi, find Phillie, She's on *Port Royal*. Tell her—" Bill's voice finally cracked. "Tell her I love her."

The helo's nose dipped dangerously close to the water, and the sling load hit the surface. The impact rocked *Tempest-One* backward, and its tail struck, followed by the entire helo spinning and crashing into the reef a couple thousand feet offshore.

"Shit! Shit!" Medlock yelled, "We have to rescue them, LT!"

Abi's heart hammered in her chest; her hands still tightly gripped the controls. "Moleka, status!"

The engineer's voice crackled through the comms. "Shaken . . .but alive. Gear's probably in bad shape, though. This hard landing on top of the previous means it'll likely buckle the next time. We won't be going anywhere after that until we fix it."

Abi cursed under her breath, her eyes darting back to Jung's chopper, now lying canted sideways on the reef. Through the dust and smoke, she saw flashes of movement in the cabin—chaos.

Her radio crackled. "*Tempest-Two*, this is Weber. You need to go. Now. You're the last run. Get your people out to *Yukon* and head somewhere safe. Go, Abi, that's an order."

"Roger, Kaneohe. *Tempest* is heading to *Yukon*," Abi said, tears in her eyes, and trying to keep a sob out of her voice. "Godspeed, Kaneohe."

"It's a different service, but I think it's appropriate, Ghostbird. 'These things we do . . .'"

"'That others may live.'" Abi finished reciting the motto of Air Force Search and Rescue. It was oddly appropriate. "Not my faith, but I'll wish you 'Until Valhalla,' Colonel." Abi whispered into the mic, knowing that the channel had already been closed on the other end.

Abi took a deep breath and powered up the engines. The Super Stallion groaned as the rotors spun to life, but the chopper lifted off the ground, but she could *feel* the uneven lift and friction as the landing gear scraped the tarmac.

"Come on, come on," she muttered under her breath, coaxing the bird higher as she watched the mob closing in. The helo shuddered but gained altitude in time for the mob to be blown back by rotor wash.

"We're up. Clear for now," Medlock said, voice tight. "Gear's not going to hold, though. Gonna be trouble later, LT."

Abi nodded grimly. "We'll deal with it when we get there, Jimmy."

The flight to the *Yukon* felt longer than it was as Abi thought on everything they were leaving behind. Finally, the dark shape of the *Yukon* appeared on the horizon as the last rays of sun disappeared under the horizon. The ship was a beacon of hope amid the chaos, but Abi knew their troubles were far from over.

"*Yukon*, this is Ghostbird. We're coming in hot—landing gear is compromised. We're going to need assistance on deck."

There was a pause, then a gruff voice replied, "Copy that, Ghostbird. We'll have Marines ready for you. Get down as best you can."

Abi clenched her jaw, steadying the helicopter as they approached the ship. The deck was crowded, but the Marines kept the landing pad clear. Abi tried to favor the broken gear as they descended the last few feet, but the helo lurched as it collapsed, causing the rotor to catch a section of railing and hurl shrapnel all around the stern of the ship. Emergency systems disengaged the rotor from the engines, but it still had momentum. It continued to strike sparks and send debris flying for a few moments until friction brought the rotor to a halt. She hit the engine shutdown procedure and the three turboshaft engines fell silent for the first time that day.

For a moment, everything was still.

"Status!" Abi barked; her voice hoarse.

Moleka groaned from the back. "We're …we're good, LT. Everyone's alive, but the bird's not flying again anytime soon."

Abi exhaled, relief flooding her. They had made it. Barely.

Medlock slumped in his seat, wiping sweat from his brow. "That was too damn close, LT."

Abi nodded, unbuckling her harness and standing on shaky legs. "We'll worry about repairs later. Right now, let's get everyone off this bird and secured."

Outside, the Marines were already approaching, their faces grim but relieved. Abi could see the exhaustion in their eyes, the same weariness that she felt in her bones. But they were safe, for now.

As she stepped out onto the deck, the reality of their situation hit like a tidal wave. The infected were spreading, the base was lost, and now they were stranded on the *Yukon* with a damaged helicopter and no way off.

But they were alive. And in this nightmare, that was all that mattered.

THE SUPER STALLION'S ENGINES were silent now, and the only sounds were from the wind, waves, and machinery of the ship. The lifeless helo sat, resting unevenly on the deck of the *Yukon*. The right-side landing gear had collapsed on landing, and the corresponding sponson was crumpled. What little fuel remained had already leaked out and been covered with foam by the ship's firefighting team.

The bigger problem had been the rotors hitting a section of the stern fencing, sending debris into the fuselage and ship's superstructure. Abi could feel the ship rocking gently beneath her feet as she surveyed the helicopter's damage. Ghostbird wasn't going anywhere soon. The hard landing had twisted the landing gear beyond anything the crew could fix with what they had on hand. They were stuck.

"Damn," Abi muttered under her breath, running a hand over her sweat-soaked brow. She exchanged a glance with Moleka, who was already checking the tail section.

"It's bad, LT," Moleka said, his tone heavy with frustration. "We'll need a full overhaul to get her flying again. At least a month's work, maybe more. That's if we can get the parts."

Abi nodded, her mind racing. The *Yukon* was their refuge now, but she could feel the tension all around her. The ship's deck was packed with evacuees, and while the Marines had managed to maintain order for the time being, the strain was beginning to show. Tempers were flaring, and every glance between people was filled with suspicion—who was infected, who wasn't?

Who would be the next to turn?

"LT!" Medlock's voice broke her thoughts. He jogged over from the communications station near the bridge, his face pale. "Captain Knox wants you on the bridge. There's a problem with Port Royal."

Abi's stomach clenched and her head throbbed. It had been a long day of too much stress and too little sleep. The adrenaline of the hard landing was still with her and would take some time to drain away. Her bird was broken, and it sounded like there was a new problem.

Ah well, hope wouldn't make problems go away, and faith wasn't about blindly wishing. She had a job to do, and the captain had called for her.

*Port Royal* was supposed to be Bill's destination. His wife was aboard, and likely hadn't gotten the news about her husband yet. *Yukon* would be struggling to deal with their refugees, and with Bill down and her broken bird, they wouldn't be going anywhere else.

When she arrived on the bridge, slightly out of breath from the climb, Knox was standing by the wide windows, hands clasped behind his back. His jaw was set, the tension visible even from the doorway.

"Lieutenant Forsyth, we've got a situation," Knox said, his eyes still fixed on the dark silhouette of the Port Royal drifting in the distance.

"What's happening over there?" Abi asked, already sensing the answer wouldn't be pleasant.

"Port Royal is in trouble," Knox said, his voice low but firm. "Infected among the bridge crew. The captain's dead, and they have a shortage of officers. I need to get a relief crew over there."

Abi's stomach twisted. "You want me to fly over and stabilize it? I can't."

Knox turned to face her, his expression hard. "Is this another can't? Or won't? I know you landed hard, but if *Tempest* can fly at all, I have a harbor pilot team that can take over for them until they can stabilize."

Abi just stood there, shaking her head.

"No? Then you are relieved, lieutenant. Get you co-pilot up here, or I can call in your wingman. Jung, was it? He's supposed to be flying missions to *Port Royal*. He'll do."

"No sir, that's not it," she said, barely restraining a sob. "*Tempest-Two* is broken, not flyable. *Tempest-One* is . . ." This time, she let the sob out. "*Tempest-One* went down in the bay. Infected in the cockpit. They had a full load of evacuees and more in a sling load. They crashed, sir. Jung's not coming; his wife's over there and doesn't know."

Knox stared for a moment, then turned back to the window. He stood stiffly for a moment, then his shoulders sank. He began to shake, then curse. "Damnit. How in the name of God could this happen? I have Marines ready to do a security sweep and a crew to take over the bridge, and I can't get them there quickly."

"God didn't do this, sir," Abi said quietly.

Knox turned to look back at her, and his gaze softened. "I know, Abi. 'Sorry for your loss' doesn't cut it. There's been too much loss, and PacFleet said this flu was man-made. Some sick fiend created this. You're right, it sure as hell isn't God's doing."

"Can you send a tender?"

"I can, but it will take too long. 'Groundhog's' drifting now. Is there any way *Tempest* can lift? Even if she gets stuck over there?" Knox waved in the cruiser's general direction.

"No, sir. She won't fly without repairs. It's not just the collapsed landing gear. If we had to, we could prop it up level for take-off. Once. Unfortunately, we struck at an angle and several rotor tips caught the rear fence. We'll have to inspect before we fly. Blade repair without a shop will take ...Actually? I don't know ...Days? Weeks? Even with minimal damage, the rotor will likely be unbalanced and try to tear itself apart when we get up to speed. She's stuck right where she is for a long time."

Knox let out a heavy breath, rubbing his forehead. He was silent for a moment, the weight of the moment hanging between them.

"I'll have to get them over by boat, then." He turned to his intra-ship comm and called the executive officer. "Henry, get them on the tender. Helo is down."

Abi stepped closer to the window, her eyes narrowing as she looked out over the water. The Port Royal was drifting closer, its movements sluggish but purposeful. Even from here, she could see smoke billowing from the midsection, flames licking at the hull. It was chaos over there.

Then she saw it—the slow, inevitable shift of the ship's course.

"Sir," she said quietly, her pulse quickening. "They're heading straight for us."

Knox followed her gaze, his face paling as he realized what she had just said. "Damn it," he muttered under his breath. He grabbed the radio, barking orders to the deck crew. "Prepare for collision! All hands, brace for impact!"

Abi's heart raced. The Port Royal was drifting toward them, its massive bulk looming in the distance. She hated this—being stuck, unable to do anything but watch as disaster unfolded in front of them. The Port Royal was now too close for any plan of relief. Even if *Tempest* could fly, it was too late, now.

The ship let out a screeching wail as it closed in, the twisted metal groaning under the strain. The flames flared higher, illuminating the night sky as it bore down on the *Yukon*.

"They're going to hit us," Abi said, her voice steady despite the terror gripping her. "There's no stopping it now."

Knox gripped the railing of the bridge, his knuckles white. "Prepare for impact," he repeated, though this time it was more to himself than anyone else. The bridge crew was scrambling, securing anything that could be thrown by the imminent collision.

Then it happened.

Port Royal collided with the stern of *Yukon*, a deafening sound of metal on metal as the cruiser tore into the oiler. The impact knocked Abi off her feet, and she hit the deck hard, the wind knocked out of her. The ship shuddered violently, and alarms blared across the deck as the collision sent a shockwave through the entire structure.

"Up!" Knox shouted to the bridge crew, pulling himself up from where he'd been thrown against the railing. He shouted into the radio. "Damage control teams now! Contain fire and assess the damage!"

Abi looked out at the stern, several small fires had broken out, and *Tempest* was leaning even more heavily, the impact had shifted it dangerously close to the railing.

Port Royal was burning as she pulled away, her bow crumpled, and starting to ride low in the water. The cruiser might well be lost. The fight was on to keep *Yukon* from going down with her.

Knox turned to her, his face set in a grim line. He nodded back to the scene at the stern, Marines and crew members putting out fires, and Moleka leading a crew to lash down the CH53E.

"See to your bird, Lieutenant. There's nothing more we can do. We'll survive this, or not."

Abi nodded; her heart heavy. They had escaped disaster by a thread, but the cost had been high. She watched the flames consuming the Port Royal, as the last light of day fled the sky. Even the lights on the distant shore had gone out, leaving only flames.

She could only think of Bill's last words to his wife.

Now she'd never hear them.

*YUKON* SAILED THROUGH THE dark waters, the soothing hum of its engines given way to the grumble and whine of overstressed engines. The rudder was damaged, as well as one of her two screws. Captain Knox had ordered the bent shaft disconnected from the engine gearing, and now the ponderous bulk was driven by a single screw, with difficulty keeping it on a straight course.

They were alone against the backdrop of the endless Pacific, cut off from the rest of the world, but still afloat. Abi stood on the stern, her broken helicopter behind her, her gaze fixed on the horizon, where the last lights of the Hawaiian Islands had long since disappeared. The silence out here was a welcome reprieve from the chaos they'd left behind.

She felt, more than heard, the silent presence of the captain as he stepped up beside her. She looked to the side, sizing up the man who, for all *human* intents and purposes, held all their lives in his hands. His face was set in a hard line, but his eyes still held a glimmer of hope. He'd been through hell, too, but still carried himself with the dignity of someone who hadn't given up.

"French Frigate Shoals," Knox said, almost to himself, his voice barely louder than a whisper. "It's not Midway, but it'll have to do."

Abi nodded, thoughts drifting as she stared out at the endless expanse of water. They had wanted to make it to Midway, to find some semblance of safety, but the damage to the *Yukon* made that impossible. The collision with the Port Royal had left them limping, struggling to maintain course. French Frigate Shoals was their best chance now—a desolate outpost far from the infected hordes. A place to shelter, to make repairs, and to figure out what came next.

"It'll do," Abi replied, her voice steady. "We'll make repairs there. It will be hard, and slow, without *Port Royal*'s hangers, but your ship has a machine shop. We just need time. We'll beat the blades with rocks and lash the landing gear with palm fronds if we have to. It's the Polynesian way."

Knox chuckled softly, though there was no humor in it. "We're off the radar and sailing into the unknown. 'Here there be dragons,' Lieutenant. "

"We'll survive, sir" Abi said quietly. "We always do."

Knox turned to face her, expression softening for the first time since she had boarded his ship. "You believe that?"

Abi met his gaze, her own thoughts drifting back to Kaneohe, to the burning wreckage of *Port Royal*, to the endless waves of infected they had barely escaped. She thought of the people they had left behind, the ones they couldn't save. But she also thought of the survivors—of the Marines, the sailors, and the refugees packed below deck, clinging to the hope that this wasn't the end.

"I do," Abi said firmly. "The Hawaiian people ...they're resilient. We're resilient. I'm not native, but I grew up here, and these people are descended from explorers—people who crossed the entire Pacific Ocean with nothing but the stars to guide them. They'll survive ...We'll survive. We must have faith, sir."

Knox smiled faintly; the weight of their shared losses momentarily lifted by her words. "Polynesian explorers, huh? I suppose we're following in their footsteps now."

Abi nodded. "We'll do what they did—navigate the unknown, find new horizons. And one day, we'll go back. Hawaii will still be there, and when it's safe, we'll return."

Knox looked out over the water again, his eyes thoughtful. "You think Hawaii can recover from all this?"

Abi's chest tightened at the thought of the islands—so full of life, now overrun with the infected. But deep down, she believed in the strength of the people, the land. "Hawaii is more than just a place. It's the people. They'll survive. They'll rebuild, one day. The islands have been through worse."

Knox didn't say anything for a moment, but she could see the hope flicker in his eyes. It wasn't much, but it was enough. The

*Yukon* wasn't just a ship—it was a symbol of their survival, of the determination that had carried them through everything. And as long as it stayed afloat, so would they.

Knox turned to go back to the bridge and deal with the next crisis. "I like your optimism, Lieutenant," he said quietly. "We could use more of that."

Abi stayed where she was, standing just inside the chain and rope that had replaced the damaged stern fence. She knew it wasn't just optimism. It was faith.

"You really believe that? That faith nonsense?" Jimmy said from the darkness. He was sitting on the open ramp of the Sea Stallion. It couldn't be closed until they powered it up, and they couldn't even start the APU until they replaced the damaged fuel and hydraulic lines in the starboard sponson.

"I do—and it's not nonsense. Faith isn't blind. It's not a gleeful ignorance of the facts, nor an unreasoning optimism. Faith is picking yourself up, grabbing your tools, and making your future with the belief that it will benefit *someone*, some place, even if we ourselves won't be the beneficiaries. Faith is motivation, not wishful thinking. It is on us to take the situation God handed us and honor Him with our attitude and outlook. Faith may sometimes be about hardship, suffering, and anguish, but it's also about determination and confidence that *you* can make a difference."

Abi looked up at the stars, imagining her father doing the same—somewhere. They'd always shared a love of the night sky, and he'd been so disappointed that she hadn't followed *his* dream of science and research.

"We'll make it, Dad" she repeated softly to herself. "Please do the same ...and have faith."

# Afterword

THESE ARE SOME OF my longer stories, firmly in the "novelette" category, and starting to nudge into "novella" territory. I sometimes joke that my default short story is 12,000 words—much to the chagrin of my editors who were looking for 8,000 words, maximum.

It's not entirely true, I have many stories that easily clock in at 5,000-7,000 words. Its just as I get into the characters, I find myself wanting to write more about them, and their setting, and their interactions...

It's a character flaw, I admit it.

Still, three of the stories are over 10,000 words, and two of the remaining are close. That makes this one of the "beefier" volumes in the Journeys Beyond the Known series, hence limiting it to six stories in this volume. I had another 10k+ story I'd wanted to include (a sequel to "No Hippocritical Oath") only to realize that anthology hasn't been published yet, and I promised Tom that particular story.

Most of these stories have been published by Baen, and some also tie into novels in the Baen Books catalog:

"No Hippocritical Oath" is part of a series of "prequel" stories commissioned by Tom Kratman for his Carrera Series: . In that series, the history of war-torn Terra Nova was shaped by the Wars of

Liberation, and Tom asked for stories based approximately 100-150 years prior to the events which start with his Novel *A Desert Called Peace*. Tom helped me with the setting which purposefully resembles the Earthly country of Panama.

"Gut Check" is a prequel to my novel *The Moon and the Desert*: . I wrote it as a short story for the Baen Website, but they chose a science article on bionics for the website tie-in to the book launch. A year later for the mass market paperback launch, I was asked if the story was still available. However, in the interim, I'd sent it to *Analog* and they bought it! I sent them "Bionic Frontier" (Journeys Beyond the Known, vol. 1) instead.

"Ghost of Kaneohe" is a prequel to my novel *Across an Ocean of Stars*: . This time, Baen asked for both a science article and story for the launch of the novel. I guess I need to figure out what to write for the MMPB launch next spring!

It's been commented that these stories, particularly "Mother" are fairly *dark* in tone. Jason Cordova, editor for *Chicks in Tank Tops* expressed surprise, since he was used to seeing technical science and humor from me.

"Hey, I can write dark, Jason!"

I feel the setting fits the theme, though. When darkness falls... When hope is lost... When it seems as if the enemy has won... a hero rises!

# Acknowledgements

It's only appropriate that I lead off this collection with a story I wrote for the first person to buy a story from me, Tom Kratman. I'd like to thank Tom, Les Johnson & Ken Roy, Tony Daniel & Chris Ruocchio, Jason Cordova, John Ringo & Gary Poole, and Toni Weisskopf for the opportunity to play in these universes.

My thanks as well for the first-rate editors and editing (I'm looking at *you,* Sandra Medlock and Griffin Barber!) who took my words and turned them into *stories.*

Elements of "World Enough" and "Mother" were heavily influenced by Anne McCaffrey's "Brain and Brawn Ship series." Thank you, Anne, and co-author Mercedes Lackey, for *The Ship Who Searched*, which introduced the germ of an idea for encapsulating a person suffering from debilitating illness—i.e. Patch in "World Enough." The book is celebrating its 20th anniversary this year. Hooray!

Both stories were also influenced by Keith Laumer's "Bolos" series. What's not to like about intelligent tanks?

Thanks again to all of my author friends and fans who keep nudging and asking for more. Many thanks to William Alan Webb and Kevin Steverson, as well as the rest of our Peacemaker Cantina writer's chat. I have learned so much about book composition, cover art, interior art, and self-publishing. I greatly appreciate your help.

Thanks to my wife Ruann, sister Sandra, Mom, Dad, and my sons, for putting up with my stories and puns.

Finally, thanks to my readers and fans. I hope you enjoy the stories.

# Connect with Robert E. Hampson

http://REHampson.com

# About the Author

Robert E. Hampson, Ph.D. is a national bestselling author and world-class neuroscientist whose stories traverse science fiction, military adventure, post-apocalyptic scenarios, speculative fiction, and even hard-SF style fantasy. Drawing from more than 40 years in scientific research, he crafts universes filled with carefully constructed ecological, technological, and political systems, infused with rich character dynamics and moral complexity.

Rob is dedicated to meticulous worldbuilding and rich characters. His stories engage readers with gripping tales that blend emotional realism with speculative imagination to create a thoughtful blend of scholarly depth and subtle wit. His stories explore themes of survival, rebellion, redemption, and legacy. His creative universe includes heroes facing complex challenges and antagonists possessing relatable depth. Worlds where hope surfaces even amidst the darkest situations.

When not dictating and refining his literary projects, Dr. Hampson continues to explore the intersections of neuroscience, technology, and storytelling, consistently delivering compelling fiction that resonates intellectually and emotionally.

For more information visit: http://REHampson.com

# Baen Books by Robert E. Hampson

**Across an Ocean of Stars**

**ISBN 978-1-964856-07-0**

**National Bestseller!**

**After the end of the world, a tropical paradise might just be the hardest place to survive.**

The virus robbed humans of their higher thought processes, turning them into uncontrollable savages. The Hawaiian Islands are separated from the rest of the world by thousands of miles of ocean, but that couldn't stop the virus. Civilization fell, and it fell HARD.

Can paradise survive the end of the world?

High atop a dormant volcano, a team of scientists preserve the last remnants of higher technology. Off the coast of Kauai, a flotilla of survivors must decide whether to return to their island, or make their way to another location, risking pirates and nature on the gamble of safer shores. On the central plateau of the Big Island, a group of ranchers want to rebuild civilization... but to do that, they'll need to reunite a people scattered across an ocean of stars.

https://amzn.to/4kZnthh

## The Moon and the Desert

## ISBN 978-1-982192-49-5

**What would it really take to make the Six Million Dollar Man? A medical thriller on earth and in space!**

Glenn Armstrong Shepard had his sights set on going to Mars as a flight surgeon, but a training accident on the Moon left him crippled. Now he has a new plan: to be fitted with bionic prosthetics and come back even stronger.

Fate and the Space Force have other plans, and Glenn is grounded. Another doctor—his ex-fiancée—takes his place, and Glenn will have to fight to prove he can be an astronaut once more....

https://amzn.to/4kYFpse

## The Founder Effect

## ISBN 978-1-982125-09-7

Anthology edited with Sandra L. Medlock

**AWARD-WINNING AND BEST-SELLING AUTHORS CONTRIBUTE NEW STORIES:** All-new fiction from Dragon Award winner and New York Times best-selling author David Weber, Dragon Award nominee D.J. Butler, best seller Jody Lynn Nye, indie best sellers Chris Kennedy and Mark Wandrey, and more. Also featuring an introduction by multi-award-winning and New York Times best-selling author Larry Correia.

It is 2185 CE. Humans now live throughout the Solar System, but their most ambitious adventure is about to begin. The starship Victoria will carry over 10,000 colonists to a new world outside the Solar System. The larger-than-life exploits of those colonists will become legendary. The colonists will build a new civilization, and the actions of a few individuals will become famous—and infamous—forever marking their new colony with the Founder Effect.

Contributors: Larry Correia, Mark H. Wandrey, Les Johnson, Christopher L. Smith, David Weber, Daniel M. Hoyt, Brad R. Torgersen, Monalisa Foster, Sarah A. Hoyt, Chris Kennedy, Vivienne Raper, Jody Lynn Nye, Brent M. Roeder, Catherine L. Smith, Philip Wohlrab, D.J. Butler

https://amzn.to/44QbcqP

**Stellaris: People of the Stars**

**ISBN 978-1-481484-25-1**

Anthology edited with Les Johnson

**THE STARS WILL CHANGE US.**

STELLARIS: PEOPLE OF THE STARS is a collection of original science fiction stories and nonfiction essays speculating about humanity's far-term expansion into the universe beyond the limits of our solar system—with an emphasis on the changes humans will undergo as a species as we make this happen. Is interstellar travel so far beyond our current imaginings that it will take a fundamental transformation of humanity in order to make it possible? And, if so, will we remain Homo sapiens or become a new and unique species—Homo stellaris (the People of the Stars)?

Herein are original science fiction stories by award-winning authors such as Kevin J. Anderson, William Ledbetter, Todd McCaffrey and Sarah A. Hoyt, supplemented by accessible nonfiction essays describing the science behind the fiction from people who should know—Sir Martin Rees (Astronomer Royal of the United Kingdom), Mark Shelhamer (Chief Scientist for the NASA's Human Research Program), and more.

This collection of original stories and essays was inspired by a gathering of scientists, science fiction authors, and futurists at a series of annual meetings held by the Tennessee Valley Interstellar Workshop. Let their speculations, imaginations and boundless sense of what's possible. Take your own journey beyond the edge of the solar system in STELLARIS: PEOPLE OF THE STARS!

**NEW STORIES AND ESSAYS FROM TOP AUTHORS AND EXPERT SCIENTISTS. Explorations of how interstellar travel may affect humanity by best-selling authors and scientists:**

Sir Martin Rees, Kevin J. Anderson, Sarah A. Hoyt, Mike Massa, William Ledbetter, Todd McCaffrey, Kacey Ezell and Philip Wohlrab, Dan Hoyt, Les Johnson, Robert E. Hampson, Mark Shelhamer, Brent Roeder, Jim Beall, Cathe Smith

https://amzn.to/4mexGr1

# The Wrogul's Oath Books by Robert E. Hampson and Sandra L. Medlock

**Four Horsemen Universe, *Seventh Seal Press, Chris Kennedy Publishing***

**Do No Harm (Hampson, Kennedy, Medlock)**

**ISBN 978-1-950420-11-7**

When Todd's critically damaged ship dropped out of hyperspace near the Human colony world of Azure, he had no memory of his past. He didn't know who he was, or even what he was, and the Humans didn't either. That didn't stop the colonists of Azure—they took him in, anyway...even though they didn't understand how he could do some of the things he could do.

Todd and his descendants consider themselves Human—eight armed and water-breathing—but Human, nonetheless. After seventy years living among Humans, Todd's descendants are going back out into the Union to make their mark—from fifteen-year-old Verne, who's a little short to be a mercenary, to Harryhausen, who wants to be the most famous PI in the galaxy. Eventually they learn that the rest of the Galactic Union knows them as Wrogul, intelligent octopus-like beings known for science and the ability to perform surgery like no other race can.

These Wrogul do more than just practice medicine, but they still intend to do no harm. Unfortunately, the Humans, whether they have two arms or eight, have powerful enemies...and the Wrogul may have no choice.

https://amzn.to/455Fx3f

## And Break It Not (Hampson and Medlock)

## ISBN 978-1-648551-92-5

The planet of Azure is nearly idyllic—there is a high standard of living, industry is booming, and the two races—Human and Wrogul—get along well with each other most days.

But underneath it all, there is tension between the races. Despite having no reason for it, the Humans don't always trust the Wrogul, and there is a faction within the Wrogul community that doesn't want its young growing up "Human."

When a large group of Wrogul move into the ocean and strange things begin happening—weird lights seen in the depths and sabotage at the mariculture stations—the Human's distrust becomes outright suspicion of treachery.

As things spiral out of control, another force enters the system—a group ostensibly sent by the UN on Earth to inspect the crops being grown on Azure—which threatens to destroy everything the Humans and Wrogul have worked for.

While the Wrogul still intend to do no harm, the Humans have powerful enemies in the galaxy, and, this time, the Wrogul may have no choice about whether to join the front lines with their Human friends. Will the threat of a common enemy break the relationship between the Humans and Wrogul...or break it not?

https://amzn.to/3GYsgBO

## As My Witnesses (Medlock, Moores, and Hampson)

## ISBN 978-1-648554-17-9

Azure Colony avoided the larger conflicts of the Omega War and Guild Wars, only to fall prey to rogue mercenaries. Now they're rebuilding, but strange forces are at work. New friends on the ground and mysterious lights in the sky promise "interesting times" for the Humans and hyper-intelligent Wrogul of Azure.

Meanwhile, mercenary leader Verne and Peacemaker Harryhausen resume their search for the ancestral home of Azure's Wrogul. They encounter distrust, deceit, and misdirection from the all-powerful guilds, but they manage to learn of sightings of Wrogul-like aliens. Their strongest lead takes them to a forgotten system where a lost Human colony coexists with a strange alien race with remarkable similarities to the Wrogul.

But when they find the colony is in the middle of a civil war, they're forced to make a choice—do they choose sides or stand by while the colonists slaughter each other?

https://amzn.to/3U036pb

## This I Swear (Hampson and Medlock)

## ISBN 978-8-893192-01-8

**Azure is a paradise—balmy breezes, lush jungles, and warm, turquoise seas. But peace is an illusion... and memory can be a weapon.**

For over a century, the Wrogul—intelligent, four-limbed cephalopods—have called Azure home. Alongside their human neighbors and a growing chorus of species, they've endured mercenaries, galactic intrigues, and a brutal protection racket bent on exploiting their world. Yet one mystery remains: the Wroguls' own past.

Aboard the starship Nautilus, a Wrogul-led crew journeys into the unknown in search of their origins. What they discover is not a lost homeworld, but a hidden colony—where Wrogul and humans suffer alike, and the villains may not be who they expected.

Back on Azure, danger multiplies. A shadowy real estate syndicate is quietly seizing land. Whispers of rebellion echo from deep-sea Wrogul colonies. The Crusaders arrive with fire in their rhetoric and warships in orbit. And an ancient intelligence offers its services—but can it be trusted?

The Wrogul are determined to uncover the truth. But it might be better for some answers should stay buried...

**From the reefs of Azure to the edge of the Peco Arm, This I Swear is a sweeping science fiction epic of memory, identity, and sacrifice—where alien legacies collide, and the cost of peace may be... everything.**

**https://amzn.to/3U0cuJu**

# Journeys
# Beyond the Known

Available from Amazon:

# Journeys Beyond the Known Series

From National Bestselling Author Robert E. Hampson comes **Journeys Beyond the Known**—collections of science fiction and science fantasy exploring the human condition through the lens of biotech, space exploration, and strange futures.

## Tinker, Tailor, Bio, Spy

*Brain & Brain Press*

**Seven tales of cells, circuits and cyborgs**

From battlefield surgeons to post-human colonists. Explore the line between body and machine, memory and manipulation. A line where humanity must embrace the future...or lose it.

Available in eBook, Paperback and Hardback editions from Amazon.

*https://amzn.to/3UbxPQg*

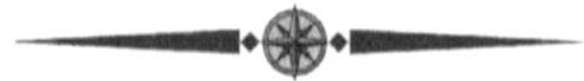

## Where the Light Still Reaches

*Brain & Brain Press*

**Eight stories from the edge of exploration**

Venture into deep space and distant futures, chronicling the legacy of pioneers, the courage of survivors, and the quiet triumph of those who refuse to be forgotten.

Available in eBook, Paperback and Hardback editions from Amazon.

*https://amzn.to/3Hjd7Lp*

## When the Stars Forget Us

Brain & Brain Press

**Eight visions from the edge of magic, and the end of science**

Wander the borderlands between science and sorcery, offering seven visions of apocalypse, myth, and transformation—where magic rises, science fractures, and unlikely heroes carry the fire.

Available in eBook, Paperback and Hardback editions from Amazon.

*https://amzn.to/4mt5C3J*

## A Hero Rises

*Brain & Brain Press*

**Six portraits of uncommon valor and courage in the face of the unknown**

Travel the paths of heroism, great, small, and everything in between—where people find a way to do the impossible—not always because they want to, but because they have to.

Available in eBook, Paperback and Hardback editions from Amazon.

*https://amzn.to/46GgjLo*

www.ingramcontent.com/pod-product-compliance
Lightning Source LLC
LaVergne TN
LVHW020708110826
845149LV00012B/2169

* 9 7 8 1 9 6 1 1 7 2 2 3 4 *